PENANCE

kristin harte

PENANCE: A VIGILANTE JUSTICE NOVEL
Copyright © 2018 by Kristin Harte

Paperback ISBN: 978-1-944336-66-0
EBook ISBN: 978-1-944336-65-3
Large Print Hardcover ISBN: 978-1-954702-06-6

This is a work of fiction. Names, places, businesses, characters and incidents are either the product of the author's imagination or are used in a fictitious manner. Any resemblance to actual persons living or dead, actual events or locales is purely coincidental.

Edited by Silently Correcting Your Grammar, LLC

Cover by Kinship Press

For inquiries, contact Kristin@KristinHarte.com

PENANCE

kristin harte

Chapter One

FINN

I knew my day would be shit the moment I saw my razor. Not because I needed a new one—I had twelve shaves left before the blades would lose their optimum cutting edge. Not because I feared nicks or burns along my jaw either. My sense of dread didn't blossom because of the act of shaving itself. Instead, it flooded me the second I saw that the razor wasn't where it should have been.

Wrong spot.

I didn't believe in ghosts or poltergeists and doubted someone had broken in to the little house my dad had left me just to move my toiletries around. Out of all the worries swirling in my head, those would be dead last. No, that razor sitting on the right side of the sink instead of hanging in the wood holder I'd carved specifically for it told me my nighttime routine had gotten off track somewhere the day before. Not surprising—I'd come back from my brother's house that afternoon too wired to sleep and too tired not to. My entire weekend had been flipped upside down because he'd needed to go out of town and had asked me to stay at his house with his girl. To keep her safe. I'd sat with his girl for three days, always on edge. Guarding. That level of energy and wariness didn't just disappear, so I'd spent the night pacing and reading and trying to burn off the stink of the past few days. And now...this.

I picked up the razor, looking it over, focusing on the details of it so I didn't give in to the pressure building inside of my chest. Wrong spot, indeed. I could fix that, though. I could make it better. So I did—I set the razor in the nook of the stand where it belonged, making sure the overpriced piece of plastic stayed put. Not wanting to disturb it again.

"So, we skip shaving today," I murmured to no one but myself as I tilted my head at the reflection in the mirror. Yeah, I could go another day or so before the scruff got to me. I wasn't a beard-wearing sort of guy—not like my brother's friend Gage. That man was covered in hair. My brothers had all worn beards as well. My older brothers, Bishop and Alder, said they stopped shaving in the winter to help keep their faces warm while working outside for the family logging company. My twin brother, Elijah, claimed the women liked him with a beard, so he'd sported some short, neat facial hair. I had a feeling it was more *one* woman who liked him with a beard. I also had a feeling that woman might have left, as he'd been clean-shaven the last time I'd been out to his place.

Details. The details gave someone away every time.

Whatever—shave or not, it didn't matter in the grand scheme of the day. Shouldn't, at least, but the placement of the razor did. Rituals, habits, structure—I needed those more than I needed just about anything else. Had to have them and follow the steps to keep any sort of balance in my life. At least that's what I told myself. That's how I got through the endless days of holding back and trying my damnedest to make up for my past mistakes. I couldn't let little things slip, or they'd snowball and turn into big things. And big things ruined lives.

Focus, Finn. Face, hair, teeth—my morning routine needed to be solid after the razor incident.

I considered it a step in the right direction when I only checked to make sure the razor was still there five times as I finished getting ready for the day, figured it was damn near a breakthrough when I only went back to the bathroom twice while making breakfast to verify I hadn't imagined the whole thing. Not too bad.

Five years ago, I would have locked myself in the house for the day, too afraid of the rest of the world coming down on my head for my forgetfulness. Two years ago, I would have checked at least ten times. Three months ago, I might have—

Shit. Three months ago, a motorcycle club had moved into town and started causing trouble. Big trouble. The sort that ended in a woman I'd known my entire life dead and her husband—one of my best friends—too distraught to stay in Justice. My rituals had gotten me through each day, each moment, every painful second of the past three months, but not easily. Not without a lot of missteps. I didn't need to think about three months ago—I couldn't risk my balance to those memories. Not today.

As I did every morning, I called my twin brother while I scrambled my eggs. Another ritual I simply couldn't break. One I actually enjoyed. Thankfully, Elijah had gotten used to my need for structure.

"Having a good morning so far?" He never said hello when I called—simply started the conversation as if we'd never stopped it. The man had his own rituals.

"Last night, I left my razor on the counter instead of putting it back in the holder."

His pause said more than his words would—gave away his need to work out why something so trivial would be a big deal to me. He could leave a razor in a totally different spot than usual and not think twice about it, while I'd think about that mistake a thousand times.

"Okay. How do you feel about that?"

The man had gone to way too many Al-Anon meetings. "Not bad. It shook me a little, but I dealt with it."

"How many times have you checked to make sure it's in the right spot since you put it away?"

"Enough to be sure it is, not enough that I'm worried about it."

"That's good. I'm sure tonight you'll go through your nightly routine and that razor will be exactly where it's supposed to be tomorrow."

One could only hope. "Yeah. I'm sure."

"So, what's on your agenda for today?"

And so we went—comparing schedules as if my working at a bar called The Jury Room and his being a lawyer and dealing with actual juries was somehow comparable. He never acted as if my life was in any way less than his, though. Never stopped asking about my tasks and my day, about the details that made my life mine. Neither did our sister. Speaking of which...

"Lainie have fun on her weekend away with that douchebag?" Because my sister had terrible taste in men.

"I'm not touching that one." Elijah laughed before yelling, "Hey Lainie, Finn's got a question for you."

I heard a soft mumble and a little static before Lainie's voice came through the speaker. "What's up, Finn?"

I hadn't talked to her in three days, and I'd missed it. Missed knowing she was safe. "How was your weekend away with the douchebag?"

I swear, if my sister could have growled, she would have. As it was, she gave an awfully loud groan. "It was utter shit. Did Elijah tell you what he did?"

"Oh no," Elijah said in the background, sounding way too pleased. "I left that for you."

"He left me in the motel room to go down to the bar and chat with another woman. Can you believe that? He set up this whole weekend trip to Vail as if time with me was something so damn important to him, then..."

And on she went. I couldn't blame her for being pissed, but at the same time, I almost assumed it was her fault. My sister, the lone Kennard female, could be a bit...difficult. She hadn't even spoken to the oldest two of our brothers in about a year without throwing some sort of fit. I still had no idea why she hated them so much, but I also never asked. Her business. I was just glad not to be on the receiving end of one of her rages.

"What about you?" Lainie asked when she was finished telling me exactly what kind of asshole this guy had been. "You dating anyone?"

Ha. I didn't even have a plant. And she knew that. "Not yet."

"Finn, you know—"

"I'll get there," I said. Because I did know. I knew all about how much they wanted to see me settled. But I had to deal with the shit in my head and my past on a daily basis. No woman needed to be pulled into my mess, and I had no space for the sort of upheaval the females of the species brought with them. Order and control—those were the words I focused on. Love and sex... well, those would likely come in time. I'd sat in a cage for seven years—I had patience.

I kept up a conversation with my siblings in Denver while I ate my breakfast—two eggs scrambled and a piece of toast with strawberry jam. Coffee with lots of cream and sugar to wash it down. Same thing every day, but I didn't complain. I liked the comfort of the routine.

An incoming text message alert pinged in the background as I washed the breakfast dishes and Elijah told me about some new computer system he'd been researching for his office. The only time anyone other than Elijah and Lainie texted me was when something went wrong, so the alert was definitely not normal. I stared at the device for a solid minute before moving toward it, before stretching to pluck it off the counter. I brought the phone to life and tapped to its home screen, letting my brother and sister keep chatting on the speaker as I switched to my messaging app. As I opened the message and read over the words on the screen.

The fact that Alder, my oldest brother and the man who basically ran this town, the one who had asked me to stay at his house with his girl this past weekend while he'd been away, had sent me a note saying nothing more than *"We need to chat—I'll meet you at the bar this morning"* only reminded me I'd forgotten to put the razor back. Only brought back all the dread I'd felt when I'd noticed. Those twelve words stole every bit of my balance and left me with nothing but what felt like a steel band around my chest.

"Shit."

"What?" Elijah asked, suddenly sounding nervous. "Everything okay?"

I headed down the hall, unable to stop myself. Not even trying. "Alder texted. He wants to meet at the bar for a chat."

"Tell the all-powerful Alder to kiss your ass," Lainie said. I shook my head, knowing she couldn't see it but too focused on the bathroom door to say anything. I couldn't have forgotten. I remembered putting the razor in the right spot, but what if I was wrong? What if my brain had decided to fill in a gap and make me think I'd put the razor away when I really hadn't? It used to happen all the time with my wallet—I'd swear I had put it in my pocket but not be able to find it when I needed it. What if I'd left that razor on the counter and only *thought* I'd hung it on the stand? What if I only thought I'd turned off the stove or used soap on the plates? I remembered, but what if...

I nearly sighed when I turned on the bathroom light and saw my razor exactly where it should have been. Sitting inside the wooden holder. The one that had taken about twelve hours to make out of a piece of beetle kill pine far too damaged by the insects plaguing the mountain for any other use.

Right spot. All good.

"It's no big deal," I said, whether comforting my siblings or myself, I couldn't have said. "It's fine, really. He just got back from Vegas yesterday, so I'm sure he wants to go over plans for the mill and town. I'll talk with him and see what's up."

"Vegas?" Lainie asked, sounding just as shocked as I'd been when Alder had told me his plans. "Why the hell was he in Vegas? Did he elope with that woman?"

Shye. And definitely not, seeing as how I'd been the one guarding her while he was gone. "No, just took a few days away with Deacon. He said he needed to recharge."

Liar, liar, pants on fire. Alder didn't recharge in places like Vegas. If he'd needed a break, he would have taken Shye up into the mountains for a few days of quiet. I couldn't even picture Alder on the Strip.

Apparently, neither could Lainie. "Well, that's one big steaming pile of bullshit."

Probably.

Ever the calm and steady force in our lives, Elijah didn't comment on the absurdity of Alder vacationing in a place like Las Vegas. He simply said, "Whatever he needs, be careful. I know you guys have a lot going on out there."

Understatement. What we had was a motorcycle club trying to kill us all and take over the town so they could manufacture meth in our woods. Talk about not normal.

A quick glance at the clock on the stove had me moving a little faster. "I will, but I have to go or I'll be late to work. Talk to you tomorrow."

"Yeah. Okay. Text me later."

"Me too," Lainie hollered just before I tapped the screen to disconnect the call. And then I stood in the hallway, and I tried to catch my breath.

Normal.

Totally normal.

Everything was utterly normal.

So why did it feel as if the earth was about to go through a major shift?

After a handful of days living out at Alder's place to guard his girlfriend while he went out and did...whatever it was he'd done, I needed to go back to work. Back to the bar where I made sure shit ran smoothly. Where order and structure could be found in liquor bottles and glassware. I needed to go back to work where I belonged, and I would. This day would not go off the rails unless I let it.

I still checked on that damned razor three times before I walked out the front door and headed for my truck.

———

The Jury Room sat on the edge of town, right off the highway that cut Justice in half. There was a small roadside motel attached—the kind of place you could rent for an hour or a month. Your choice. Deacon Manns, former Army Special Forces officer and best friend of my oldest brother Alder, owned the place. He ran a tight ship, demanding a lot of his employees but giving just as much as he asked from us.

Deacon had hired me at a point when no one else in town would even look at me. Good folk didn't really want to support a drug-dealing ex-con, after all. Deacon had, though. He'd helped me figure out the rituals I needed to work through every day as a free man with a mental cage, too. He'd dragged my ass to NA meetings when I'd felt too weak to force myself to go and patted me on the back when I'd made the right decisions and stayed strong. He was another brother to me, and I owed him everything.

But it wasn't Deacon who caught my attention when I walked into the bar. It was my brother Alder. And his smile. His huge grin. *What the hell?*

"You see this shit?" Deacon asked, pointing at a grinning Alder. "What the fuck is wrong with his face?"

Those two might as well have been an old married couple—stuck together forever but not letting the other get away with anything.

"I don't know, boss. I've never seen the man so... Are you *happy?*"

"No, you jackasses. I'm engaged."

Well, shit. My own grin couldn't have been stopped. Smart man to lock down a girl like Shye, and smart girl to see how much my brother loved her and not want to let that go. "Congratulations to you both."

Deacon grabbed a bottle from the cabinet below the bar.

The one where he kept the good stuff we never actually sold. "Well hell, man. I just figured you'd gotten a good slap and tickle or something. Engaged...tied down...locked up with the old ball and chain." He shook his head in an almost solemn sort of way. "This calls for a memorial toast."

Deacon poured two glasses of scotch then grabbed a rocks glass and filled it with ginger ale. For me. I'd never been a drinker, but there was no sense in tempting the beast within me. I accepted the drink with a nod of thanks.

My boss held up his glass. "To my best friend, the brother I never wanted, and the latest victim of a good woman with big enough blinders on not to notice all your ugly bits. May your marriage be a happy one."

We all sipped our drinks, Alder still grinning around the rim of his glass. I couldn't blame him. Shye, his new fiancée, was a good woman. A great one, really. Pretty and kind, she'd been a waitress at the truck stop in Rock Falls since she'd moved to town. At least until trouble had come calling for her in the form of that murderous motorcycle club. Same one that wanted to turn Justice into the meth-making capital of Colorado. They'd burned down her trailer before we'd even known they'd hit town. Luckily for Shye, Alder'd been in love with her since the first time he'd met her. He'd taken her in, protected her, and now he would be marrying her.

Smart, smart man.

"So, how soon until this shindig happens?" I asked.

Alder's grin grew impossibly wider. "One month."

"A month?" Deacon said, nearly choking on his scotch. "Fuck, man. She saving the pussy until you put a ring on it or something?"

Alder threw a coaster at the man. "Don't be a jackass, jackass.

My girl said she wanted this to happen quickly, and I'm good with that. I'd marry her tonight if she'd let me."

"You're locking that down."

"Completely."

"Smart man," I said. "So, what do you need from me?" Because he needed something. This wasn't a social call or a chance to share the good news. He could have done that over the phone. Making sure I'd be at the bar meant there was more to his visit.

Alder lived up to my assumptions. "I need everyone to step up. We might be getting a visit from the national head of the Soul Suckers, and I don't want any sort of shit heading Shye's way."

Motherfu—

Deacon knocked on the bar top, giving me a weighted look. "What the kid said. Whatever you need, man. You've got us."

"Yeah," I said. Trying hard to keep my voice level. "Whatever you need."

Even though what he'd need would fly straight in the face of what I needed. His needs would bring more disruptions. Alder and this war with the motorcycle club had wreaked havoc on my normally orderly schedule, but I'd been handling the upheaval. Sort of. Barring the whole razor thing. That had come out of the blue, though. Security details and guarding Shye wouldn't. With enough planning, I could handle just about anything. Alder and Deacon were planners—I could do this.

"I knew I could count on both of you." Alder looked my way, his smile dropping a little. "Have you met our guests yet? Jinx and Parris?"

I hadn't. He'd told me two new people were in town, but they'd already been holed up at the motel when I'd stopped at the bar the night before. "No. Why?"

Deacon nodded toward the front of the bar. "Because you're about to."

The door swung open, and a man and woman walked through it. The guy reminded me of my brother Bishop—big, mean-looking, and full of the sort of swagger that came from military training. His high and tight haircut and the Semper Fi tattoo on his arm told me he was a Marine. The glower on his face told me he was trouble.

But the girl was the one who stole my attention. Short, blond, and curvy in all the right places, with ink and scars decorating her skin. Lots and lots of skin—those were the shortest damn shorts I'd ever seen in my life. Hell, even dressed in a gunnysack, she'd have stood out in a crowd. In a room of just four men, looking like sin and sex and temptation personified, she might as well have been standing under a spotlight. One that shone a light on every instinct I had for self-preservation.

Alder had said her name was Jinx, as in curse, and it fit her to a T.

That girl was trouble. Dangerous trouble.

And I couldn't tear my eyes away from her.

Chapter Two

JINX

Finding myself in a strange room—in a strange bed, even—without a stitch of clothing on my body had become far too normal at that point in my life. Which was a really fucked-up thought to wake up to.

I rolled over carefully, keeping my weight off my injured back. Letting the sheet tangle between my legs and the pale sunlight pull my mind from the dark place where it had wallowed overnight. Nightmares galore. They never ended, never gave me a break. I couldn't remember the last time I'd slept without having one.

I also couldn't get up—couldn't put my brain into gear or my muscles to use just yet. I needed to shake off the fear and the pain radiating off my body. It'd been a long night. Hell, if I were being honest with myself, I'd say it'd been a long few days. Maybe a long few years. And I wasn't anywhere close to being done with—

The door swung open, rebounding off the wall as I yelped and sat up. My back screamed in protest, the skin pulling tight and likely opening up one of the scabs there. Parris walked into my space just as he always did—as if he owned me. Which, technically, he might have. But that was a whole other shitshow I didn't have the energy to deal with.

"Get out." I tugged the sheet up my body, not really hiding much. The man had seen me naked before. He'd seen me a lot more naked than simply being without clothes, too.

"Get up," he said, just before he tossed some clothes on the bed. His eyes never left my face as he stood and waited for me to do what I'd been told. He crossed his thick arms over his broad chest when I didn't, making him look even more solid and wall-like than before. I'd once told my mom Parris reminded me of a tree. She'd said, *"No, honey. Trees stay still. They're tall and broad, visible from miles away. Parris is more like a shark—huge and dangerous and able to hide until it's too late to get away from him."*

She hadn't been wrong.

"Not happening." I flopped onto my stomach, tugging the sheet over my head. Keeping the fabric off my back and letting him see the damage that Soul Suckers crew had done. The ones Parris hadn't been quick enough to save me from. *Broken promises. All just broken promises.* "Get out. I can't deal with you today."

"I said get up."

"And I said no."

He yanked the sheet off the bed, leaving me with nothing to hide behind. Nothing to stop him from looking over every inch of me. Seeing every cut and scar. Every mark from the damage of the past few months. I lifted myself up, making sure he saw the slashes across my back, at the blood probably dripping there, before turning around and sitting up. Glaring at him.

"I need time to rest and heal. Or did you forget I was tied to a cross and whipped by your friend yesterday?"

His voice wasn't as rough when he said, "He wasn't my friend. And I know you need to heal—your back looks rough as fuck—but I brought you a dark shirt so you wouldn't..."

"Bleed through it and scare the locals," I said when he couldn't, unable to hide the sneer in my voice. "How thoughtful."

"Quit being a brat, Jinx. We've got shit to do."

We always had shit to do. Usually, it was the kind I didn't want to be involved in. Being under Parris' guard meant dealing with every sort of rider the Black Angels Motorcycle Club had to offer. Good and bad, leaning heavily on the bad. This time, though, we had new people around us. Non-club type people. Men who might be good, though the jury was still out on that. It was easy to fake being a decent human being for a day or so.

When Parris' glare grew too dark for me to ignore for another moment, I rose to my feet and stretched, making sure the man got a good, long look at the bloody mess of my back. At the slices that had burned and itched and ached all night long. At the punishment I'd received for his mistake. I found more than a small bit of satisfaction in the way Parris' jaw clenched and how he couldn't keep his eyes on the palette of blood and torment my back had become.

Good. "The only shit I need to do today is whatever Church tells me to."

That brought his attention back to me. "Church?"

"Yeah, you know. Deacon. Church."

He scoffed. "Jesus, Jinx."

"Heard that before." I grabbed the clothes he'd so generously thrown at me and tugged on a pair of shorts—the shortest damn Daisy Dukes I'd ever laid eyes on—and a shirt that had big block letters across the front, spelling out the word "savage" in capital letters. SAVAGE, as if with teeth. Fitting. I was feeling a little savage, even if I was way too underdressed for the weather outside. I was going to freeze—not that I'd tell Parris that. "What's so important that you have to come wake me up anyway?"

"We need to head over to the bar. See what sort of trouble these fuckers have gotten into already so I can figure out how to get them out of it." He handed me a toothbrush and travel-size toothpaste. "Here. Your church guy said the clothes and this was the best he could do for now."

I clutched that toothbrush in my hand, remembering the time I'd begged Parris for one. The time I'd been without for too many days to count because some club member had decided I didn't deserve to be clean. The time he'd picked me up off the floor and had brushed my teeth for me because the cuts on my arms—the ones his so-called brothers had given me—had hurt too much to move.

Still, I refused to be indebted to a man like Parris. "You don't need to take care of me."

"Yeah, kid, I do." He headed for the door, pausing as he swung it open. "I'll be outside. Move your ass—it's cold out there."

Then he was gone, and I was left wanting to throw something at his big, blocky head. I wasn't a kid. Not by a long shot, but Parris liked to toss words like that at me. Words that reminded me he'd known me when I *was* a kid. When I'd been too young and naïve, thinking he was a tree, big and safe to rest in the shadow of. Not old enough to see the shark before me, even with my mom warning me of what to expect.

There were days when I hated him more than I'd ever thought it was possible to hate another human being. Today was one of them.

Teeth brushed, face washed, and hair...well, sort of tamed, I headed into the cold to meet up with Mr. Shit To Do so we could walk across the parking lot to The Jury Room. Cute name for a dumpy-looking bar. No, that was wrong. Dumpy implied it was a shambles—the place looked clean and kept up, with rocks in the flower beds and actual windows in the walls instead of blacked-out, bulletproof glass. Even the front door to the bar seemed pristine, as if no one had ever kicked the thing or pushed on it with their keys in their hands. The slab of metal didn't have a scratch on it. The bar and motel didn't look like dumps. They looked cared for and clean, but poor. Simple in a way that implied better wasn't going to happen. Like the homes I'd grown up in.

God, I missed those trashy apartments and run-down rental houses. Or maybe, just maybe, I missed my mom. Which was not the path to go down right then.

Still, The Jury Room looked a lot better than places I'd been hanging out. And the men I'd met—the owner of the bar and his buddy who'd saved me from the hell I'd found myself in just twenty-four hours ago—they seemed better than the guys I'd been hanging around, too. Kinder. More honest.

Which made them dangerous. An unknown risk. I'd rather cling to the danger I knew.

"You sure about these guys?" I asked as Parris led me toward that way-too-perfect metal door. Just one flaw—it needed a dent or a scratch. Could it even be a bar if the door didn't have a little grime on it? If I weren't about to die of hypothermia, I might have worked out a plan to make that door more normal. Maybe. Right then, all I could think about was that my back felt as if it was on fire and my arms were going to fall off if I didn't get them warmed up soon.

Note to self: find a winter coat. And pants. Pants would be good.

Parris paused when he reached the front walk of the bar, giving me a chance to catch up with him. Pinning me with a solid glare when I didn't move fast enough. "As sure as I can be. We've got a few mutual friends I trust with my life, and they say these guys are legit. Don't fuck with them."

I held up my hands. "I've got no intentions to. I only want to make sure I'm not walking into what I just got pulled out of."

He grunted, heading for the door again. "Let's hope they're better than that."

Sure. Hope. That and a banana would get me...nothing but a banana. And I hated bananas.

Parris opened the door and walked inside as if he'd been there a thousand times. Maybe he had—it wasn't as if I could keep track of the man.

I followed, relishing the warmth of the place and keeping close to Parris' hip. I might not always like the guy, but he had a wicked fighting style and an annoying need to defend me that had come in handy once or twice. Bonus points for the fact that he was big enough I could practically hide behind him. And right then, as three men turned to look me over in varying degrees of interest and concern, I felt the need to hide.

Church was there along with tree guy—the big boss man. Alder, if I remembered right. A new guy stood nearby, tall and lean with straw-like blond hair cropped close to his head and blue-gray eyes that reminded me of the sky right before a storm came. Eyes that were taking in every inch of me. And there were a lot of inches to see—damn shorts might as well have been underwear, which I didn't have on because I had no clothes of my own with me. I should have been grateful church guy had been able to find anything at all for me on such short notice, but with Storm over there practically trying to absorb me with his look, grateful didn't come easy. Uncomfortable did. Scared did. Interest was a bad thing in my world. It was way better to be invisible. Storm had just made things clear—no way would I be invisible to him.

Trouble. That man was nothing but trouble.

"Good morning, sunshine," Church—Deacon—said, looking from me to Parris and back again. "I hope you slept well."

Parris took that one. "Slept fine. Thanks for the room."

"Plural." I shrugged when he shot me a glare. "Rooms. Plural. I got my own."

His growly voice deepened, a sure sign of his frustration with me. "Rooms. Thank you for the *rooms*."

Score one for Jinx in the pissing off Parris game.

Deacon either didn't notice Parris' crankiness or didn't care. "Well, I was happy to oblige. Can I get you anything to eat or drink?"

My stomach was practically eating itself, I was so hungry, but I'd learned a long time ago not to ask for anything I wasn't willing to earn. And since I still had no idea who these guys were, I kept my mouth shut. Parris wasn't so cautious.

"I'm fine, but maybe Jinx wants something. I don't think either of us had dinner."

"That's our fault," Alder said. Looking so damn tall and confident. This was the man in charge—I could sense it. "We were on a tight schedule to get back, so we didn't stop to eat. I'm sorry about that, Jinx."

Apologies were really rare in my world. Like, really, really rare. As in nonexistent. It took me a few seconds to remember how to respond to one. "Oh no, you're fine."

Storm cocked his head, his brow furrowing. "You're Midwestern."

No question. No doubt either. All said in a voice that could have been made of warm caramel or something equally as thick and smooth. "No, but my mom was from Wisconsin... How'd you know?"

Everyone in the room focused on Storm, something that would have made me want to squirm. He didn't seem the least bit uncomfortable, though.

"Only in the Midwest do people reply 'oh no, you're fine' to an apology."

That couldn't be true, but I didn't call him out on it. Parris opened his mouth, though.

"She also says *ope* when she bumps into things. And pop— she always says pop."

"What the fuck's a pop?" Deacon asked, looking all sorts of confused. "Do I need to learn a whole new language?"

Meanwhile, Storm hadn't stopped looking at me. Inspecting me. His attention both lit a spark inside of me and turned my blood cold. The clothing I wore left little to the imagination. My scars were on full display, the remnants and memories of the past year of living a false life right there for him to see. To judge.

I couldn't take it, so I shifted my focus to Deacon. "Pop is soda, but I'm actually smart enough to switch to whatever other people say. Parris just likes to be an asshole sometimes."

"Only sometimes?" the man in question asked, obviously making fun of himself.

"It's really a permanent condition, but we don't like to remind you of that. Gotta have hope for a cure, you know?"

Deacon huffed a laugh. "Cure for being an asshole. Hell, if

you ever find one, let me know. This guy—" he hooked a thumb toward Alder "—has been needing a fix for a decade or so."

"Point that finger at yourself, son."

But it was Storm who took the next swing. "Alder's kind of assholery is genetic, I'm sorry to say. There is no cure."

The weight of the pause that followed seemed pregnant, as if no one had expected him to say that. No one had expected him to be sarcastic.

"Well, I'll be damned," Deacon said, grinning. "The kid's getting feisty with us. I like it."

Alder frowned. "I don't. The last thing I need is a Deacon-copy walking around busting my balls. Speaking of which—"

"You have to go home and get your balls busted by your pretty new fiancée?"

If looks could kill, Deacon would have been toast for that one, with Alder as the man behind the mission. "Fuck off. I need to get to work. Shouldn't you all do the same?"

"Definitely." Parris, who'd been broody and silent as he was wont to do, tucked his phone into his pocket and headed for the door. "You good on your own for a bit, Jinx?"

As if. "Yeah. Of course."

"I've got her," Deacon said, giving me a wink. "No promising you can have her back, though."

"She's not mine."

"Only in the literal sense." I shrugged as Storm and Deacon looked my way. "He bought me fair and square. Isn't that right, Parris?"

He ignored that question. "Behave. And try not to cause any trouble."

Again...as if. "Yes, sir."

Deacon waited until the door closed behind the hulking biker before asking, "You okay, Jinx?"

The concern in his voice nearly undid me. Nearly made me open my mouth and spout truths. Lies were easier, though. And safer. "Totally. Put me to work, Church. I'm ready."

He held my gaze, staring hard. His face impassive and unreadable. I could play that game too, though. Could lock my emotions deep down into a place no one could use them against me and put up a front. I'd been doing it for years. I was a damn expert at it.

Proven when Deacon nodded once, accepting my lie. "Church. I like it. Okay. Well, first, you need a better shirt...and maybe some pants. Not sure why Parris grabbed those. Aren't you cold?"

"I'm fine," I said even though the cold had definitely gotten to me.

Storm pinned me in his gaze. "Somehow, I doubt that."

I didn't even get a chance to answer before Deacon said, "I figured. We've got other clothes in the back for when accidents happen or customers have wardrobe malfunctions in the bar."

I couldn't just let that go by. "People get naked here often?"

"Often enough to need to keep a stash of clothes," Deacon said. "There's not a lot in terms of sweaters or long pants, but I'll get some for you on my next trip to Rock Falls. Take what you want for now. Finn can help you find everything."

So, Storm was Finn. Like a fish. Fish guy.

Storm fit him better.

"C'mon," Finn said, tipping his head toward a door behind the bar. "I'll get you set up."

I followed him through the door without thinking about where it led, a mistake on my part. Hallways tended to be traps in my world—dark, quiet spaces where bad things happened. Could happen. Always seemed to happen. And I didn't know Finn from anyone.

As the walls seemed to close in around me and the shadows crept closer, ice spread into my chest and up my spine while my vision blurred. *Not now, not here. Don't panic. I am okay. I am safe. I am—*

"Hey." Finn's soft voice in the dark stole my breath and made me jerk backward. "Are you all right?"

"Fine." The word exploded from my mouth, an almost instinctual response to a question that could reveal a weakness I didn't have the luxury of showing. "Where are we going? And why are there no lights?"

He stayed quiet for a long moment, watching me. Shadows hiding his eyes from me even though I could feel them. Then he pointed to a door. "There're lights in there along with the clothes. Go ahead. I'll wait out here for you."

I wanted to say thank you, but words were hard, and my emotions felt too raw, so instead, I slipped past him and slammed my hand against the wall, trying to find the light switch. After five or six pats, Finn leaned in and grabbed a thin chain hanging over my head, pulling hard. Flooding the room with light.

"Still okay?" he asked.

"Yeah. Fine."

But I wasn't—not by a long shot. Ink. The man had ink on his arm—a tattoo I'd seen a time or two before. One that held meanings to certain kinds of people who'd been in specific situations. The cobweb around his elbow was also a trendy design, but not usually in such dark colors. Not usually so unrefined and heavy. The kind of tattoo Finn wore was one I had experience with. The sort that implied he'd lived a life that didn't fit what I thought I knew about him.

Had he been to prison?

That wasn't a question I wanted to ask, though, so I kept

quiet as he shut the door behind me, giving me privacy, it seemed. Or trying to get away from me. Most women didn't exactly have panic attacks from walking down a hall or being unable to find a light switch. I wasn't most women.

I was a little bit broken.

Chapter Three

FINN

Wait. Alder brought another woman home with him? From Vegas?"

If Lainie's surprise had been any more evident, it would have reached through the phone and grabbed me by the shoulder.

"Technically, I guess." I poked at the remnants of my breakfast—the one I'd eaten while talking with Elijah before he'd had to leave for work. "There's a guy with her."

"What's big brother doing? Picking up strays?"

"Lainie." The harshness of my voice took me by surprise, but her insinuating Jinx was a stray didn't sit right with me. "They seem nice enough, and it looks like the girl needed a little help to get on her feet. Just because you hate our brother doesn't make him some sort of devil."

Silence. Lainie didn't like talking about Alder. Bishop either, really. At least not unless she was complaining about something regarding them. Then she could talk all day. I wasn't in the mood for it, though.

"Fine," she finally said, sounding anything but fine. "What are you carving this week?"

Carving. As in wood. My stress reliever and the only hobby I'd ever really been able to keep up with. "I'm making a statue of a man and a woman for Alder and Shye. Something they could use as a cake topper if they want or just stick on a shelf somewhere."

"I still can't believe he's getting married."

"You should come home. Spend more time with Shye. You'd like her."

"Does she kick Alder in the knees every few hours?"

Hardly. "No, but she makes him smile. A lot. It's grinapalooza over here."

I chuckled as she laughed, moving to wash the dishes. I couldn't concentrate this morning. My razor had been in the right spot, my house as clean and orderly as I'd expected it to be, but something had felt off all night and morning. Something had been missing.

I didn't want to think about what that could mean.

"Okay, Finn. I need to get to work. You steady?"

She meant was I craving something. Was I struggling. Was I likely to start using today. Probably not. "I'm good. Be careful out there."

"You too. Love you."

"Love you too." I ended the call and headed for the sink, ready to wash up and get my day started even if my thoughts were stuck in a loop. One I hadn't been prepared for.

Half an hour later, I turned onto the highway toward The Jury Room, trying hard to focus on the drive. The scenery. The sound of the wheels eating up the concrete and the music playing softly in the background. Anything but Jinx and those nearly gray eyes looking my way.

I failed miserably.

Elijah and Lainie had both asked me about the newcomer—the girl Alder had brought back from Vegas. I'd struggled to answer because the words wouldn't come. Anything I'd have told them would have been too simple, too easy and light. Jinx couldn't be described with mere words. Well, except for one.

Disruptive.

The only word that came to mind when I thought about Jinx—and I thought way too much about the woman—was disruptive. But how could I explain that to my sister and brother? You couldn't tell someone about a woman like Jinx—they had to experience her. Just like I had.

All day—every damn minute yesterday—she'd taunted and teased, directing conversations with snark and wit when she'd wanted to. Almost disappearing into herself when she hadn't. If I had to guess yesterday, I'd have said she didn't like talking about herself. But after a night of not being able to get that blond hair or those smoky eyes out of my mind, I had come to the conclusion that not liking to talk about herself wasn't quite right. Her aversion went a smidge deeper. She didn't like revealing anything *about* herself.

Jinx had worked my entire shift at The Jury Room, inventorying the bar and learning how to place orders. She'd been a good student—attentive and interested in what Deacon was teaching her. But I'd seen that veil she kept between her and everyone else, had noticed it drop into place whenever anyone—boss, customer, man, woman—asked her something personal. That sweet smile she gave the customers walking through the door at the bar, the front of confidence she'd throw out there, pretending to be all loud and brash.

Fake.

Others might have bought it, but I didn't. I'd watched her snap at herself when she couldn't get something right. Had seen that wide smile fall into a scowl when someone greeted her in more of a flirtatious way. I'd watched that confidence crumble when she'd thought no one was looking. But I'd looked. I couldn't stop looking, it seemed. Jinx was hiding something, and it had eaten at me all night not to know what. Which had led to another problem.

Thoughts of Jinx and her secrets had come with thoughts of bending her over and smacking that tight little ass. Of pulling her into my lap and feeling her weight on my cock. Thinking of Jinx had led to jacking off to thoughts of Jinx, which had led to more guilt and confusion than I cared to admit to. I hadn't thought about a woman in that way in a long time. Not a specific one, at least. Sure, I masturbated while imagining a partner with me, but they were always slightly blurry in my head, leaning toward looking like some random celebrity. Jinx wasn't random and wasn't a celebrity, and she hadn't been blurry at all. Those damn shorts she'd worn the day before needed to be burned so she could never wear them again.

I walked into the bar with my head still buzzing, unsure if I wanted her to be there or not. Unsure what I should do about this certainty that Jinx wasn't who she'd said she was and my attraction to her. Both seemed far too dangerous to sit on.

Deacon met me at the door. "Good afternoon, sunshine. You ready for an exciting day slinging beer and serving burgers?"

I'd once wanted to be a doctor. It was moments like this that reminded me how far from that idea I'd slipped. "Absolutely."

I turned to head for the back room—because today was Wednesday, and that meant I needed to check-in yesterday's liquor orders and make sure the back room was stocked—but Deacon cut me off.

"She already did it."

"Did what?"

"The inventory of the back. Putting the orders away. She did it before I could stop her."

My hands itched to work with something, and my chest grew tight. Those were my tasks, my job. Counting bottles in the back was how I started every Wednesday shift.

"So...what do you want me to do?"

"Keep an eye on the kitchen for now." Deacon eyed me hard, looking more concerned than I wanted him to. "I'll make sure to separate tasks for the two of you so there's no overlap."

As if I couldn't function without my routines. Which... sometimes, I couldn't. The razor yesterday, the way I'd forgotten to rinse down the shower this morning and had needed to spend an extra twenty minutes washing the walls because the idea of soap scum made my skin too tight, how my breakfast call to Elijah had been late and he'd had to drop off early, leaving me to chat with Lainie alone. Routines and rituals ruled my days, and I hated to have them disrupted. But I'd have to deal with this particular change, this Jinx in my space. At least for today. "Yeah. Great. That's fine. Just let me know if you need anything."

"Sure thing, kid."

He strolled off as if he hadn't just set my world on a different axis. Me? I headed for the bar. For Jinx. The girl wore a long-sleeved shirt today, covering the scars I'd gotten an eyeful of the day before. I knew cutting scars for what they were, knew the rings around her wrists were from restraints, too. Hell, I'd even spotted and catalogued the burn marks on her upper arms. I'd noticed, logged, and memorized every one.

I hadn't asked about them, though.

Today, those arms were covered, but her stomach was on full display as she'd apparently cut off the bottom of the shirt. Ridges peeked from under the shadow of the fabric as she stretched and twisted, as she glided along the length of the bar, wiping down the top. Looking completely at home. And sexy. My God, did she look sexy.

"Morning, Fish," she called as I approached, tossing me a casual sort of smile. One that didn't quite reach her eyes.

Calm down. Breathe. Don't get a hard-on at work. "The name's Finn."

"I know." She raised an eyebrow, one side of her mouth ticking up just a smidge more than the other. "Want a beer?"

Yes. Always. For fuck's sake, yes. A beer, then a joint, then... well, more. Every day I wanted to drown myself in the chemicals that would make me feel then take all the hurt away. And every day I denied that need.

"No thanks. I'm good."

"Suit yourself."

Easy. Simple. She didn't know I was an addict, that I'd made too many mistakes to count. That I'd been in prison. She knew nothing about me, and she showed no interest in finding out. I was a non-issue to her. A thought that hurt a little more than it should have.

I beelined for the kitchen, needing to get away from her. Half wishing she'd never stepped foot in Justice. Half wishing she'd show me something real.

"How many days?" Parris stalked the length of the prep counter, his phone tucked against his ear and a vicious snarl on his face. He caught me watching him but didn't stop, just gave me a head nod before saying, "There're too many opportunities for collateral damage in town. We'll need to deal with it on the road."

The man talked like my brothers did, like Alder and Bishop, even Deacon and Gage. All former military, which meant Parris likely was as well. His Semper Fi tattoo and all that added into the mix meant he was likely an ex-Marine. Though Camden—who'd joined the Marines while I'd been incarcerated—would have said, once a Marine, always a Marine, so maybe the ex wasn't fitting. Those sorts of details muddled my mind. I'd been stuck in a cage many of the years my brothers and friends had served—seven of them. Three years using, seven spent inside, only five out. I had a long way to go still in terms of making up for lost time. A damn long way.

I changed direction, heading for the back office. Needing a quiet place to settle my thoughts. The entire bar, what had become my second home, suddenly felt different. As if I didn't belong there anymore. All because two people had infiltrated it.

When I turned the corner into the room Deacon used for bar business, I found my boss sitting in his chair tossing a red ball in the air. No, wait. Not a ball. An apple.

"Don't you know you shouldn't play with your food?"

He cocked an eyebrow my way. "Don't you know not to sneak up on a man when he's alone?"

"Yeah. I do. Learned that one pretty damn quick."

Deacon's face didn't change—he didn't look at me with disgust or pity. Didn't try to push me to forget or talk about those years spent learning entirely new rules and ways to survive in a ten-by-ten cell. He knew more about that time in my life than most people.

He was also really fucking good at giving people the privacy they needed. "Parris still jawing away on the phone?"

Subject change: achieved. "He was when I came through the kitchen. Why? You need him?"

"Nah, just wanted to chat for a few. I'm worried about Jinx."

Every instinct in my body lit up, as if I needed to run, fight, protect, and defend—all at once. Funny thing was, I couldn't tell if I was supposed to run away from Jinx or toward her; defend myself from her or jump between her and whatever was coming. Because something was coming for her —of that, I had no doubt. Alder and Deacon had shown up with her out of nowhere, and no one would forget about a woman like Jinx.

"What's going on?" I managed to keep my voice steady for those three words, managed to banish thoughts of the little blonde needing me. My sort of trouble was the last thing she needed.

"I want to make sure she's comfortable at the motel, but if I ask *her* that, she'll say she's fine. She's always *fine*." He tossed that apple again, staring up toward the ceiling with a scowl on his face. "I fucking hate the word fine."

"Maybe she really is fine." She wasn't, but I wasn't about to tear away that veil she relied on. Not just yet.

But Deacon had a way of seeing through things even better than I could. "Or maybe she's never learned to ask for better than the scraps people have handed her."

That... Yeah, okay. I'd met people like that. Had known men inside who were grateful for the bullshit life the state had given us. For three meals a day and a place to lay their head down, even if the cells were dirty, the building infested with rats, and the other inmates a danger we couldn't control. The idea of Jinx being like one of those guys, the thought that she could possibly be so simple, didn't fit in my head. Those puzzle pieces didn't go together.

"That's not Jinx's issue."

Deacon whipped his head in my direction, the apple gripped tight in his hand. Stationary. The words hung between us. I hadn't meant to say them, hadn't even given them any thought, but no way could I—or would I—take them back.

"What's her issue, then?" Deacon asked, still staring hard. Watching me.

"I don't know." I didn't, but I knew that wasn't it. "I've barely talked to her, but I have a feeling she'd ask for what she needed."

"Huh."

That single syllable sounded more dangerous than it should have. "What, huh?"

"I've just never seen you interested in a girl before. It's...different."

"I'm not interested in her."

"Could have fooled me."

"Apparently I did, because I'm not interested in her." Not her blond hair, her scars, her curves, her soft smile when she thought no one noticed...none of it. "I don't date."

"You say that." He tossed the apple again. Still paying more attention to me than to his edible projectile. "Someday, maybe you'll stop punishing yourself."

That day felt a long fucking way off. "Someday, maybe I won't deserve the punishment."

Deacon sat up with a sigh and rested his elbows on the desk, looking equal parts bartender and therapist. "You're allowed to have a life, Finn. Past mistakes don't negate that truth."

"I have one. A nice, calm one. I don't need chaos brought into it."

"Life *is* chaos. And you deserve to have one."

"Yeah. Okay. I'll get right on that." I took a breath, nearly apologizing for my sarcasm. But not. This was Deacon—he hadn't known me back before the drugs. Hadn't decided how my life should be and then watched me destroy those ideas in a storm of bad decisions and even worse luck. He'd only ever known ex-con, addict Finn. That fact actually made our relationship easier. "I'm heading over to The Baker's Cottage to see if Katie's got any soup ready."

"It's not Thursday."

"What?"

"It's not Thursday. You buy her cream of chicken every Thursday, but she won't have that today."

He was right on both counts—I went to the restaurant in town every single Thursday for that cream of chicken soup. I also went to the diner on Saturday afternoons for huckleberry pie and ate spaghetti on Monday nights. Structure, rigidity, attention to the details—that's what had gotten me through treatment. What had helped me go from addict to...whatever I was now. Former addict? Recovering addict? Neither felt as if they fit, but I wasn't using, so maybe they were right and I was the one who was wrong. I was the one who couldn't fit in the definition.

"I just want soup," I said, the argument weak.

Deacon didn't push, though. Simply reached into his back pocket and pulled out a fifty-dollar bill. "Why don't you ask Jinx what she'd like and grab her something too?"

I didn't take the money. I couldn't even look at it without my chest tightening in a way that felt an awful lot like humiliation. "I can buy her lunch."

"I'm her boss. Just take it."

Fuck and no. "I've got it."

Deacon smiled, the lift of his brow a warning. "That's what I thought."

"What?"

"You don't like the idea of another man paying for her."

"No," I spat, the word exploding from my mouth. "That's not what this is."

"Sure, it is. Your pride won't take that hit."

"Shut up, Deacon."

"You shut up."

"No, you shut up."

"Why don't you both shut up?" Jinx said, strolling into the office and frowning at the two of us. "What the hell is going on here?"

"Nothing," I said, refusing to look her in the eye. "We were just talking about lunch."

"Oh good, that's why I came back here." She fidgeted for a second, a minor movement most people wouldn't have noticed, but I did. "Do you mind if I make myself a burger or something? I can pay for it out of my tips."

Asking for what she needed—I'd been right about that aspect of her, at least. Deacon looked me square in the eye, eyebrows raised. Questioning. And fuck if the man wasn't going to win this one.

"I was just about to head to the restaurant in town to grab food," I said, taking out my phone and tapping to open the browser app. "I'll pull up the menu, and you can pick something."

"But we can make food here."

"Shitty food."

"I resemble that remark," Deacon said, finally sitting back in his chair.

"You can resemble whatever you want, but burgers and fries do not make for a well-rounded diet. You need to eat some vegetables."

He huffed. "Sure thing, Mom."

"Be thankful I'm not your mom. I'd have drowned you at birth."

"Are you two always like this?" Jinx asked.

"Yes," we both replied at once.

"Good to know. So, food. Yeah. I'm in on that. I can chip in a few bucks from last night's tips."

My gut burned, and my chest tightened again. Like the fucking bastard he was, Deacon stared at me, waiting. Giving me just enough rope to hang myself.

And I did. "No, you keep that. I've got this one."

Jinx looked a bit skeptical, while Deacon suddenly grinned like the cat who ate the...whatever bird that saying mentioned. Me? I sighed and accepted the fact that something about this girl had thrown me for a loop. One my mind apparently had taken a liking to and wanted to stay on. One that was likely going to make me throw up at some point.

It was going to be a long fucking week.

Chapter Four

JINX

There was nothing quite as sad as watching the last patron of the night stumble their way out of the bar. Headed for a hookup, recovering from a breakup, or chasing something they certainly would never find at the bottom of a bottle of whiskey —no matter the reason, the view always sat heavy on my heart. That was the only bad thing about working at The Jury Room. The customers were nice enough, everyone seemed relatively respectful, and Deacon kept a tight rein on his clientele, so things never got out of hand. A huge change from other places I'd worked.

Another change? The owner didn't try to force me to my knees at the end of the night. Didn't demand I show my gratitude for him allowing me to work there. Deacon wasn't that way, wasn't the type of man to take what wasn't offered. He didn't need to be either. Kind, funny, confident—he might as well have been an example of the type of guy to chase after. He was a total hottie in that slightly older, got-his-shit-together sort of way too. A true catch.

Deacon didn't catch my eye, though.

That honor went to the man washing glasses in the back.

The one I'd been trying to avoid since he'd popped into my life.

The one I was about to have to work next to as we closed down the bar for the night.

Once I'd locked the front door and turned off the neon lights decorating the windows, I headed to the kitchen. Arms on full display, Finn stood hunched over the sink, viciously working the glassware over the brush that scrubbed the insides clean. Up and down, up and down, wrists strong, forearms flexing, biceps bulging. I'd seen him mopping, sweeping, scrubbing, and now washing dishes. Lord help me, but a man who knew how to clean was hot.

Time to distract myself. "Need some help, Fish?"

"It's Finn."

"I know."

"Yeah, I know you do." He finished loading the glasses into the racks and slid them into the industrial washer before turning my way. "Why do you do that?"

I tossed the bar towels into the basket for the laundry service. "Do what?"

"Call people by the wrong name."

No one had ever asked me that before, so it took a few seconds to put together an answer. A mostly true one. "There's nothing more dangerous to the men I usually deal with than a smart woman paying attention. I learned quick to play dumb. Why do you?"

"Why do I what?"

"Call people by the wrong name. You called that Mack guy Mike like four times tonight."

He turned away, wiping down the sink and avoiding my eyes. "My memory's not so great."

"Have an accident or something?"

"Or something."

That tone, the emotions behind the two words—hurt, anger, embarrassment—I'd heard it before. Too many times to count. Heard it from my own mom before she'd disappeared on me. Heard it from patrons at bars I'd worked at and from friends I'd made who'd lost their way. The prison tattoo, the forgetfulness, the orderly way he moved through his tasks—Finn fit the pattern to a T.

And I was an idiot. "How long?"

He glanced up, brow furrowed as he asked, "How long what?"

"How long were you using?" No scars on his arms, no telltale burns on his fingers, and he certainly didn't seem the coke type. "Meth, right?"

"Yeah." He tossed his rag into the service basket and leaned a hip against the counter, looking at me with more inquisitiveness than I was comfortable with. "How'd you know?"

Because my entire life has revolved around other peoples' drug habits. "My mom uses."

Present tense, not past. My word choice made my heart stutter. I shrugged and turned my back on Finn, needing a second to pull myself together. To push down the grief and fear that seemed to strangle me on a daily basis. The obsession that I knew was destroying my life but that I couldn't let go of. Bury it all good and deep so no one else would see it. No one else would know.

Sneaky, sneaky, Jinxy girl.

Before Finn could try to dig any deeper into my past, Deacon exploded into the kitchen, tossing his keys in the air and looking far too excited for two in the morning. "You guys about done? I'd like to get out of here before the sun comes up."

That was...new. "What's the hubbub, Church? Got someplace to be?"

Finn chuckled and hung up his apron. "He's got a date."

"Like...with a woman? Or are you and the big boss man finally cementing your place in each other's lives?"

"Oh, Jinx—my place in Alder's life was cemented decades ago. But yes, I have a date. With a woman. And I'd like to get to it."

I nodded to Finn. "It's well past the dating hour. Sounds more like a booty call."

"Totally," Finn said, coming up to stand beside me. Two against one. Game on. "Are you sure this is a date?"

Deacon looked ready to fight us both. "It's a fucking date."

"Oh, a *fucking* date." I nudged Finn in the side. "So there will be fucking going on."

"Seems likely."

"For the record, it's just a date with a friend. And I should fire both your asses," Deacon said as he turned and headed toward the front of the bar. Not that I was about to let him escape so easily.

"Just a friend? Is there kissing involved, because that's a good sign it's more than friendship."

"There's been kissing," Finn said, right on my heels. "There's definitely been kissing."

Deacon slammed through the front door harder than he needed to. "Fucking fired. The two of you."

Winter air bit into my skin as I followed him outside, not that I was about to stop. Never let it be said that I didn't know how to push someone too far. Or sing them there. "Kissing friends are the best friends. Deacon and..."

Finn jumped right in. "Felicia."

"Felicia, sittin' in a tree..."

"Fired," Deacon hollered before jumping into his truck and backing out of his spot. He paused only long enough to roll down the window and yell, "But you'd better lock the fucking bar up before you leave for good."

Finn waved. "See you in the morning, boss."

"Fired!" And then Deacon was gone, heading off to who knew where to do who knew what with some chick named Felicia. And leaving me alone with Finn for the very first time. In the cold. Without my coat.

Crap. "So..."

"Inside first. It's fucking freezing."

Totally. I rushed back inside the bar, my fingers twisted together and goose bumps all over my skin. I needed a few minutes to warm up before I braved the walk across the lot. Even with the winter coat someone had dropped off for me, I'd likely freeze. I'd grown up in the desert—cold and I didn't get along.

Silence didn't like me much either. Which was why I couldn't help but ask, "What do you usually do after a shift?"

Because there was no way a person could fall right to sleep after working in a bar all night. It simply wasn't done. Everyone I'd ever worked with had had some sort of post-work life.

"Go home. Watch a movie. Eat ice cream."

That sounded...almost blissful. "Ice cream?"

"I reward myself with a treat for making it through the day."

"I like ice cream and rewards."

"Yeah." He ran a hand over the back of his neck, looking anxious, and I suddenly felt like the world's biggest loser.

"Oh god, I'm sorry." I shook my head and laughed, trying

hard not to sound as awkward as I felt. "That wasn't an invitation. I'm perfectly capable of getting my own ice cream as a reward." Without a car, that was unlikely. Finn knew that.

"I guess we could—"

"No," I said, putting my hands up and shaking my head. "That was super rude of me. There's no need to accommodate me just because I decided to insert myself into your life."

"It's okay. I just... I don't usually have people over." His teeth appeared, embedding themselves in the soft, pink flesh of his bottom lip for a second. "The truck stop has the best ice cream sundaes around, though. Not that there are a lot of options, especially not this late at night."

"Justice does seem to be lacking in business open past dinnertime."

"The whole county is lacking those." He huffed, his expression determined. "Want to take a drive with me?"

"You don't have to—"

"I know. The not-having-to part. This isn't some sort of pity invite, Jinx."

Well then. "The best ice cream, huh?"

"I like ice cream—you can trust me when I say this sundae is the best."

Temptation, thy name was Finn. "How can I turn down the best?"

We locked up the bar, grabbing our coats from the hooks by the door, and walked outside together, him leading me to an old pickup truck I'd seen in the back lot a handful of times. The inside was neat as a pin, and the engine started without a second of hesitation. Well cared for, Finn's vehicle. Which didn't surprise me. What did was the music that came blaring through the speakers.

"Never took you for a Parrot Head."

Finn turned onto the highway, staring diligently at the road ahead. "I'm not. Not really. I like the idea of life on a beach, though."

"Sand and surf and all that?"

"Yeah. And no snow. I'm anti-snow."

I pointed out the window where winter seemed about to explode all over the mountains. "I hate to tell you, but you're sort of living in the wrong area if you hate snow."

"Hence why I like the idea of beach life."

"You can't live forever with your toes in the sand."

"Sounds like you have some experience."

"Just...something my mom used to say." When we had still lived in Vegas. When I'd had no worries except what time I could sneak out of the house to meet my friends. When I'd known the guys on bikes coming around but not how much trouble they would bring with them. Seemed like a lifetime ago, felt more like twenty.

We made it to the truck stop without issue, both of us ordering sundaes from the dessert menu instead of actual food. If I was going to do bad things, I would do them to the fullest degree. Extra hot fudge, please.

"Warm enough?" Finn asked, pulling me from my silent perusal of the mountains outside the big windows behind him and my dreams of whipped cream.

I tugged on the sleeves of my shirt, covering my wrists. "Yeah. I'm good. Church has been bringing me longer shirts and stuff to wear, so the weather isn't really bothering me too much."

"Deacon has?"

"Sure. Or else there's some sort of clothing fairy dropping off long-sleeved shirts and jeans every night at my motel room. Shit, that might be more realistic than to think Church would do something so nice."

"Oh no, it sounds exactly like something Deacon would do. He'd also crow about it every chance he got since he likes to be the center of attention. I would have assumed Parris was bringing you clothing, though."

I nearly snorted. "Parris isn't so great at thinking of anyone's needs besides his own. Besides, he's been gone."

"Gone where?"

"Riding." I shrugged one shoulder. "I'm not really sure where to, though. He said he had work to do and took off on his bike."

He sat back in his seat, frowning. "I didn't know you'd been alone at the motel."

"Does it matter?"

"I don't know. Does it?"

"Not to me."

"You're not scared?"

"To be alone?" I huffed a sarcastic laugh. "I'm safer alone than with anyone else in the world."

And I was, though I had to admit to feeling a little lonely the last few days. And to not sleeping so well. I was used to sounds at night—cars, trains, planes, men fighting, motorcycles rolling through. But Justice wasn't a city like the ones I'd been in. It was quiet until it wasn't—the hooting of owls and baying of animals off in the hills waking me from even the deepest of sleeps.

All thoughts of wild animals disappeared when the waitress brought over the biggest darn sundae I might have ever seen, though. "Whoa."

"Worth the drive?" Finn asked as he looked over his own massive pile of sugar and cream.

"Definitely. Thanks for bringing me."

The man might have blushed. "You're welcome. Now eat before it melts. That hot fudge is literally hot."

I dug in, filling my spoon with ice cream, whipped cream, and plenty of the hot, hot fudge. "Cheers," I said, raising my spoon to Finn. I practically moaned when I took a bite. Nearly orgasmed too. "Oh my god."

"Told ya it was good."

Good was an understatement. "I will never doubt you again, Fish. At least not when dealing with food."

"I'll take that."

We ate our sundaes in relative silence, though not an uncomfortable one. I didn't know if there was such a thing as being uncomfortable around Finn Kennard. He was quiet and kind, easygoing and not at all adversarial. In other words, almost completely the opposite of every other man I'd ever met. That had to be what made me so interested in him—the differences. The uniqueness. It couldn't be true interest because I didn't date. Ever. It was a rule that had kept me alive and sane for a number of years. Finn Kennard wouldn't make me break it. Not even for the best darn hot fudge sundae I'd ever had or those killer blue-gray eyes. Nope, not happening.

No matter how much I might have wanted to let him in.

"Thanks for coming with me," Finn said out of the blue as we were finishing up.

"Thanks for bringing me."

"Anytime." The look on his face, the strength in his words— he meant that. Anytime.

Be still my heart. "Don't tempt me, Finn Kennard. I might just make you cart my butt all the way to the grocery store for my popcorn and flavored water addiction."

"What kind of popcorn?"

"Any kind. Any flavor. It's an addiction." Open mouth, insert foot. "I mean, not like that kind of addiction. Not like—"

"Hey, Jinx?"

"Yeah?"

He reached across the table and covered my hand with his. "It's okay. I understand what you mean."

Easy. Finn was the sort of man who was way too easy to fall for. I should have put the brakes on thoughts like those. Should have pulled away and put distance between us. Should have protected myself and him from the reality of my life.

I didn't let go of his hand.

Sundaes finished and bill paid—by Finn, something that would need to be remedied as I wasn't about to be indebted to the man—we headed outside together. I was tired but happy, overstuffed with ice cream but totally content about it. I didn't even mind the cold...much. My coat kept most of the cold at bay, and having Finn beside me helped as well. Kept me warm and happy, comfortable in my own skin and with the person opening my door and placing his hand on my lower back. It was as if we were an actual couple—normal people on a real date. I almost relaxed for those first four steps outside.

Just four, though. On the fifth, I happened to look up.

Three thirty in the morning at a truck stop wasn't exactly the busiest time of day, but across the lot, I couldn't help but notice the headlights lined up.

Motorcycles.

Lots and lots of them, all blocking the one and only exit. All awfully close to Finn's truck. There was no escaping without being seen. No way to avoid them. I had to assume that was intentional.

"Fish."

"I see them." He tugged his phone out of his pocket and tapped on the screen for a few seconds before putting the device away. Then, without asking, he grabbed my hand, gripping me tightly as he pulled me into his side. "Stay with me, Jinx."

As if I would leave him to face these guys alone.

"Finn Kennard," one of the guys toward the middle yelled. Not the leader—he would have been dead center on a ride. I couldn't see their colors yet—couldn't tell what group they were from—but all clubs worked the same. Hierarchy within the positions, respecting those above you and following the leader of the pack. Still, the spot in the lineup was one of power. Not a good sign if he knew Finn. "Long time no see, man."

"Too bad we couldn't keep it that way. Seen Coyote lately?" The anger in Finn's voice, the strength, took me by surprise. This wasn't the sweet guy who'd taken me out for ice cream. This was the man who'd beat back an addiction to drugs and survived a stint in prison. A side of his personality I doubted he let out very often. And he sounded pissed as hell.

The biker, on the other hand, was obviously playing a little cat-and-mouse game. "Coyote's been out of touch, man. I know you had a little spat with him, but we had a good partnership all those years ago. So what, because of that asshole, we can't be friends anymore?"

"I'm not interested in friendships right now, Monk. Not unless you can tell me where Coyote is."

"Like I said—I don't know where he's at. Now, if you were still a customer …" The guy—road name Monk, apparently—shrugged, letting that unspoken offer hang there. Giving Finn the tease of getting whatever information he was seeking if only he'd play ball. Finn didn't respond, though, which was good. These men had no honor and wouldn't come through on such a thing. I knew that from experience.

Monk finally looked away from Finn, giving me a once-over instead. "How you doing, sweetheart?"

I hated him already. "Just peachy." I squeezed Finn's hand tighter. "But I'm getting tired. We'd better get going."

"Back to The Jury Room?" Monk grinned, even though I did my best to keep from reacting to his words. To the fact that he knew such things about Finn and me. "Yeah, honey. We know where Finn here works. Only a dumbass amateur shows up in town without doing research first."

I never heard a step, not a single scratch of a shoe on pavement, but suddenly Deacon slipped in next to me, almost blocking my view of the bikers. And he looked pissed as hell.

"Then it sure seems like you've got some dumbass amateurs on your team."

Parris walked up beside the older former soldier, the two forming a wall of muscle and male bravado between me and the bikers. Finn joined right in with them, making sure to hang on to my hand as he blocked me. Keeping me tight to his back. Obscuring most of my view. Most...but not all.

Monk grinned in a smirk-like sort of way. "The Green Beret to the rescue. I hadn't been expecting to meet you so soon, Deacon Manns, but I can't say I'm unprepared. I've got a few Special Forces soldiers on my team as well."

"If they're riding with the likes of the Soul Suckers, they're not Special Forces. Maybe they're yours, Parris. Got some chump-ass ex-Marines in that club?"

Just as I would have expected, Parris grumbled, "Once a Marine, always a Marine. There's no ex about it, but if anyone was stupid enough to come rolling up into Justice unannounced like this, they're not Marines. No matter what you grunts like to say, we're not all dumb jocks."

Deacon coughed a harsh sort of laugh. "These guys aren't proving that to me."

"Nope. Sure not."

"You're wearing colors, son," Monk said, eyeing Parris hard.

Staring intentionally at the Black Angels vest he wore. "Shouldn't you be on this side of the lot?"

"We may all ride, but you're not my crew. I'll stick to this side."

"See? That's the problem with other clubs. They accept this sort of behavior." Monk sat back, looking almost lethal as he glared at Parris. "Us Soul Suckers, we don't take kindly to traitors."

But Parris didn't seem the least bit intimidated. "And I don't take kindly to threats. Neither does my boss."

Monk glanced to his left, as if looking for some sort of approval. As if thrown off by Parris' reply. "And who would that be?"

"The big prez. I work directly for the man at the top of the national club and answer to no one else. And that's all I'm giving you." Parris grabbed my arm as he passed behind the other guys, giving me a rough push. Forcing me backward and away from Finn. "I think it's about time to call this meeting of the mindless over, don't you, Deacon?"

But Finn had other ideas. "They know Coyote."

Deacon stood firm and strong, not saying anything. Eyeing the men across the lot with no emotion on his face but an aura of malice about him. Ready to fight. Ready to kill. The moment lasted far longer than I'd expected, the tension increasing like humidity before a storm. Pressing in and making it harder to breathe with every second. No one moved; it seemed as if no one even dared to breathe.

But then Deacon laughed, breaking the moment in a casual sort of way that belied what had just happened. "Yeah, I think it's about time to call it a night, boys."

Finn whipped in his direction. "Deacon—"

"We end it. For now." He raised an eyebrow at Finn, who

seemed even more pissed than earlier. Whoever this Coyote guy was, Finn wanted to find him.

The bikers, meanwhile, all looked to one man—a big, mean-looking guy on the end. A position of a rookie rider, yet he didn't look like any rookie I'd ever seen. He looked like a man trying to go unnoticed. A leader in hiding. Which was dangerous.

The leader—because there was no way he wasn't the one calling the shots—gave a single chin nod. "Think that might be a good idea. We just rolled into town. Need to find a place to hole up, but I've heard there's only one motel in Justice."

"Aye," Deacon said. "But we're all full. Might want to keep on riding to Rock Falls. There're a few no-tell-motels out that way."

He got another nod for the effort. "I figured as much. C'mon, boys. Let's leave these guys to their plans. Good folk aren't usually out this late, after all."

Message received—we were good, and they were the big, bad wolves at our doors. Typical posturing, but still a warning to remember.

We stood in a half circle, watching as the bikers peeled off and headed for the highway. I inspected each one, cataloging their features. Making sure I would recognize them if I ran into them again.

It was on the third to the last that a biker took any interest in me. The dark-haired man stared back hard, eyeing me with a familiarity that made my blood run cold. I knew those eyes, the scar on his jaw, the way his chin jutted out in a hard square. Knew the roughness of his hands too. The cruelty behind them.

If there hadn't been a literal blockade of masculinity in front of me, I might have started shaking. Instead, I inched closer. Not to Parris or even to my new boss, Deacon. No, I skipped the military men and moved myself closer to Finn. He leaned into me, gripping my hand in his. Anchoring me as the man finally stopped looking and followed his brothers.

We stood in the lingering silence, not talking. Not moving. Likely each dealing with whatever residual feelings we had after we'd faced that threat. At least, that was what I did—tried to cope with the fear that man being anywhere near me instilled. No way was his showing up here a coincidence.

It wasn't until the taillights had all faded into the distance that anyone broke the silence.

Parris took that honor, focusing his obvious anger on Finn. "You put this girl in that sort of danger again, and I'll slit your fucking throat, Kennard or not."

Deacon spat out a quiet, "Parris—"

"Understood," Finn interrupted. Cutting off his friend and boss. Letting go of my hand and not even bothering to give me a glance before promising, "It won't happen again."

Why those words hurt so much, I didn't want to think about. Why Finn not anchoring me to him anymore hurt more, I refused to ponder. Good thing the guys didn't give me a chance.

"You said a hundred bikers would come," Deacon said, turning on Parris. "That wasn't a hundred."

Parris looked ready to kill. "They weren't local either. Those were Soul Suckers from Vegas—two had patches of blackjack chips."

I could have confirmed one of their identities. I didn't, though.

"So, the rest are still coming," Deacon said, making the words a statement and not a question. Because we all knew more would come. This was only the beginning.

Parris confirmed my thoughts with a single word. "Yup."

Deacon huffed and ran a hand over the top of his head. "How soon?"

"I don't know for sure, but I'll find out." Parris nodded at me. "Let's go, Jinx."

Finn glanced my way but said nothing. Letting Parris make the decisions on my behalf.

I wasn't down for that. "Maybe I don't want to go with you."

Apparently, my opinion on the subject didn't matter. At least, not to Parris. "Too damn bad. You shouldn't have left the motel to begin with."

"I'm not a prisoner."

"You really want to push me on this?"

No. I didn't. I knew how demanding he could be, knew how much of a bastard he was. This fight didn't matter enough to me to continue it.

My past did, though.

Specifically, my past with the biker who had definitely recognized me. Who had once lived in the same house with me. Who had shared a bed with my mom.

The one I believed likely had something to do with her disappearance.

The one I definitely needed to stay the hell away from.

"Fine. Let's go."

But Finn had other ideas. "I'll take her."

Parris froze, looking hard at the man standing up to him. "You sure you want to do that?"

"Absolutely. I'll get her back to the motel safely." Finn didn't flinch when Parris stepped into his space, a fact that made my heart stutter just a little bit. Maybe letting go of my hand wasn't as big of a deal as I'd thought. Maybe I should stop jumping to conclusions.

Maybe I should cut it with the maybes.

"Good," Deacon said, patting me on the shoulder and pushing me closer to Finn in a casual yet demanding sort of way. "Because Parris and I have a few things to discuss."

Such as how to deal with a band of bikers because running away wasn't an option.

At least not for the men of Justice.

Or so it seemed.

Chapter Five

FINN

Y ou don't have to do this."

Third time. That was the third time Jinx had told me I didn't have to take her back to the motel, that I didn't have to stay with her until Deacon and Parris made it back from following the bikers out of town, that I didn't have to protect her. Good thing I had a hard time following orders.

"I'm doing this, so how about we stop arguing about that fact."

She crossed her arms and gave me the meanest glare she could, which reminded me of some sort of angry kitten because she was just so cute. "Fine."

I might not have had much dating experience, but I had a sister. Any woman who said *fine* in that tone was never fine. Not even close to fine. She was the antithesis of fine.

I leaned back against the wall, keeping my eyes on the door and my mouth shut as Jinx paced and mumbled to herself. I thought I heard her say she could take care of herself. I definitely heard her say stupid man.

Angry. Fucking. Kitten.

Thankfully, I was saved from any further insults and language booby traps by a knock at the door. Jinx jumped and spun my way, looking more nervous than I'd seen her. I had an urge to hug her, to wrap her in my arms and hang on. Instead, I lifted my finger to my lips to indicate we should stay quiet then snuck over to the window to peek outside. Deacon stood in the light outside the motel room, looking anxious and wary as he kept his eyes on the parking lot.

"It's Deac."

"Did he bring beer?"

Funny chick. "No. Do you need one?"

"Maybe. Open the door, Finn."

So maybe I was okay at following *some* orders. "Yes, ma'am."

"Hey, Finn," Deacon said once the door was open. He glanced over my shoulder into the room. "Everything okay here?"

"Just peachy," Jinx said, sounding more than a little irritated.

Deacon's mouth lifted just slightly, and one eyebrow joined it on that higher plane. That eyebrow spoke volumes. It begged the question *what's up with her.*

"It's fine," I said, stressing the word to indicate just how not fine things were. "Jinx is dealing with a sugar crash."

"Am not." She pushed past me. "I'm not a child. I don't need a babysitter."

Babysitter? That was how she saw me now?

Deacon looked almost as irritated as I felt, though he hid it well. "He's not a babysitter, Jinx. He's a guard."

"I don't need one of those either."

"Well good, because I want Finn to come talk with Parris and me. We'll leave you alone like you want."

"Good." Jinx sounded tough but looked a little pale. A little more afraid than she would ever admit. Tough little kitten.

Unable to leave without clearing one thing up, I leaned close so I could whisper in her ear. "Babysitter? Really? And here I thought I was just being a friend and keeping you company. My mistake."

Her face fell, but I didn't stick around for an answer. I didn't need to hear an apology from her...or not hear one. I'd give her a little time to settle down, to find her way to a real fine instead of a not-fine-at-all fine. Maybe then we could have an actual chat. One could dream.

I followed Deacon across the parking lot, shivering the entire fucking way. The temperature had dropped as the hours had passed, and dawn was still far enough away to know it would only get colder. I should have left an extra blanket with Jinx.

Too much—quit trying to do too much. She'd ask for a blanket if she needed one.

I quickened my steps and rushed into The Jury Room to get out of the cold. Forgetting about Jinx all alone in that motel room along the way.

Okay, not forgetting at all. Just tucking those thoughts away. For the moment.

Parris sat at the bar, shoulders up and back stiff. He looked ready to explode. At me, apparently. "What the fuck was Jinx doing at the truck stop?"

Easy enough to answer. "She wanted ice cream."

Parris blinked, then frowned. "She what?"

"She wanted ice cream. I took her to get some ice cream."

"At the truck stop."

"There aren't exactly a lot of options out this way at two

thirty in the morning. The only other one was taking her back to my place, and that didn't seem like a good idea."

"No, it wasn't. Though neither was taking her out in public. Those guys could have recognized her."

"They seemed to have recognized me instead."

His glare sharpened. "Want to talk about why that is?"

I glanced at Deacon. He didn't flinch, didn't issue a single tell. He knew more about my time away than anyone, so if he wasn't stopping me from telling Parris anything, I had to believe the guy was trustworthy. To a point.

"I'm a former addict," I said, hating that term. Hating the past tense of it. Once an addict, always an addict...just like the Marines. "I bought from a couple Soul Suckers for a while."

Parris didn't seem surprised by that news. "Meth?"

"Yeah. Spent a few years inside because of it. But that gave me time to get good and clean, so it wasn't for nothing."

"They'll use that against you."

My drug addiction. The fact that it never truly lets go of anyone. The weakness that everyone knew was inside of me. "I know."

For once, Parris looked almost...concerned. "You sure you're strong enough to handle that?"

This time, it was Deacon who answered. "He's strong enough."

"Good, because we don't have a lot of options here. Alder is all Mr. Wedding Bliss, Gage is attached at the hip to his woman, and Bishop is off in Vegas playing bodyguard to the psychic. It's just the three of us to deal with this shit right now."

"You got a plan?" Deacon asked.

Parris picked up a glass of what looked like beer and took a pull before answering. "We go on the offensive against the Soul Suckers."

Well, damn. I hadn't been expecting *that* option. "You sure that's the best idea?"

Parris stared me down hard. "It's the only language these fuckers understand. Violence and aggression. If we don't take them out, they'll come for us. There are two clubs in town—my crew, the Black Angels, and the Soul Suckers. I can deal with my guys, try to work from the inside to keep them out of Justice until we can handle the others. But even without my team backing them up, those fucking Soul Suckers outnumber us. They'll win just about any war they start. We can't give them that advantage."

"I'm not military," I said, not for the first time feeling the shadows my older brothers and their friends threw. "I'm not trained like you guys."

Parris just shook his head. "You survived time in prison and made it out alive. You'll do fine."

Okay then. "Then let's do this."

"We need to verify where they're staying," Parris said, looking to Deacon.

My boss shrugged. "There's only one place big enough around here. I'll double-check, but my money's on one of the campgrounds in Rock Falls. Most have at least a few cabins and lots of open space for campers. It's too cold for most tent camping, but not too bad for an RV."

"The Black Angels are staying at one just over the river. There're no Soul Suckers there, though."

"There are a few different camps. Maybe they're at one of the other ones."

"Confirm it. I don't want to come rolling up to find Jim from Accounting on vacation with his family, you know?"

Deacon nodded once. "No worries. It'll be checked."

"Good." Parris took another long drink from his beer before

settling his gaze back on me. "Do you think they recognized Jinx?"

Deacon jumped in before I could answer. "Should they have?"

Parris paused—a subtle, almost invisible hold before he responded, but it was there. Noticeable to me. I'd had to study people in prison to make sure I didn't end up on the wrong side of some arbitrary line. Had been forced to read people the way others read books. That tell didn't just whisper, it screamed. His lack of trust and things he didn't want us to know telegraphed themselves around the room in a split second.

Yeah, the bikers would recognize Jinx. Why, I had no idea. But I'd find out. I had to.

"No," Parris said, likely lying to us. "But she's been around the clubs a long time, and a few of them were from her town. Someone could."

Deacon shrugged. "So, we keep her out of the spotlight."

"Agreed," I said. But I didn't agree. Not yet, not without knowing all the facts. Because Parris definitely seemed worried that those guys would recognize Jinx. Thinking back over the interaction at the truck stop, Jinx had stiffened up toward the end. One guy—he'd stared at her. I'd assumed he'd been trying to intimidate her for some reason, but maybe not. Maybe he'd recognized her as Parris feared. And maybe, just maybe, she'd recognized him too.

And not said anything about it to me or the guys.

That seemed like trouble for sure. A weakness in our tenuous little bubble of a team.

"So, what's the plan?" I asked, unable to take my mind off of Jinx. Wanting this session of the testosterone carriers to end so I could make sure she was okay.

Parris ran a hand over his shorn head. "It's on us to fix this. The three of us."

"Plus Jinx."

"I want her out of it," he said, tapping his fingers on the bar top. "She's been through enough. Besides, if they realize who she is, we'll have more trouble than we're ready for."

I kept my mouth shut, not revealing she'd likely already been recognized. Not yet at least. I'd tell them soon—maybe once I worked out what the situation was. With her. For her.

"When do we hit?" Deacon asked.

"Maybe a week. We need some supplies, verification of where they're staying, and a solid plan. That takes time."

"You're not worried about them hitting us first?" I asked.

Parris shook his head. "These guys are here to intimidate us. Don't get me wrong, they'll burn the whole town down if they feel the need. But first, they'll play a little cat and mouse."

"So, we let them," Deacon said, looking like a man with a plan. "Hide your children, hide your wives, deal with the jabs. Then cut the legs out from under them."

"Exactly."

Which was all fine and good, except for one thing. "Where will Jinx hide?"

Deacon looked my way. "We'll have her stay with Alder and Shye."

"Without telling him the real reason why?" My brother wouldn't like that. He was also too smart to fall for it. "You know there'll be blowback if you aren't up front about why Jinx is there."

That might have been the first flicker of doubt I'd ever seen from Parris. "I'll take the hit on the decision, but it's the only way to keep her out of harm's way."

It wasn't, so I looked to my boss. "What about bringing Bishop or Gage in with us? Letting them watch over Jinx."

"It's decided," Parris said, interrupting whatever Deacon might have had for an answer. "They're not reliable right now because they've got pussy on the brain. This mission is on us, and I'm not bringing in extra people just because Jinx might find herself in trouble again. I wouldn't lead us on this mission if I didn't think we'd come out okay. That includes her."

That didn't prioritize her, though. Parris' plan might as well have been bare minimum when it came to Jinx. She needed better. Deserved it, too. But there wasn't much I could do or say right then. Not without knowing more about the situation, about her past and present. About her in general. Bishop and Gage had pussy on the brain, and I had Jinx distracting me, but I couldn't admit it. Instead, I'd buckle down. Focus on what could be done, what needed to happen, and how to save the town I'd grown up in while learning everything I could about the girl. Easy enough, right?

Deacon looked almost excited—ever the mission planner. "So, what do we need to do first?"

Two hours and a ton of ginger ale later, we had a plan laid out. One where Deacon stalked the enemy, cutting them down one by one. Where Parris rode in like a man possessed and took them on headfirst. One where I was relegated to keeping watch and making sure none of the bikers slipped away. My position as lookout stung, but I understood it. I wasn't military like they were—I didn't have the experience with the weapons and tactical maneuvers the way they did. I was basically backup.

I never talked much about my time in prison, so most people didn't understand the lengths a man would go to survive in there. The deals and negotiations, the delicate balance of acting tough and not attracting the sort of attention that made people want to take you down to prove they were tougher. I had a feeling those skills would come in handy with this mission, though I might not get the chance to use them.

Story of my life.

"We good?" Deacon asked as we wrapped things up on the plan. "I've got a woman in my bed that I'd like to get back to."

"You hadn't left too much before us," I said, working out the timeline in my head. "That's a quick date to end up in bed together."

"Being in bed together *was* the date." He winked my way. "Sometimes, the whole wine them, dine them thing is simply not necessary."

I snorted a laugh. "My sister would call you a pig for that comment. Then she'd likely rip your balls off."

"I've never met the fairer Kennard, though she sounds quite pleasant."

Parris choked on his beer. "Getting your balls ripped off sounds pleasant?"

"I'm more concerned about him calling Lainie fairer. She's in no way fair—unless you count her hair color. Word to the wise—don't let the blond locks fool you. She's a bitch on wheels, and she's proud of it."

"Well hell, son," Parris said, leaning back on his stool, elbow resting on the bar. "I might want to meet this ball-ripping, blond hellcat."

Deacon just laughed. "Get in line, bud. I've known Alder Kennard for seventeen years, and I've never met the woman."

"And I doubt you ever will. At least not unless it's on her terms," I said before standing up and stretching. Damn, those chairs needed some padding. "If we're done here, I want to go check on Jinx to make sure she's okay before heading home."

"I'm sure she's fine, kid," Parris said, looking as if he wasn't unseating his stool just yet.

"Maybe she is, but if I were in her position, I'd appreciate someone checking on me." I nodded to Deacon. "Need anything, boss?"

"No, sir. You go on then and get yourself home. Text me if you run into any problems."

"I will. G'night."

I hurried out of the bar, needing to get away from them. To recenter myself a little. Every muscle in my body itched to jump in my truck and go on home, to seek the warmth of my shower and then my bed, but I headed for the motel instead. Wanting to make sure Jinx was okay.

Needing to figure out why I'd just kept info from Parris and Deacon in some instinctual desire to protect her.

Chapter Six

JINX

Motel rooms were sucky places to need to pace. There was never a good distance between any obstructions, so pacing became more akin to spinning, which made me dizzy, which cut my pacing time into odd little chunks of walking, spinning, then holding my head as the world righted itself once more. My back burned from all the pacing, the slashes Pistol had laid on me healing painfully. At least they'd stopped weeping, stopped soaking my shirts and sheets with grossness I had trouble hiding. They tugged, though. A constant reminder that I wasn't free. Never would be.

A foreshadowing of what was to come.

And still, the clock ticked on. Most people—good people—were fast asleep in their beds. Me? I was busy stumbling around a motel room with the curtains wide open and the door cracked just enough so I could keep an eye on the parking lot. Cold, be damned.

With every pass of my path around the room, I did my best not to trip over my beds. I had two to choose from, and yet neither interested me in any way other than a place to rest and make the world stop spinning around me. I was far more worried about what was happening over in the bar and why Parris had refused to let me join him there. Because that was totally a Parris thing to do, not a Finn or a Deacon one. Only Parris would undermine my value like that, as if I weren't an asset. As if I were some delicate petal who needed protection.

"I'll give them delicate," I said as I rose to my feet to resume my pacing pattern. "I'll give them my delicate foot right up their asses."

"Sounds a bit on the painful side for me."

I spun, my heart jumping in my chest at the voice coming out of nowhere. Pounding even harder when I saw the man it belonged to. Finn Kennard stood in the doorway to my room, not entering. Just...leaning. Watching. Looking all sorts of kind and sexy and...I needed to stop that train of thought right there.

"It's cold out there."

He nodded. "Yeah, it is. Can I come in?"

My entire body pulsed at the thought. "Of course."

He stepped in a little more, closing the door behind him. Blocking out the cold air that had permeated my space. "Why'd you have the door open?"

"To keep an eye on you three. Meeting over?"

He shrugged, seemingly uninterested in the subject. "Mostly. I have a feeling Parris and Deacon will hammer out a few more details. The sort us non-military folk don't know enough to chime in on."

That sounded a lot like irritation. "So, I'm kicked out for not having a penis, and you're kicked out for not having an old uniform in your closet."

Finn considered me for a long moment before he said, "Simplistic, but it works. Yeah."

Silence fell between us, and the space neither of us occupied seemed to grow. Most men barged right into my life and took over—their world, their rules. Finn stood just inside the door, obviously interested in coming to see what I was up to, but refusing to infiltrate my space. Having asked permission to even cross the threshold. I had no idea how to take that.

"What would you have done if the door had been closed?" I asked, mentally trying to put the pieces of this man together.

He frowned. "What door?"

"That one. Mine. My motel room door. I'd left it open to be able to know what was going on outside, so what would you have done if it had been closed?"

"Your light was on."

It was my turn to frown. "Huh?"

"Your light"—he indicated the table lamp in front of the window—"it was on. I could see you walking around the room because of the light, so I came to make sure you were okay after tonight. If your door had been closed, I'd likely have knocked. But if I hadn't seen your light on, I wouldn't have stopped by."

"Why not?"

"Because I would have assumed you'd been sleeping. Do you sleep with the lights on?"

"No. I don't."

"Neither do I, and no one likes being woken up in the middle of the night. So yeah, if the door had been closed, I'd have knocked, unless the light had been off. Then I'd have left you alone."

He wouldn't have just barged in. How novel. "I'm glad I had the light on."

"Me too."

"You can come in farther, you know. You don't have to hold up the door."

His eyes darted around the room, landing back on me. "I didn't want to intrude."

As if. "Come on in and quit being so polite. Parris intrudes all the time, but I haven't put my foot up his ass." I gave Finn a grin over my shoulder. "Yet."

"Well, let me know when you decide to make that a reality instead of just a possibility. I might enjoy the show."

"Deal." I sat on the bed farthest from the door as Finn took a seat on the other, both of us facing one another. There were a couple of feet between us, yet I could practically feel the warmth coming off him. Or maybe that was simply a "being around Finn" thing.

"How'd you know that guy?"

The subject change knocked the warmth right out of the room and chilled my blood to the point of goose bumps rising along my arms. "I don't know what you're talking about."

"Yeah, you do." He sighed and sat back, resting his weight on his outstretched arms behind him. "You knew those men."

Never let it be said that Finn Kennard wasn't observant. "I knew one of them."

"How? I'm going to go out on a limb and say it's not from Sunday school."

How I could almost laugh during this interrogation was beyond me, but I did. I almost laughed. "Never went to Sunday school. I knew the guy from my time with the Soul Suckers."

He sat up straight, his brow furrowing hard. "You rode with the Soul Suckers?"

This time, I really did laugh. Out loud. Hell, I practically cackled. "Dear, sweet Fish. You have no idea how clubs run, do you?"

"Not really, no."

"Well, let me be clear about a woman's place in them, then—there aren't a lot of clubs that let females ride."

He scowled, likely at the fact that I'd called out the sexism of the clubs. Or at least, I assumed that was the reason. "Why not?"

"We're the weaker sex."

It was his turn to laugh, though the weight of the sarcasm in his chuckle was strong enough to practically have a physical presence. "If women are the weaker sex, then men must be useless."

I could have kissed him, if that was something I'd wanted to do. But it wasn't, or at least it shouldn't be, so I didn't. *Focus, Jinx.* "You said it, not me."

"So, if you didn't ride, why were you there? You don't look like the sort of person who'd be club pussy."

The word "pussy" coming from those lips should have been obscene. It should not have sent a tingle up my spine. "Really, Fish? Club pussy... Pulling out the MC terms, are we?"

The man had said pussy like he used that word on a daily basis, but he flushed when I said it. He also stumbled over his words a bit as he said, "I know a little about the clubs."

"How?"

"What?"

"How do you know a little? Big *SOA* fan, are you?"

His brow dropped, an almost confused expression forming on his face. "What's *SOA*?"

Color me shocked. "*Sons of Anarchy.*"

He stared blankly, as if the title of the show meant nothing to him.

I finally had to ask, "Do you not watch TV?"

"No. I don't own one."

I blinked. Again. Three times. "You don't even own one?"

"Deacon always has one on at the bar, so by the time I get home, I've had enough of the noise." He shrugged, all casual and calm, even as I could tell he felt uncomfortable with the conversation.

"Interesting," I said, though whether that was in regard to his words or his reaction to me asking him something, I wasn't really sure. "I don't watch a lot of TV, but I studied *SOA* like my life depended on it."

Which it had. Still did. I'd studied every TV show, documentary, and novel written about club life, had learned the history and structure of motorcycle clubs in our country. I'd learned everything I could when my mom had started hanging around bikers more and more.

None of that knowledge had helped either one of us in the end, though.

Finn shrugged. "I'll have to watch it sometime to have a frame of reference, though that won't answer my question."

About why I was at the Soul Suckers' clubhouse. About how I knew them and they knew me. I didn't usually like going with honesty, but I figured Deacon and Alder already knew this part. It was only a matter of time before the rest of the Kennard clan heard the story. Besides, my time with that club was far easier to explain and deal with than what I'd done with the Black Angels. "I was a prisoner of the Soul Suckers club, not a member."

His lips flattened into a thin line. "They held you against your will?"

He made it sound as if he was shocked by the news. He shouldn't have been. "It's really not all that unusual in those circles."

"Why?"

"Because assholes like the men in the Soul Suckers think women are nothing more than property."

He nodded, looking almost distracted. "They treated Alder's fiancée like that. Shye—they hung a debt around her neck that she could never pay off, then tried to come grab her and take her away. As if she belonged to them."

"She did." I shrugged when his head jerked in my direction. "That's how they see us, Fish. We're not humans—we're objects that have no free will or agency. I made a deal with a club that chose to hand me off to another. Not my choice, not my plan, not my place to say no."

"I just don't get it."

"How men can be such pigs?"

"No, I get that. Men can be awful," he said, which brought a choked sort of laugh from me. At least the man recognized his gender's faults. "What I can't understand is how you got mixed up with them. You don't really fit the club girl sort of mold."

How I got mixed up with the Soul Suckers would lead me down a path of explaining how I ended up going to the Black Angels. And that really wasn't a story I wanted to tell. "That's not your business."

"You're right—it's not." He leaned forward, closing the distance between us and softening his voice. Soothing me with his words as he said, "That doesn't mean you can't tell me, though. That you can't talk to me. I'm a good secret keeper."

I wished. Wished hard. Sometimes, I just wanted to lay out everything I'd been through—every step I'd taken—to someone who could help me figure out where I'd gone wrong. Help me find what I'd missed. Who could simply listen to the tale and tell me I wasn't insane, and everything really had happened.

But that was an impossibility. "It's not safe to talk about such things."

Rough. My voice came out so rough, but Finn heard me.

"For you or for me?" he asked, all low and quiet. Still

soothing. Still pulling honesty from me when I knew better than to give that to him.

"For everyone."

He inched closer, shifting all the way to the edge of his bed, reaching slowly across the space between us toward me. Raising his arm bit by bit and extending it until his fingers brushed mine as they sat in my lap. He'd held my hand earlier in the evening at the truck stop, so the touch shouldn't have surprised me. But it did. It shook me, too. Sent sparks of energy shooting up my arm and brought a shiver to my spine. His lips parted slightly, drawing my attention. So pink and full and soft-looking, so perfect. I'd never wanted to kiss someone so badly. Never wanted to know what they tasted like so much. For one moment—one second—I thought maybe I could have that. One taste. One kiss. One moment of more.

But that one second passed.

Finn ran his fingers along the length of the scars on my wrists —the ones that had only one story to tell—causing my body to lock down. My fear to explode within me. I tried to pull away on instinct, fear of more hurt and pain and mess driving my actions. Finn didn't let me run from him, though—hanging on with a gentle touch as he raised the sleeves of the hoodie I wore. Staring at my scars in a way that made my eyes burn.

"Are these from the Soul Suckers?"

Yes. No. Sort of.

"Partially," I said, finally succeeding in pulling my hands away. I crossed my arms, trying to hide my wrists. The lines around them that screamed restraints. That proved I'd been a prisoner. And in that moment, as Finn allowed me to retreat, as he settled farther back on his bed and gave me my space, I allowed one tiny crack in the wall around my truth. "Some are from my mom's old club."

"Your mom rode?" He shook his head when I cocked mine. "Wait...not rode. She was involved in a club?"

"Yeah. That's how I met Parris."

That definitely got a reaction, though not a brash one. The man was nothing if not subtle. He was also confusing, as he didn't ask me the question I'd been expecting. Nothing about Parris or our history. Instead, he went with, "Why'd they restrain you?"

No one who'd seen my scars had ever asked that, and I couldn't do anything but answer honestly. "Because I tried to run after I'd sworn I'd stay."

He kept his eyes on my wrists. Kept his voice so gentle in tone as he asked, "Why'd you try to run?"

Because I hadn't belonged there. Because I'd been terrified. Because I'd given up all hope of finding out what I'd wanted to. Because the new president hadn't honored my old deal. "Because I didn't want to do what they told me to."

He shifted forward again, coming closer. Pressing his knees against mine and his hands on my thighs. "What did they want you to do?"

So close. So very close and warm and smelling of man. Of safety. Of home. "Likely the same thing you want me to do right now."

His eyes darted to mine, and he shook his head. "I would never make you do anything you didn't want to. I would never push you like that."

"I know." And I did. I trusted him...as much as I could trust anyone. With my body but not my heart. Or my secrets. "But you want something from me. I can tell."

Finn inched closer, running his fingertips along the length of my hand. "I do. I'll admit to that. But I'd never hurt you, Jinx. I'd never take without asking."

"I know that, too." That wasn't in Finn's nature, the taking. The abusing. He'd ask for what he wanted and respect my right to turn him down, not that I planned on doing so. In fact, I had a feeling I wanted the same thing as he did. Maybe more. Maybe a lot more. "Ask me, Finn. Tell me what you need, and I may feel the same way. You know you want to."

"What I need doesn't matter."

It did, but I wouldn't argue with him. "What about what I need?" I leaned closer, bringing our faces only inches apart and licking my lips before whispering, "I want you to ask me, Finn."

His breath caught, and he bit his bottom lip for just a moment before he finally voiced the question I'd been hoping for. "Can I kiss you?"

"Yes." I closed my eyes as his hands slid around my hips, as he dropped to his knees on the floor between us and gently brought our bodies closer together. As he breathed over my lips before pressing his to them. Soft, so soft and sweet and gentle. Just as I'd thought they'd be. Unlike anyone else. Uniquely Finn and so damn perfect, those lips. That kiss. Simple and graceful and easy.

But way too short.

"Thank you," he said after he broke the kiss. As if I'd given him a gift or something.

"You don't have to thank me."

"I feel like I do." He sighed, moving back to meet my gaze. To stare up at me. "I liked that."

So honest, this man. So sweet. How could I do anything but reciprocate? "Me too."

He pushed my hair over my shoulder, keeping his eyes locked on mine. "I want to know more about you."

I swallowed the dread those words inspired. I could trust Finn. Sort of. "Ditto."

"Quid pro quo?"

"What's that mean?"

"It means I ask you a question, then you ask me one. We take turns."

What a terrifying thought. "Can I go first?"

"Sure."

I grabbed his arm and tugged, twisting as gently as I could until I had access to the place I wanted. To his elbow where a black and gray cobweb radiated from the joint. Until black ink stared back at me. The same black ink I'd seen that first night at The Jury Room. The spider web tattoo that told me Finn wasn't as innocent as he seemed.

"What were you in prison for?"

Chapter Seven

FINN

The tattoo. Jinx had been around bikers—some of them likely criminals. Of course she'd see the tattoo and know the meaning of the symbol. The real meaning. I didn't usually have to explain the art to anyone. Most people assumed it was nothing more than that—art. A common design likely found "on the wall" at the shop I'd gone to. They didn't know I didn't get the art in any shop. They also didn't know the symbolism behind it. That spider web had a long history in prison culture. It meant I'd been an insect trapped in the web of the penitentiary system for a long time. Long enough to have earned the dark, rough lines drawn on my arm. Too damn long.

"Those years…" I licked my lips, suddenly hot and dry and in desperate need of something more than a ginger ale. Jinx was pure chaos even in her calmest state, a disruption I shouldn't be playing with. One I didn't want to walk away from just yet, though. "That's really not something I talk about."

"Cool." She nodded, looking at me as if things were decidedly *not* cool. She might as well have said fine. "So that ends this whole quid pro quote thing."

"Quo." By her glower, my automatic correction of her misspoken word didn't help matters. "Sorry."

"It's fine—"

"It's not." I reached for her hand, unable not to. Needing some sort of connection to her, even if only for a few moments. "Talking about that time in my life is hard, and you knowing that the tattoo was a prison one threw me off. Most people don't know or don't ask."

"I'm not most people."

"Trust me, I've figured that out." I took a deep breath, letting go of her hand so I could sit on the edge of the bed closest to the door. The one I assumed she didn't sleep in. I couldn't handle the thought of being in *her* bed at that moment. I also couldn't break my word—we'd made a deal, and I'd stick by it. "I went to prison for possession with intent to sell methamphetamines."

She rose to her feet and walked out of our little hallway between the beds, leaning a hip against the dresser at the end, putting extra space between us and looking so damn disappointed. "You sold drugs."

"Nope. Not once."

"Then why—"

"I'm not innocent," I said, knowing there were no truer words. "I would never claim I didn't do things that were wrong, but I didn't do *that*."

She didn't look convinced. "I'm confused."

"Yeah. I really suck at this." I took a deep breath and dug down deep for the right words to say. The ones that might tell my story without this entire thing blowing up in my face. "I wasn't bad, you know? I wasn't a troublemaker, and I didn't come from some messed-up family. I was a good kid with solid grades, a close family, and a future all planned out. I was a *good kid*."

"Until you weren't."

"Until I wasn't." Until that first summer. "It started almost as a joke—my friend's mom had a bunch of prescriptions, and some of them made you feel pretty loopy. Or pretty relaxed. I didn't really think much about taking them because she didn't seem to need them, and they weren't illegal or anything. They came from a doctor."

A doctor with a total disregard for his patient's health and an overactive prescription pad, but I was too far gone by the time I figured that part out.

Jinx sighed, shaking her head. "Fish, you don't have to—"

"Those drugs led to painkillers, which led me to things that were harder to get my hands on." I clenched my fingers, my hands nearly shaking. I'd have given anything to be able to have something to do with them—to have a carving project to work on or a piece of wood to whittle. I hated when my hands didn't know what to do with themselves. "At least until I found a doctor willing to write me my own prescriptions."

Her eyes zeroed in on mine, pinning me in place. Making my hands go still again. "You found Oxy."

Bull's-eye. "Yeah. There was a doctor over in Whitman who—I thought—would write anyone a prescription for it without them being a patient. Turns out, his medical assistant was writing the orders and selling them. She got busted and my supply line dried up, so that's when I moved on to Special K."

Ketamine. A powerful disassociative drug that had seemed like a gift at the time. A gift of distraction.

Jinx must have known about it already. "And the bikers who dealt it."

I shook my head. "Not at first. There was a local guy, someone I'd grown up with. He would go outside Justice to buy and then sell to the rest of us. It wasn't until my addiction grew strong enough for me to want to cut out the middleman that I met the Soul Suckers."

"I bet they loved seeing you coming."

There was no holding back my snort of laughter. "Dumb, rural kid who had parents with a little money? Already addicted and needing my daily doses to get through life? Yeah. I was a wet dream of a customer for them."

Jinx nodded as if she knew exactly where this story was going. "And they got you to sell to your friends?"

"No." I shrugged at her confused expression. "I wasn't kidding or trying to soften what I said earlier. I never once sold drugs. I only bought them."

"But...you went to prison for dealing." She couldn't have sounded any more surprised or filled with doubt. And I couldn't blame her a bit.

"I did. I'm sure you've heard this from anyone who ever went to jail, but I was innocent of the charges brought against me." Man, I hated that word. "I may not have been *innocent*—I was an addict, after all, and had done some shady things to get my hands on my drugs. But I never sold. Not one time."

"Then how did you end up in jail?"

Two words...Sheriff Fucking Baker. Okay, three. "The county sheriff had a beef with my family, and I took the brunt of his anger. Sheriff Baker came at me hard with a bunch of trumped-up evidence and some major exaggerations about my past. He made me out to be some serious degenerate who would murder your kids to get what I wanted, and I was too stupid to figure out a way through him. I refused to let my parents hire some expensive lawyer and lose their retirement money, so I used the public defender. And I went to jail."

She looked horrified—not unexpectedly. But there was sadness there as well. Pain in her expressive almost-gray eyes as she asked, "How long?"

I sighed, deep and loud, and lay back on the bed. Hands behind my head, I stared at the ceiling as I said, "Simple possession of Schedule II drugs is a level four drug felony and carries a penalty of six to twelve months plus a fine. Judges can also knock that down to a misdemeanor if you complete a treatment program and don't violate any conditions of your parole."

"How long, Finn?"

"Baker pushed and got the DA to charge me with possession of a Schedule II drug *with* intent to sell. Nine grams—two over the limit for a shorter sentence."

Jinx was nothing if not persistent. "How long?"

The sound of my father's gasp when the judge sentenced me was something I would never forget, something I would never not hear. Something that would haunt me for the rest of my life. "I did seven years of an eight-year sentence."

"Jesus."

"Trust me, Jinx—he wasn't at that sentencing."

Memories of those first few nights in jail, of the fear and the sickness and the anger—at everyone around me because of how unfair life was, but not at myself...not yet—clogged my mind. I'd hated the world but had hated myself more for needing that fix. That way to make the world around me fuzzy and hide inside myself. All these years later, and I still itched for something to help me cope when my emotions came into play. When everything around me suddenly felt like *too much*. When I couldn't put my hands on a piece of wood or a stick or a knife that would transform the ordinary into more and take over every thought in my muddled brain. Carving wood kept me sane when the world tried to make me crazy, but I couldn't carve all the time. So I took a few deep breaths, searching hard for some sort of balance. Shoving the memories to the back of my mind to deal with later.

The mattress dipped as Jinx sat beside me, her very presence stealing every bit of my attention and making my chest tighten. I rose a little and turned her way, watching. Needing. So close. I could smell the soft, floral perfume that clung to her. Could almost taste it on the air.

I suddenly wanted to taste it on her skin instead.

"I'm sorry that happened to you," she said, her voice quiet and soft. Her eyes locked on to mine. "That asshole sheriff deserves to be shot for what he did."

Irony, thy name is Sheriff Baker. "He was."

She blinked. "They shot him for pressing fake charges?"

"No. Someone shot Sheriff Baker for trying to kill his girlfriend." I lay back on the bed, staring at the ceiling. Needing a moment to calm my thoughts. "Either way, he's dead."

She opened and closed her mouth as if to speak but seemed unable to find the words. I totally understood that. Baker's treachery in my arrest and subsequent trial, how he'd padded every piece of evidence to make sure my charge was just harsh enough for such a rough penalty, his constant threats hanging over my head, how he'd helped destroy what little life I'd had— all of that ended the moment someone else had pulled the trigger. If I'd have been man enough—if I'd been as tough and badass as my two older brothers with all that training and experience in war—maybe I would have been the one to do it. Maybe I would have shoved a gun in his face and pulled that trigger. Going back to jail hadn't seemed worth the satisfaction that act would have brought me, though. And really, I'd never been given the opportunity.

I would never know what I'd have done if I had, though.

"So," Jinx said as she lay down beside me and inched closer. Bringing our shoulders together and forcing me to stop breathing. "How long since your release?"

"Five years."

"Still sober?"

The carefulness of that question, the obvious concern, gutted me. I was proud to say, "Absolutely."

She nodded, almost seeming to hold her breath for a moment before whispering, "I'm sorry I always ask if you want a beer."

I hadn't expected that. "Don't be. Alcohol wasn't my thing, but even if it had been, you didn't know. It's my job to turn down temptation."

"Yeah, but there's no sense in tempting you even more."

With alcohol. Not with her body, which was the sort of temptation that had me sliding ever closer to her. Moving so our arms, legs, and hips touched as well. "I'm okay with you tempting me. I've actually grown almost used to it."

She bumped me with her shoulder. "Quit being so charming."

"I'll try, but since I don't know how to be charming, it might be difficult to turn off."

"I'll tell you when you're charming me. That way, you can learn how to be a regular loser guy instead of someone sort of great."

This girl. "Perfect. Thanks. It's what I've been wanting—a crash course in how to be a loser. I appreciate the help."

"You're welcome. Just doing my part to save the world from falling for the local fish."

"My name's Finn."

"I know." She turned toward me, grinning. "But you'll always be my fish."

Hers. I shouldn't like the sound of that as much as I did already.

"So," I said, turning on my side to face her as she mimicked my movements. "Quid pro quo. Tell me something about yourself."

Her smile fell, and her eyes grew wary. "Like what?"

How you got those scars. Why you're messed up in motorcycle clubs. Where you're from. What you want out of life.

Can I take you to dinner sometime?

"Like...what's your favorite color?"

"Orange." She gave me a sourpuss sort of look. "That one was too easy."

It was. Intentionally so. I had a feeling if I went for anything deeper, she might shut down. I couldn't have that. "True, but I want to circle back to your answer for a minute. You really like orange? No one likes orange."

"That's a second question. I don't have to answer you."

Trickster. "You asked about prison. I should get at least ten easy ones for that mammoth discussion."

"Five."

"Eight."

"Deal. And yes, orange. I like orange. It's...happy."

"Yellow is the color of happy."

"Ugh." She recoiled, her face twisted up as if something stunk. "No one looks good in yellow. Orange is way better."

I had no way to argue that one, so I didn't even try. "Okay then. Let me see—question number two."

"Three."

"No, two. I asked your favorite color."

"True, but then you asked me to confirm my reply. That counts as a question. This is question number three."

"You cheat."

"At almost everything. Keep up."

Damn, this girl was fun. "Okay. Question three." I traced a pattern down her arm toward her hand, nearly biting my lips as she flinched when I reached her wrist. She wasn't ready to talk about those scars, the ones around her wrists or the ones stacked in lines along her inner arm. That was okay—I wanted to know more about her than that. "What is the meaning behind your favorite tattoo?"

She stared at me for a long time, her breath evening out. Her eyes locked on mine as she held stock-still. And then she sighed. "My favorite is a promise to my mom."

That was it. Her only answer. And she didn't move. "You're not going to show me which one it is?"

"That would be another question."

I pursed my lips and gave her a fake but hopefully effective glare. "Sneaky."

"No. Literal. You asked the reason behind my favorite tattoo, not which one was my favorite. You were the sneaky one thinking I'd show the tattoo to you and then explain it."

She had me. Fun and smart—I was a goner. "Fine. Question four. Would you punch me if I hugged you?"

Her eyes widened, and a slow smile tugged at the corners of her mouth. "Probably not."

"Probably not. Okay." I sat up, nodding. "I'll take that."

"Now?" she asked, sounding almost panicked as she bolted upright.

"Now what?" I rose to my feet, stretching as I did.

She blinked and dragged her eyes up my torso. "Are you going to hug me now?"

"Not unless you want me to." Because I wanted her to want it, wanted her to ask for it. I wanted her to make that move. I'd been the one to reach for her hand tonight. Twice. She'd accepted the advances, but I didn't want to push. This girl didn't need me to take... She needed to make the call.

But it seemed she wasn't quite ready yet. "Then why did you ask me if I'd punch you?"

"To be prepared in case you asked."

"So, you think I'd ask you to hug me then punch you for hugging me? What sort of women have you been hugging?"

"None."

"None?"

"None. Not since my mom died."

Her mouth fell open. "That's..."

"Don't say sad."

"I wasn't going to." But she blushed. A definite tell that, yes, she thought my non-hugging state was sad.

My groan nearly rumbled through the room. "Now you think I'm some loser."

"Mission accomplished."

"What?"

"I said I would help you stop being so charming so you could be a loser again." She grinned. "Mission. Accomplished."

This girl. "You're cruel."

"Sometimes. What's your next question for me?"

Interested. Excited. She was both, and I wanted to keep her that way. Give her time to trust me a little more so she might actually answer a few tough questions. Not tonight, though. "You know, I think I'll hang on to them."

"What do you mean?"

I headed for the door, smiling at her urgency. "Yeah, see—I have to be at work in a few hours, so I'll just hang on to these last four questions until I have more time to get good answers from you."

"That doesn't seem fair."

I nearly stumbled as my body came to a complete stop, and the words my mother had intoned so many times over her life that I heard them in her voice no matter who was speaking fell from my lips. "Life isn't fair."

"Yeah. I get that," Jinx said, oblivious to the pain I'd fallen into. The sense of loss drowning me. She didn't know—couldn't —how much the idea of anything deserving fairness bothered me. How much the very word lied.

"Sun's coming up. I'm going to head home," I said, trying hard to pull myself back together. Working my thumbs against the tips of my fingers as my thoughts slipped to what I could carve tonight. What pieces I had in my workshop. What I could turn from a hunk of death into something pretty and new.

Jinx wasn't ready to let me go, though. "Hey, Fish?"

"It's Finn."

"I know. And someday I might actually stick to calling you by that name, but today is not that day."

Smartass. "Fine. What do you want, Jinx?"

Her voice might not have been as strong as I would have liked, but her words were clear and her consent plain as day. "Will you hug me please?"

Done. I had her in my arms before her question was all the way out, had her off the floor and pulled against me by the time she hit the last syllable. So soft and warm, this girl. So wonderful. And still such a mystery.

I nearly let go when she gasped in what seemed like pain, though. "Jinx?"

"Tighter," she said, curling around me even more. "Just hold me tighter."

There was no saying no to her. I clutched her to me, listening to her breathing slow, feeling her heart thump against mine. Sharing heat with her. There was no greater feeling in the world, no higher high. The world could have stopped right then, and I'd have died the happiest man in it just because I had this woman in my arms. I never wanted to let her go.

"Don't think this means I won't ask you tougher questions," I said as I buried my face in her neck and just...held on. Breathing her in. "I'm taking it easy on you."

She chuckled, wiggling against me. "If this is easy, I'd hate to see you hard."

And that was the moment I almost dropped her as a laugh exploded out of me. Jinx laughed right along with me, keeping her forehead on my shoulder as I set her back on her own two feet. As we both cracked up at her innuendo.

As I did my best to make sure she didn't notice how *hard* I really was.

"I should go," I said once I'd caught my breath.

"Yeah. Okay. I'm not on for another couple of hours, but I may pop over before then for something to eat."

"Let me know what you need. Or if there's something special you want in the kitchen that we don't serve—I can bring it in with me since you don't have a car."

She stood staring at me, considering. Weighing her options, it seemed. Thankfully, she must have come to the conclusion that she could trust me enough to ask for something.

"Green stuff," she said, wringing her hands together. "I miss vegetables and things."

Green. I could do green. "Anything in particular?"

She grinned, leaning out of her door and looking deliciously bright-eyed in the deep pink of the morning glow coming over the eastern hills. "Surprise me."

Challenge accepted.

Chapter Eight

JINX

There wasn't much I couldn't handle at that point in my life—I'd been kidnapped, held hostage, beaten, and far worse. But when a blond woman with a big slow cooker in her arms and a bigger smile on her face showed up at my motel room door, I'd have to admit I was stymied. I'd been hoping to see Finn... She definitely wasn't him.

"Can I help you?"

Her grin faltered as her eyes took a quick trip from my hair to my tattoos to the scars on my arms before darting back up to mine. "I'm Shye Anderson. I heard we had a new resident in Justice and thought I would stop by." She recovered well, that smile kicking back up, raising her arms as if offering me the small appliance. "I brought pot roast and homemade bread for sandwiches."

No way was I turning down that. "Come on in."

Shye moved past me to set up the pot on the chest of

drawers. She then pulled a couple packets of silverware wrapped in napkins from the bag slung over her shoulder and started setting the little round table in the corner. The one I never used for anything more than storage. The one I was apparently about to have lunch on.

"So," I said, drawing out the word. Feeling useless as the woman bustled around my motel room, moving piles of stuff from one place to another to give us room to sit at a real table. "People are talking about me being here?"

"What? No." She frowned my way. "Why would you think that?"

"You said you heard we had a new resident."

"From Alder." She looked up, that smile back on her face. "He told me he brought you back with him from his...*Vegas* trip."

Vegas. Huh. So apparently that was the story he'd gone with. I guess I understood the need to lie—it wasn't as if he could come right out and say, "I went to Boulder to murder your brother because he was a threat to you and happened upon him whipping another woman so, hey—meet Jinx." That might be awkward. But by the way Shye had accented Vegas—had spoken the word with an inflection that made it stand out—I had a feeling she knew there was no Vegas.

Didn't matter—I'd back up his lie. The man had saved my life—I owed him at least that. "He and Deacon brought me back, yeah. They helped me out of a really bad situation."

"They're good folk, these Kennard men. That includes Deacon and Gage as well. Have you met Gage yet?"

"Unless he hangs out at the bar, I doubt it."

Shye snorted a quiet laugh. "There's no way he's been hanging out at the bar. He's got himself a girl in town. Katie—

she owns The Baker's Cottage. You may have gotten food from there—it's the only restaurant in town."

"Finn brought some soup in the other day and shared it with me. Maybe that?"

Shye pulled soft, golden bread rolls from her bag and set them on a napkin in the middle of the table. "On Thursday."

I calculated back, remembering the smile on my face when he delivered the container of soup. The day after our crazy ice cream date. Just a few hours after he'd hugged me the way he had. So much warmth and strength. So much—

Focus, Jinx. "How do you know it was Thursday?"

"Because Thursday is always cream of chicken day, and that's his favorite. You could set a watch off him picking up an order of that and some pie. He's got a bit of a sweet tooth. And a memory issue—he never remembers to bring his wallet with him."

From the drugs—addiction transfer and memory issues were things that happened when you finally sobered up. Or so I'd read. My own mom had struggled with loss of cognitive function over the years of using, growing forgetful and confused whether high or not. It didn't feel right to mention that, though. Seemed like Finn's secret on his end, and mine on my mom's.

Still, I had to smile about one thing. "I noticed the sweet tooth."

She glanced up, looking almost confused. "You did?"

"We went for ice cream in the middle of the night."

"Sounds like Finn." She motioned to the chair nearest me. "Sit. I'll just grab the meat, and we can start."

"Thanks." I lowered myself onto the chair she'd indicated, suddenly unsure of protocol. Was I supposed to pretend as if I knew nothing going on in town? As if I didn't know about the Soul Suckers. Did she? She had to, right? It was her brother

Alder had killed in Boulder. What was I supposed to say and not say?

"You look like a woman about to go into an interrogation." Shye set a plate piled with chunks of roast in between us before taking the opposite seat. "You can relax. I swear, this is just a social visit."

Sure it was. "I'm not usually the most social person."

"Me neither, but Finn said you and I might have a few things in common."

Finn. Every ounce of my attention funneled her way even as I fought off showing it. "Finn told you about me?"

"Just that you were new here, that you and I might have had a similar life growing up, and that I should stop by." She smiled and shrugged. "I would have been here earlier this week, but Alder gets a little overprotective of me. He's really busy with some big order at work, so I had to wait for a day when Alder's brother Bishop was in town so I could have two babysitters."

"Alder isn't with you?" That was surprising as all get-out. I'd taken from his own words and Deacon's that Alder rarely left Shye's side. These Justice men seemed a bit...territorial.

"No, he was needed at the mill. Deacon and Bishop are outside keeping an eye on the motel, though." She gave me a look, the kind that said *I know you're up to something* without words. "Alder's not stupid, you know. He's sure something's going on, but he's letting Deacon and Parris handle it all since that's the path it seems they've chosen."

And apparently, that look was accurate. "I can't really talk about that."

Can't. Won't. Same difference.

"Yeah, I figured. But it's okay—so long as things are under control." She darted a look my way, one that looked calm enough. But the sharpness of her eyes, the depth of that stare—she knew, and she was worried. "Are they under control?"

I held her gaze, giving her the only answer I could. "As much as I think they can be."

Her lips tightened, but her smile never broke. We had a lifetime of conversation in that moment—words exchanged that could never be spoken. An understanding agreed upon that would never be known outside that room. Shye knew a lot more than she let on, as did I. We were two peas in a pod.

Finally, she sighed. "That seems about as much as I could hope for. Alder would step in if he needed to, I think. But he could use a break from running the world of Justice for a bit." Her smile grew, her eyes brightening. "We've got a lot of planning and stuff going on."

"You're getting married, right?"

She practically glowed as she said, "Yes, in just a couple of weeks."

"Congratulations," I said before biting into my sandwich and moaning. "Oh Shye, this is amazing."

"Thanks. It's one of Alder's favorites."

I nearly died with my second bite. "How is this so good? There's nothing here but meat and bread."

"Simplicity is key sometimes. You can fancy that sandwich up with all sorts of stuff—veggies, chutney, aioli, sauces made from ingredients you can't even buy in Rock Falls—but in the end, good meat and fresh bread will knock it out of the park every time."

She wasn't exaggerating. "Well, thank you for bringing this over. Simple or not—it's amazing."

"You're welcome," she said, that ever-present smile softening, almost falling a bit. "I don't want to pry, and I especially don't want to bring up any bad memories, but I have to ask."

Shit. "Ask what?"

"How's your back healing?"

I nearly choked on my food, nearly emptied my stomach all over the cheap little table she'd worked so hard to make into a place to eat. My hands shook as I set my sandwich down. "You know about my back?"

"We have a few things in common, remember?" She kept her eyes on mine as she rolled her arm, showing me the small circles that matched the ones I'd been forced to endure. The burn scars from cigarettes being put out on our flesh. Then she turned slightly and pulled the back neckline of her top a little lower. Tugging it down until mottled flesh appeared. Long, deep scars.

What my whip marks would become.

I had to take a deep breath before I could even think of opening my mouth. "Those Soul Suckers have a particular repertoire, it seems."

"Not the whole club. Just one guy." She cocked her head, that hard stare back. "My stepbrother."

Pistol. The man whom I'd been given to after the Soul Suckers won me in a card game. The man who'd stripped me naked and tied me up. Who'd laughed while he'd whipped me.

Who'd also, apparently, whipped her. "Yeah," I said. "That's the one."

"Do you know what happened to him?"

How to answer that without giving anything away? Without breaking the secrets Alder and Deacon had trusted me with? "I'll say this—he deserved what he got."

She nodded, looking toward the window with unfocused eyes. "He did, whatever it is that he got. Alder doesn't want me to know specifics."

"But you do, don't you? Want to know."

She met my gaze, not flinching as her voice hardened around every word. "I want to be sure he's dead and gone."

Not who killed him or how, not the details. Just the surety. "He is. There's no coming back from what happened. Even a zombie wouldn't have made it through that."

"Good," she said, nodding twice. "Now, how's your back healing? Do you need anything for the pain?"

"Mine doesn't hurt much anymore, and it stopped weeping pretty quickly. The skin just...tugs sometimes."

"When you move in certain ways or stretch," she said with a nod. "That'll happen until the scar tissue forms over the lash marks."

Until I moved into the mottled flesh stage. "Did yours itch?"

Her eyes grew wide and she leaned forward. "Oh my god, horribly. But mine wept for months. He must not have had you on the cross as long as me."

My mouth went dry as her smile fully dimmed and her eyes lost their focus. I'd seen people trapped in memories. That girl wasn't over what her stepbrother had done to her. Not by a long shot.

"I'm sorry," I said, trying hard to keep from wanting to smash the table at the unfairness of it all. "Your stepbrother was an asshole."

"He was. A huge one. I really am glad you don't have to suffer the way I did." She patted my hand. "I remember what it was like to be alone and in pain all the time. I wouldn't want anyone else to have to deal with that."

"And now you don't, because you have Alder."

"Yes," she said, that smile tugging its way back onto her face. Not as bright as before, but there. "And the people of Justice are so nice. Give them a chance—you might find some really good friends here."

If I stayed after this mess with the Soul Suckers was over. A picture of Finn popped into my head, but I pushed that away. I wasn't about to stay in some town for a man. Not even one as kind and funny as the fish.

We spent our lunch chatting about our favorite meals and recipes, swapping tips and laughing over some of the complete failures that had come out of our kitchens. We were in the middle of one such story when a knock sounded on the door and Deacon poked his head inside.

"What's so funny in here?"

"Shye was just telling me about the time she tried to make s'mores in the microwave." Tears had started running down my face from laughing so hard, and there was no way I'd be catching my breath anytime soon. *In the microwave* would forever be embedded in my mind as one of the funniest things I'd ever heard.

Deacon obviously had no idea why that would be funny. "What's a s'more?"

Our laughter stopped, and Shye frowned. "Are you being serious?"

"Yeah," I said, unsure whether to run to the grocery store right then or smack him upside the head. "How could you have never had a s'more?"

He shrugged, seemingly unaffected. "I don't know what they are, so figuring out where in the lexicon of my life things went wrong is an impossibility. Why is it funny to make them in the microwave?"

"They have marshmallow on them." A blank face met Shye's answer. "Are you telling me you've never put a marshmallow in a microwave?"

"I don't know that I've ever had a marshmallow outside of something already made."

I suddenly wanted to know a lot more about this guy. "You're a mystery, Deacon Manns."

He grinned again, looking charming as all get-out. And handsome. The man had a roughened movie-star quality to him. "I'm just a guy. One who was sent to deliver clothes to you."

He handed me a bag before leaning down to press a kiss on top of Shye's head. "Thirty minutes, then I have to get you home or—"

"My carriage will turn into a pumpkin?"

"More like your prince will turn into the beast and decimate the town to find you."

Shye actually giggled. "Sounds about right."

Deacon rolled his eyes before stepping outside, closing the door behind him with little more than a nod in my direction. Shye didn't even wait to tackle that little bag of clothes—just reached inside and started yanking out stuff. Folding shirts and pants then placing them on the bed behind her as she went.

"You don't have to do that," I said, collecting our garbage from lunch to toss in the can outside.

"It's fine. I like to keep busy."

As did I, which was why I had the room cleaned in no time. Trash cleared and clothes folded, I sat down to face the woman who had shown up unannounced. The one I had a feeling I'd like to have as a friend. "Thanks for all of this."

She waved me off. "It was nothing."

It was definitely *not* nothing. Not to me. "Seriously, don't downplay this. You have no idea how nice it is to have real food after living on burgers and protein bars for a week."

I felt like an ass complaining, though. I hadn't been in Justice long, hadn't been out of the Soul Suckers' hold for more than a matter of days really, yet I'd gotten a job, a place to stay, food, safety, and now a possible girlfriend to commiserate with. Plus Finn. I had a lot to be thankful for.

"Sorry," I said, not wanting to seem too greedy. "I know I should be grateful for—"

"My dad—who was president of the Boulder Soul Suckers—used to tell people to be glad they got anything at all." Shye looked at me as if she could see deep down into the darkest hiding places in my mind. "Alder tells me that's accepting scraps and that it's okay to want more. To even ask for it."

And...yeah, she knew. Understood exactly the sort of mentality that had been forced upon me. But the genesis of that sort of thinking wasn't just from the Soul Suckers. Having a mom who worked the clubs for a living didn't exactly make for a stable living environment, and sometimes food wasn't the priority for a night's wages. My mom had tried when I was younger, but things had never been easy for us. I had to be grateful for what little I got because there wasn't much to go around. And now, I worked in a bar mostly for tips. I didn't see things changing.

When I didn't say anything in return, Shye sighed. "Look, Jinx, you don't know me yet, but I think we have a lot in common. I grew up in the MC world. I know how bad being involved in a motorcycle club can get."

And still, I said nothing, thoughts of my mom and my childhood whipping through me like a tornado. Stirring up the dark and dirty of my past. Of hers. Of a life that had started off bad and slid downhill fast. Too fast.

Shye didn't push—simply nodded, not looking at me as she said, "You need all these dark cotton shirts because the lash marks on your back may keep oozing. Wear a tank top under them to keep from showing on the outside. That way no one wonders what's wrong. The skin will feel tight for a few weeks, I hate to say. They'll also burn and itch, but that means they're healing. Use some aloe vera to keep everything moisturized. I'll have Finn drop some off to you."

"Great," I said, trying hard to come back from the bad places in my head. "Thanks."

"And when you're ready, we can talk about the rest." She glanced my way then darted her eyes to her hands as she refolded the pants she'd already straightened. Avoiding me. "Our histories are likely the same. The clubs, the men, the...stuff."

Stuff. She couldn't even say the word, let alone talk about what made up stuff. I had a feeling her stuff was far different from mine. I gritted my teeth as I said, "That won't be necessary."

"No, really. I'm here if you want to—"

"Did they sell you like cattle?"

She looked as surprised as I felt at my outburst. "Sorry?"

In for a penny, in for a pound. "Sell you. In an auction. Did they strip you down, stand you on a dais, and sell you to the highest bidder?"

Her face paled. "No. I—"

"Did they ever use you as collateral in a card game? Throw you in like some plastic chip or hundred-dollar bill?"

"Jinx, I don't—"

"Did they? You were brought up in the clubs, right? Your daddy was a member, so you were a girl on the periphery. Accepted and considered one of their family, but not allowed inside, right?"

"For most of it, yeah."

Figured. "Well, I wasn't. You were raised as if you had value to those men, even if they turned on you later. I never held any status within their club. You *don't know* how bad things can be inside. So, while I'm sure your story is similar to mine, it's not the same. My mom hung out at the clubs, but I wasn't a member's kid. I didn't have any value to them other than my body from the time I hit puberty, so I stayed away. Ran away, really. It nearly killed me to throw myself into their world."

Shye's expressive face fell a little, her brow tightening and her lips pursing. "Why did you, then?"

Any possible words disappeared. *Open mouth, insert foot.* Why did I go to the Black Angels MC? To find my mom. Why did I stay with them? Because I was an idiot of epic proportions and bought their story. Big mistake. Huge.

And not something I ever talked about. "That's not your business."

Thankfully, Shye didn't push. She also didn't drop her smile as she collected her slow cooker and utensils. "Okay. This may have turned in a direction I hadn't intended, but I had fun today. Thank you for letting me invade your space and for being so kind. I think it's about time for me to get home before Alder comes looking, though. You come see me real soon, okay? Bring Deacon—I need to rile him up a little every now and again."

I followed her to the door, my eyes burning. This girl had been kind to me, and I'd shot down her words. Had tossed up a wall between us that I had no way to tear down. I felt like an asshole.

And yet, as Shye left, she turned and gave me another one of those soft, sweet smiles. "You're in a safe place now. If there's one statement of mine that you can believe in, it's that one. These men won't let bad things happen to you."

I'd heard that before. "And when I'm of no use to them anymore?"

"That's not how they operate."

Yeah, well...I'd have to wait to make a determination on that one.

And I would—wait, that is. I'd hang around Justice for a while. I liked working for Deacon, and the rest of the townspeople who came into the bar all seemed nice. Plus, Finn was here...somewhere. Not at the bar yet today for sure, but he'd turn up. He always did—seeking me out to say hi and see how I was doing. Watching me work or jumping in to help me. Hanging around the bar until my shift ended so he could walk me back to the hotel and give me a hug. Sweet, kind Finn. Even just thinking his name made my heart do weird somersaults in my chest. Made my body respond in a way it never really had before.

He made me want things that would hurt to lose.

And that would have been the most terrifying thing of all.

Chapter Nine

FINN

Being able to talk to Lainie and Elijah every day was definitely a deterrent to the low-buzz anxiety I endured. Sometimes, though, I just needed my brother. My twin.

"It feels as if nothing is happening."

A scratchy noise came over the speaker of my phone, likely the sound of Elijah sighing. "As much as I agree with Lainie that Alder can be a controlling asshole, he's not going to let some biker gang take over the town. I'm sure he's doing something."

I flicked a chunk of sawdust off the piece of wood I'd started carving the day before. I still wasn't sure what it would become, but the swirls in the grain spoke to me. The smoky-blue color making it impossible not to turn it into something more than firewood. "He's not really involved in this one."

"Wait," Elijah said, his voice no longer calm or steady. "Are you saying things are happening in Justice that Alder doesn't have his hands in?"

I snorted. "You sound like Lainie."

"That's because I spend way too much time with her. I need a life."

"You have one."

"A better one."

"You can always come home."

That earned me a full-on guffaw. "And what? Defend people against traffic tickets?"

I could see his point. "Retire young. Come back and live a nice, slow life of fishing and hunting and—"

"I haven't fished or hunted in over a decade."

"You might enjoy it."

"I might bludgeon you to death with a fishing rod before the first week is out."

Truth. "Fine. Stay with Lainie and suffer your non-life of espressos and fancy cars and big trials."

"And long nights and empty beds and microwave dinners. Don't leave out the highlights, Finn."

I held up the hunk of wood, squinting as I brought a chisel to a particularly intricate pattern. Wanting to follow the curves. "My kingdom for a night in yours."

"Anytime, brother. Come on out to Denver, and I'll show you the town. Take you to a good restaurant."

"We have a good restaurant."

"So you say. You also think the truck stop has fine food."

The truck stop. Where Jinx and I had shared sundaes. Where I'd held her hand for the first time.

Things I shouldn't be thinking about and that even Elijah didn't need to know about. "I could go for some of their huckleberry pie right now."

"I know, and you'll be bemoaning the short huckleberry growing season for the next nine months."

My twin knew me well. "Just as you'll be complaining about how boring your life is until the next woman comes around to give you something to do."

He huffed a laugh. "Fine. Maybe. Hey, I think I might come home for Christmas this year. Want some company?"

That got my attention. "Is Lainie coming too?"

"Doubt it."

"You know you both have to be here for Alder's wedding."

"I know that. She does as well. We'll be there, but I was thinking I'd come see you for Christmas also. Hang with my favorite brother for a bit."

Unusual. That decision was definitely unusual, but I'd never turn him down. "You're always welcome here."

"Good. I'll make plans. I have to get to work, but you text or call if you need anything."

"I will. Same to you."

"Always."

I tapped to end the call, rolling the wood in my hand as my mind wandered. Home for Christmas. Elijah hadn't come home for the holidays in...four years? Maybe five. This would be a treat, though it got me worrying that there was a reason for coming home twice in as many months. That there was something wrong. He'd tell me, though. We didn't keep secrets.

Except I hadn't told him about Jinx. The sundaes, the hand-holding, the kiss...none of it. I'd kept all of that to myself.

Maybe he had a few secrets too.

"Okay, wood," I said, focusing back on the project at hand, knowing there was nothing I could do to figure out what was up with Elijah until he was ready to tell me. "Maybe you're about to become a Christmas present."

There were some things that were simply bound to set off my need to have control of my world. Things that ignited the chaos inside my head. Things that reminded me of painful emotions I'd much rather have forgotten completely about.

Dealing in any way with the woman I'd been dating when I'd started using drugs all those years ago was definitely high on that list. Seeing her name on the screen of my phone as I was getting ready to walk out the door for work? Sent my entire world teetering.

I'd barely spoken to Mercy Bell in fifteen years—intentionally so. The only time I'd initiated any contact with her had been when I'd been working my twelve steps. I'd written out all of my apologies and had mailed them to the people my addiction had affected...including Mercy. I couldn't have handled a face-to-face at the time, plus asking her to come to the prison where I'd been incarcerated would have just made things more difficult for her, so letter it had been. She'd sent me a reply that had said something to the effect of *I forgive you. Get better.* Done and done... Yet somehow, the guilt that had eaten me alive back when I'd been inside still gnawed at my gut when I thought of her. Because of that, I'd pretty well avoided her since she'd moved home with her young son in tow.

There would be no avoiding her today.

I tapped to answer the call. "What's up, Mercy?"

"Hey, Finn. I hate to bother you, but I can't reach either of your brothers, and I wasn't sure who else to call."

If she was looking for my brothers, this definitely wasn't any sort of social call. "No problem. What is it you need?"

"Are you anywhere close to town? I think there's trouble over here, and I can't go check because I've got Beckett with me."

Her son. One of the few kids in Justice, and someone who

definitely needed protecting. "I'm about six minutes out. Stay put—I'll be there."

"Okay. Hurry."

I tapped to disconnect the call then sent a quick text to Parris before rolling onto the highway. No way was I calling Deacon for backup—he needed to stick close to Jinx in case she needed help. Parris responded immediately with an *already on my way* text that settled at least a few of my nerves. Whatever was going on, I wouldn't have to deal with it alone.

The drive to town passed faster than it should have, mostly because I slammed my foot on the gas and hauled ass the whole way there. Speed limit? No such thing. I needed to get to Mercy. Not because I still had feelings for her—those had been long gone for well over a decade. No, that number coming up on my phone made *me* the Kennard in charge for the moment, the one who needed to take care of Justice and its residents. If Mercy had seen trouble, that meant it was close enough to The Baker's Cottage to possibly involve Katie, which meant Gage would be involved because he didn't leave that girl's side. Three adults and one child were definitely in harm's way, plus anyone else who happened into town at the wrong time.

I'd never wanted to take on the yoke of the Kennard legacy—the responsibility of running the business or the town—yet there was no slowing me down. A Justice resident needed me, and I sure as fuck was going to show up. Alder was working to keep the whole town employed, Bishop was off in Vegas, and Gage—an honorary Kennard, for sure—was likely distracted with Katie. This was on me to handle. Me and Parris.

The man's bike sat outside the hardware store when I rolled up, though he wasn't on it. Nothing else looked out of the ordinary—just a random, quiet weekday on an almost dead Main Street. I parked and hopped out, heading for the entrance to the storefront the Bell family owned. Had always owned as far as I was concerned. Bell's Hardware had been on this same corner my entire life, had actually been there for close to a hundred years. They'd upgraded a few things along the way, but the place still had that look to it. That small-town Americana style. Nothing much had changed over the years except for the name over the door. The sign that once had called out her grandpa and later her dad now showcased her name. Mercy Bell, Store Manager.

A chime dinged as I walked in, though the two arguing by the counter certainly didn't seem to notice.

"I don't know you," Mercy said, glaring hard at the big, hulking biker on the other side of her counter. The one I knew well enough to know he wouldn't like some woman pushing him around.

"Well, you'd better get to know me, sweetheart. Think of me like the local cop—you have trouble, I'm your 9-1-1."

"The Kennards are my emergency number. That's who I called." Mercy finally spotted me, looking all sorts of pissed until she locked eyes with me. The relief I saw there nearly knocked me to my knees. I was a Kennard, a protector of this town, and she acknowledged that with one look. I'd always let Alder and Bishop command those roles because they were the big, bad soldiers and I was the trouble they likely would have tried to keep off our streets. Not this time.

"What's going on here?" I asked, moving up beside Parris. "I figured you'd wait outside for me."

"Thought I'd jump right in, but Beauty here doesn't seem to want my help."

If looks could kill, the glare Mercy sent Parris would have melted him into nothing. "The name is Mercy."

Parris leaned closer, practically growling his words. "Be thankful I'm not calling you Beast."

"Are you saying I'm ugly?"

Jesus. We didn't have time for this. "Hold up. Before we fall down the rabbit hole of name-calling and fairy tales, can we talk about what's going on?" I paused, letting both of them refocus for a moment before looking to Mercy. "What did you see that made you call me?"

Mercy glanced at Parris, at his motorcycle vest, then back at me. The woman had a smirk that could peel paint off a wall, and she unleashed it as she said, "Bikers. Lots of trashy bikers in town."

"Aw, Beauty," Parris said, placing one hand over his heart as if wounded. "You're breaking my heart calling me trashy."

"If the boot fits—"

"Okay." I took a deep breath, trying hard to keep them focused. "So, you saw a group of bikers. How many? And where?"

"Ten, maybe twelve. They drove down Main Street this morning heading toward the highway."

Which would put them on a path to pass by Katie's restaurant. "You seen Gage this morning?"

"Not yet, but I'm sure he and Katie are at the restaurant. You know he won't let her open that place alone."

He sure wouldn't. There was a protective partner, and then there was Gage. The man might as well have been Katie's personal bodyguard for all the time he spent watching out for her safety, and part of that meant she was never alone in the restaurant she owned. Especially not for the before- or after-hours time she spent prepping and cleaning. Everyone in town knew that, though outsiders likely didn't. That would work in our favor.

Mercy didn't have a Gage to be with her—at least not that I knew of. "Was it just you and Beckett this morning?"

"Yeah. Just us."

"And the bikers—they didn't come in here?"

"No, they just rode past me. I would have followed them to see where they went, but Beckett's upstairs and—" she glanced at Parris again, her eyes hardening "—I don't trust bikers around my son."

I jumped in before Parris could even open his mouth. "We should head over to The Baker's Cottage. Make sure Katie and Gage didn't have any trouble. We can loop through town on the way back to be sure they're all gone."

Parris never took his eyes off Mercy. "Sounds good."

Mercy nodded, flatly ignoring the man staring at her and keeping her gaze locked with mine. "Thanks, Finn. I appreciate you coming so quickly."

"Anytime. You can call me whenever you need to."

"Or me," Parris said with a grin. "Like I said before, I'm your personal hero."

She finally looked his way, her face twisting into a sneer. "More like my personal zero."

"You wound me, Beauty. You really do." He knocked on the counter once, as if purposefully grabbing our attention before he said, "You'll change your mind eventually."

"Why don't you hold your breath and wait for that moment?"

"But then I'd miss breathing in that pretty perfume you wear." He leaned over the counter, sniffing audibly as Mercy's face flushed. "Yeah, that's what I thought. You like my attention."

"Back off, Parris," I said, not sure whether Mercy was about to punch him, about to kiss him, or about to run. I wasn't even convinced she knew how she wanted to deal with the man in her face.

Finally, she took a step back and crossed her arms over her chest. Protecting herself. "You are insane. Finn, he is insane."

"Nah, I'm just a man who knows what he wants." Parris moved away from her, giving her room to breathe again. Backing toward the door even as his mouth kept moving. "I'd say see you later tonight, my beauty, but I've got plans already."

"I'd say this playboy attitude is overcompensating for what you lack, you presumptuous asshole, but I prefer to be unique and not follow the trend of every woman you've ever met."

Parris laughed, looking totally at ease with the insult. "You'll give in eventually."

"Never going to happen."

"We'll see."

"You can just keep on looking because the only thing you'll see is my middle finger." Which she showed him. She even arched an eyebrow to go with it. Tough as nails, that woman.

"Do you not want me to leave, or are you just the type of woman who has to get the last word?"

Mercy's mouth fell open before she slammed it closed with a click of her teeth. She stared at Parris for a long moment, silent and still, looking downright rage-filled. Then she turned to me. "It's good to see you, Finn. Tell Katie to pop over if she needs anything. And try to keep your guard dogs chained up, would you?"

And then she stormed out through the door to the stock room, leaving us alone in the store.

It had to be said, and I was the only person around to say it. "That did *not* go well. She hates you, Parris."

"Nah. She's going to fall in love with me. She just hasn't

accepted it yet." Parris gave me a cool look as we walked outside. "You two have a history?"

Fuck. "Yeah. An ancient one."

"Planning on keeping it that way?"

I nodded, sudden thoughts of stormy gray eyes, ink, and scars on arms that I wanted wrapped around me again knocking out any and all other women in my life. "Totally."

"Good. I'm laying claim to that woman."

"I don't think you can just claim a woman. She has to choose to be with you."

"Like I said—she's going to fall in love with me. She just doesn't know it yet. She's a momma, that makes her defensive and protective. I get that. I can work with it too. I just need a little time to make her see how perfect I am."

"And humble. Don't forget humble."

"Perfect for her, jackass. We'd be perfect together."

I shrugged because what the fuck could I say to that?

Parris wasn't finished, though. "You chasing Jinx's tail?"

And that...was a hard question to answer. "We're friends."

"Son, men and women can never—"

Thankfully or not, we were interrupted by Gage as he threw open the door of The Baker's Cottage and stepped onto the sidewalk between us. Tall, thick, and intimidating, with a glower hidden behind the bushiest beard in Justice, he was a mountain of a man suddenly blocking our path. And he wasn't happy. At all.

He stared for a long, quiet moment. Looking from Parris to me and back again before asking simply, "Could Katie be in trouble?"

So he'd seen the bikers roll through town. No sense in trying to sugarcoat things. "No, but I wouldn't leave her alone."

He grunted, a slight shifting in his heavy beard the only visible reaction. "Got a reason Alder isn't involved in this?"

"He and Shye got engaged."

Another grunt. "Heard about that."

Parris said, "We're handling shit while he gets his plan on."

"Makes sense. I don't like it, but it makes sense." He nodded once and held up his fist for bumps from Parris and me before saying, "You know how to reach me if you need anything."

But he had Katie to protect, and that seemed more important than having him as backup. At least for the moment. "We do."

"Good." That beard moved enough for me to know he was grinning. A scary thought, for sure. "But if anything could possibly come Katie's way and you don't give me a heads-up? I'll cut your fucking balls off."

Parris didn't respond. He must have been used to being threatened with castration. Me? I nodded and said, "Understood."

"Nice to be on the same page. Now, go check that those fuckers aren't holing up in the alley or something, then come in and eat." Gage opened the door to head back inside. "Katie will be thrilled to have butts in the seats. She likes feeding people. Besides, it's Thursday. She'll expect you, Finn."

Cream of chicken soup day. The one day of the week I always showed up for lunch. It was a little early for that, but I was already in town. Might as well eat. I'd taken some of the soup to Jinx last week, and she'd liked it. I'd definitely take her more today. And some good, homemade bread. Maybe Katie had green stuff I could bring her. I still needed to get her green stuff.

Fuck, I needed to get that girl out of my head for a few

minutes. Or maybe get her in my arms for longer. "Give us ten, and we'll be there."

The walk around the block of Main Street took almost no time, even with Parris jawing the entire way about Mercy. I had to interrupt him though because my mind was on a totally different woman.

"Think we should call the bar? See if Deacon needs us? Or Jinx?"

Parris grunted, not looking at me. "Jinx is fine. She's got company today."

Company. That word tightened my gut. "Who?"

"Deacon convinced your brother to let his little blondie head over for a visit."

Brother and blondie...Alder and Shye. "Alder let her be at the motel alone?"

The snort Parris gave could have put my own to shame. "He's got two layers of security on her. Deacon and Bishop."

"My brother's in town?"

That got his attention. "You didn't know?"

Nope. Not surprising, though. Bishop and I hadn't talked since the last time we'd seen each other. The day he'd punched me in the jaw for my part in Anabeth's leaving Justice in high school. One more apology owed, one more thing to feel guilty about. I'd deserved that hit. I deserved a lot more.

"Bishop and I don't really talk much."

"Huh." Parris turned into the alley, pulling a gun from under his coat. "You really are the weak link in the Kennard chain, aren't you?"

"I guess so." The words came easy, but my mind revolted at the notion. I wasn't the weakest link—not by a long shot. I knew that, but I doubted anyone else would have. The frustration of that burned, and yet I knew it was my own fault. I chose to keep certain things private, to not burden my siblings with my past.

We continued on our hunt for anything out of the ordinary, Parris leading the way and me following along. Distracted by my own thoughts. No bikers laid in wait, thankfully. Everything was as quiet and empty as I'd expect in the post-lunch, pre-dinner hours we were in. Most of the men in town were busy working at the mill, and there wasn't anything in town for people to do unless they were going to eat or in need of something from Bell's. Downtown Justice sat empty.

Once we'd made sure the bikers had moved along, I headed inside the restaurant with Parris on my heels, finding my favorite seat at the bar and hopping up. Gage gave me a head nod before rising from his seat and lumbering into the back, while Parris took the stool next to mine.

It didn't take him long to fill the silence. "I'm surprised you're not a military guy."

Not something I heard often, or ever. "Why's that?"

"You're regimented. Orderly."

More like slightly compulsive. "I need to be."

"Learn that skill inside?"

Inside. As in prison. Deacon wouldn't have told him that about me, and I doubted he'd spent much time with the others. That meant Jinx had likely taken what I'd told her in trust and spread it. That hurt a lot more than it should have.

"Yeah, prison. Jinx tell you why?"

"Jinx doesn't tell anyone shit, so get that thought right out of your head. If you talked to her, those secrets are safe. I saw the tattoo and put a lot of puzzle pieces together is all."

My ink. Twice now people had recognized it for what it was. A virtual calling card to a number of years spent inside, being caught in someone else's web. "It's just...not something I usually talk about."

Except with Jinx. And now with Parris.

"I can understand that. But you've taken the best part from it, seems like. The regimentation."

"And then some. A lot of the same shit, different day, you know?"

"Yeah," he said with a sigh. "I do."

That sounded literal. "You did time?"

"A nickel."

Five years. Less than me but still long enough to leave a mark on you. "That's a good chunk of time."

"And what got me thrown in there was worth every second." Parris sat back and smiled as Gage brought out our soups with a basket of crusty bread. "You a waiter now, man?"

Those black eyes pinned my seat neighbor in place. "I'm whatever that woman needs me to be, and right now, she needs me to run orders so she can finish the meatloaf for tonight's special."

Parris grinned. "Smart man."

"No shit." He set everything down in front of us, even retrieving packets of silverware from under the bar. "Need anything else?"

"Nah, we're good." I grabbed my bowl and pulled it close. "Tell Katie thanks for this."

"You bragging on that soup and coming in every week to eat it is thanks enough, but I'll tell her."

Parris sat quiet as Gage walked back into the kitchen, only making a noise once he tasted the soup. A noise very much like a groan of satisfaction.

"That's fucking amazing."

"It is. This is why I come every week for it." I took a bite, practically sighing and sinking into the bowl in pleasure. "Don't doubt my love for good food."

"I didn't doubt you. I doubted something as simple as soup could be this good. Color me wrong."

We ate in silence for a while, both of us seeming to enjoy the fresh bread and soup combo that had become my staple lunch on Thursdays. I was just starting to think about what pie I might order for dessert when Parris spoke up.

"I heard you've been asking around for a Soul Sucker named Coyote."

Coyote. The man who'd killed Camden's wife, Leah. The man we owed a visit to. "What about it?"

"Just wondering what you wanted with him."

"I've got a friend who owes him something."

"Like what?"

"Like something that isn't your business." I took a sip of my soda, side-eyeing the man. "It's Justice business."

Parris just chuckled. "Son, I'm all up in Justice's business already. But really, if you want Coyote, I might be able to help you find him."

"At what cost?"

"A favor to be named later."

Dangerous. That was definitely dangerous, and yet... "I'll take you up on that. You get me info on Coyote, and I'll owe you one."

"Sounds good." Parris set down his spoon and sat back, looking far from done with this conversation. "Jinx tell you about her mom yet?"

That question left me in an awkward position. If my secrets were safe with Jinx, hers should be safe with me. And with Parris. I didn't want to learn anything new about her from him.

"No. And I'd prefer if she tells me whatever it is you're thinking about."

"Trust me, son. I wasn't about to spill her secrets any more than she'd spill mine. But a word of advice? Ask her."

"About what?"

"Her mom. It's definitely not my story to tell, but you need to know it. So, ask her."

"You think she'll tell me?"

"Probably not. Ask anyway. And keep asking until she does."

I had a few questions left from our quid pro quo night. Maybe asking something more personal would work in my favor. Or maybe she'd clam up and never talk to me again. Either way, it was time for a subject change.

"We hitting that club anytime soon?"

Parris grunted. "Definitely. I'm waiting on one last bit of intel before we strike."

"They're obviously playing a little cat and mouse with us, coming into town like they did today. I don't like that."

"Me either, but I'm not going in unprepared."

"Now you sound like Alder."

"The man was Special Forces—that's a compliment even for an old Marine like me." He tossed his napkin over his bowl. "You'd have made a good Marine."

"My best friend spent a few years serving as a Marine, but with a brother in the Army and another in the Navy? The Marines wouldn't have been an option for me." The fights between Bishop and Alder over Army versus Navy were bad enough. Add a third branch in there, and we might have had our very own war, Kennard-style. "Besides, I never wanted to join the military."

"What did you want to do before you got caught up?"

I shrugged one shoulder, thinking back over all the things I let go of while off chasing a high. "Go to college. Maybe med school. Have a life."

"You've got one."

Hadn't I just said the same thing to Elijah that morning? I suddenly understood why he'd argued with me about it. I didn't have a life—I had an empty house, a routine that left me mostly alone, regrets that could have filled the Grand Canyon, and no one nearby to talk to when things went bad.

Except Jinx. Lately, at least. "Maybe."

"Not maybe, son," Parris said with a shake of his head. "You've got friends here and family that most people would kill for. It might not be the life you'd planned, but it's an attractive one nonetheless."

"I guess so."

"Talk to Jinx. Compared to hers, your life looks like fucking Disneyland." He stood and stretched. "I need to hit the head. Can you ask for the checks?"

"Yeah. Sure," I said, nodding. Knowing I'd left my wallet in my truck as I always did. The one thing I let myself forget without worrying over it since I would always remember where to find it.

But my mind wasn't on checks or paying Katie or wallets I simply couldn't remember to hang on to; it wasn't on anything in Justice, really. It was on Jinx and the scars that covered her arms. The pain in her eyes and the way she shut down whenever anyone tried to get close to her. Anyone but me.

Maybe I would ask about her mom one of these days.

And maybe, just maybe, I'd try to find a way to bring a little extra light to her life since she'd brought quite a bit to mine already. That meant I needed to make a trip to Rock Falls before heading into work for the night.

Chapter Ten

JINX

Working in a bar meant eating bar food. The greasiness and lack of options really hadn't been bothering me that much until Shye had come over with that pot roast sandwich. *Don't know what you've got until it's gone...* That pot roast was gone, and I wanted more. With extra potatoes this time. And carrots. I might have been hungrier than I'd thought. I needed to grab something before I started drooling on the bar.

"Hey, Fish," I hollered, catching the man in mid-lift. He'd been fiddling with the chairs all evening—cleaning them, flipping them upside down on the tables to replace the little metal feet, adjusting them until they were as solid as an oak tree in the forest. I'd never seen someone take such care of furniture in my life. And while watching him had been fun—the man had some serious muscles in those arms of his—my stomach needed not to be empty any longer. "I'm taking a break. I need to eat something."

"Sounds good." He nodded, moving around the table to get the best angle on the chair he'd set his sights on. Not hurried in his movements. Casual and cool and altogether far too sexy.

"You keep staring at that boy that way, and he's going to come looking for what you're offering." Rhonda, a past-the-point-of-middle-age woman with a permanent football helmet haircut and some wicked eyeliner winging skills, took a sip of her Old Fashioned and gave me a wink. "Though maybe that's what you're wanting."

"We're just friends." The answer came automatically, but the words felt wrong. Sounded wrong, too. Were we friends? Only friends? We talked a lot at work, and he'd kissed me. A good kiss. A great one. But that hadn't been repeated since. For days, I'd been expecting him to show up at my door and ask for more, but he hadn't. So...maybe friends it was.

Ugh.

Rhonda was far more perceptive than I'd given her credit for. "Friends don't look at friends like they want to hump them through the floor."

"Rhonda."

"What?" she said with a raise of her shoulders and an exaggerated innocent expression on her face. "I call them like I see them."

"Well, you can call them however you see fit. Silently. Or at home. When's your ride coming?"

She frowned and looked at her watch. "He should be outside already. You behave, girl." She finished her drink and pushed the glass toward me before rising from her stool. It took her a little longer to put her coat on, her fingers shaking against the thick fabric. Rhonda was a good drunk—kind and sweet—but she was still drunk at four drinks in.

There was no way she'd make it to the door without stumbling. "Why don't I—"

"Hey, Rhonda." Finn swooped in, giving Rhonda a smile that made her eyes go unfocused and her own thin lips turn up. "I'm sorry I didn't get to talk to you tonight. How are you doing? How's Rusty?"

The woman beamed—positively beamed—at Finn as he subtly and yet determinedly led her to the door. "Oh, Finn, you work too much. You should have more fun. That's what I always tell my Rusty. My grandson is going to go to the grave without having a lick of excitement in his life. You know he's working for your brother, right? Out on the mountains cutting trees just like his daddy and my dear husband did. Such strong men."

The two walked slowly to the door, Finn obviously holding her up at times and keeping her on her feet. All the while, she chatted and laughed, the social side of her loosening up under the lubrication of all that alcohol. And Finn never missed a beat —patting her arm, grinning, responding to her questions. He'd make sure she got to her ride's car just fine so she could make it home. A good man, that Finn Kennard. A real good one.

Friends. Ugh.

I headed for the back, my thoughts trapped in a cyclone of Finn. Sweet, kind, strong, protective Finn. My friend. I'd called us friends. I hadn't considered anyone a friend in a long time, but the label seemed to fit our relationship. Maybe. Friends hugged, right? I could look past the kiss—though I didn't want to—because it seemed to be a one-time thing. Friends didn't kiss. But they did hug and look out for one another. They thought about the other when they weren't around. I mean, sure, thinking about Finn naked may have been a bit over the friend line, but that was normal too, right?

"Food. Just get food, then back to work." I beelined for the chest freezer to grab a frozen burger patty before hitting the small walk-in refrigerator at the back of the kitchen. Cheese. I needed cheese to complete the burger. And maybe a pickle. Pickles counted as something green, right? A vegetable? I missed those.

But when I stepped into the fridge, what stood before me was not the usual potatoes and condiments and stacks of processed orange cheese product. Oh, no. The refrigerator had become a virtual forest. Green lined every shelf of the one side, creating an almost patchwork art piece of fruit and vegetables. Apples, celery, plastic boxes of lettuces of all kinds, cucumbers, asparagus, Brussels sprouts, even avocados. So much green—way too much.

Green stuff...surprise me.

Finn had remembered my casual request. And he'd definitely surprised me.

I wrapped my hand around an apple all slow-like, as if the thing might disappear before I could grasp it. As if it was some weird part of my imagination. But the flesh felt cool and smooth against my skin, the apple heavy with the moisture within. Nope —totally real.

When I'd been a kid, I'd asked my mom for more vegetables in the house, and she'd laughed at me. Had said only her Jinx would want more vegetables instead of fewer. She'd supplied them, though. Nothing like this—nothing extravagant. I'd gotten canned veggies and whatever had come out of the gardens of the old ladies at the club. I'd eaten every bit of it, knowing how much effort my mom had put into bringing all those things into my life.

This was...ten times the effort. And a hundred times the result. "I will never be able to eat all this."

"Good thing I come with an appetite."

I spun, holding that bright green apple to my chest as if to hide the thumping of my heart behind it. Finn stood in the doorway, looking completely casual again with his shoulder resting on the jamb and his feet crossed at the ankles. I'd have called it a pose and wondered if he'd practiced it at home, but Finn wasn't that type of guy. He wasn't fake. This was just him being...all Finn-like.

I liked it. A lot. "This is too much."

"You wanted green stuff."

"Yeah, but—"

"I got you green stuff."

"And then some." I looked over the wall of green again, an unfamiliar burn in my eyes making it hard to see. He'd listened to me, remembered something I wanted, and had gone above and beyond my simple request. He'd just rocked my entire world off its foundation...with produce. "No one has ever done so much."

"It was just a trip to the grocery store."

I faced him, shaking my head slowly. "No, it wasn't. Not to me."

We were silent for a long moment, both of us staring at the other. Neither moving. I wanted to, though. Wanted to run to him and throw my arms around his neck. Wanted to press my body to his and steal some of his warmth. I wanted...and that desire might have been more terrifying than anything else. What if he didn't feel the same? What if he did?

"Hey, Jinx?"

"Yeah?"

Finn looked down and took a breath before refocusing on me, his eyes intense. Determined. Was he nervous?

"I'd really like to hug you right now."

Blunt. Honest. I could only respond in kind. "I'd really like it if you hugged me right now."

He was on me in a heartbeat, had wrapped his arms around my waist and picked me up off the floor in the next. I clung to him and that ridiculous green apple, refusing to let go of either. Needing the security of both to keep me grounded, as just touching Finn might have sent my heart soaring into orbit.

My body moved of its own accord, enveloping him. My legs lifting without my intention to wrap around his waist. My hands sliding up into his hair, gripping tightly to lock him to me. Every inch of me pressed against every inch of him. And Finn, he never faltered. Never loosened his hold or stumbled. He simply gripped me just as tightly, wrapped himself around me just as completely, and breathed into my neck as if he'd been suffocating without having me to hang on to. I knew that feeling. That tightness in the chest that came with being apart from him. I'd been living with it since the last time we'd hugged.

I was tired of fighting the need.

"Finn." I kissed his neck, running my nose along the length of it and letting my lips follow. Letting them drag along his flesh. "Finn, please."

Finn met my whispered plea with a small groan as he slid his hands down to cup my ass. As he pressed our hips together tighter. Closer. I couldn't hold back my own throaty moan as I answered his grip with a rock of my own, as I pressed against where he was so hard.

But then he stiffened.

"Sorry. I should have asked first," he said, his voice tight as he moved his hands back up to my waist.

That wasn't what I wanted, though, so I did the only thing I could think of to tell him without words. I pressed another wet kiss to the base of his neck, licking him there as well. Moaning against him as I wiggled in his hold.

"Touch me, Finn."

"Fuck," he hissed, those hands coming right back to where I wanted them. His body responding to mine as I continued to kiss and lick and even bite his neck. "You're killing me, Jinx."

"Same." I reared back, needing to look into those eyes. To see his face. Needing to watch his expression. "You can kiss me."

He didn't need to be told twice. In typical Finn fashion, he dipped slowly, keeping his eyes on mine. Giving me a chance to back out of my request. Not that I needed one. I arched into him, closing the distance so he could finally—finally—press his lips to mine in a kiss that I felt all the way down to my toes. Sweet but firm, his lips moved against mine. His hands held me up as he moved us to the shelves. As he pressed my back against that beautiful wall of green and softly traced my bottom lip with his tongue.

As I hissed and jerked away from the pain that shot through me.

"Sorry," Finn said, spinning us around so his back was against the shelves instead of mine. "Are you okay?"

"Yeah. Just...my back—"

"Is hurt. Yeah, I picked up on that. I should have been more careful."

Sweet, sweet Finn. "It's fine." I kissed him again, wanting to get back to that feeling. Back to that place where nothing mattered but him and me and the heat of our bodies coming together. "Don't stop, Finn."

"Are you sure?" he asked before once again teasing my lips with his. "I don't want to push you."

"You're not." I opened my mouth and let my tongue meet

his. Just a brush—a tease. A single taste. That was all I needed for my body to burn from within, though. "More, Finn."

He answered my request, groaning into my mouth as he tangled our tongues together. As he kneaded the flesh of my ass and pressed his body against mine. As he drove me to the edge of desire and threw me right over it.

"Finn," I whispered as he moved those wicked lips to my jaw. "I want—"

But I didn't get to finish my sentence. Didn't get a chance to even think about what was coming next in that statement. The entire room began to vibrate, a rumble growing louder throughout the bar. I knew that sound. Knew the base of it, the melody. Knew exactly what to expect outside.

Motorcycles. Lots and lots of motorcycles had just pulled into the parking lot. And there were just the two of us in the bar.

"Is that—" Finn looked toward the door, a frown marring his face. Tugging down those kiss-swollen lips. These guys had the worst timing in the world. "Are those motorcycles?"

"Yup."

He set me down and straightened the waistband of his jeans. "You should stay in here."

As if. "I'm not hiding from them."

The look on his face, the grit there, made him seem ten times as tough as usual. "They might be here for you."

I'd already assumed that. "We need to call Deacon." I pulled away from Finn, running for the front of the bar. Better to meet them outside than have them come in. "And Parris. Get Parris on the phone."

Finn followed right behind me, phone in his hand and thumbs flying over the screen. Likely texting Deacon and Parris. Maybe even one of the Kennard brothers. Good. We needed all the help we could get.

I slid into the workspace and crawled underneath the counter, grabbing the handgun Deacon kept there for emergencies. I didn't like guns, but I certainly knew how to use them. Parris had made sure of that. Well...mostly.

"Is this thing loaded?" I asked, wishing I'd taken the time to learn how to tell instead of just how to shoot.

Finn grabbed my hands and took the gun from me, looking meaner than I'd ever seen him. "I've got that. You should go lock yourself in the office."

Oh, hell no. "You don't get to be some sort of martyr."

"And you don't need to throw yourself in front of me." He clicked off the safety and held the gun as if he knew what he was doing. "Deacon and Parris are on their way. You go hide while I stall these guys."

"I don't like this plan."

"You got a better one?"

"Yeah." I pressed myself against him, rising onto the balls of my feet to plant my lips against his. To kiss him strong and hard, sliding my tongue inside when he opened for me. Hanging on to his arms as I moaned and melted into his hold. At least until he brought the hand holding the gun to my hip. I followed the length of that arm down, down, down until my fingers brushed the bones of his wrist. And then I broke the kiss. "I'm sorry."

"For what," he whispered, his voice rough and his breaths coming fast. Distracted. How I wanted him.

"For this." I yanked the gun from his hand and jumped away, heading for the front door. "Stay inside. I'll deal with these guys."

But, of course, he wouldn't do that. He was a Kennard, after all, and they all seemed to have some sort of protector complex. That whole knight in shining armor thing. Hot, for sure, but stupid as well. Club guys would rip right through that armor then use it as serving plates to cook his entrails over a fire. You couldn't play fair with them—they didn't understand the concept.

"Damn it, Jinx." Finn grabbed my hand just before I opened the door, stopping me. "We go together, okay? I've got your back, you've got mine."

"No, Finn—"

"I mean it—you're not going out there alone."

There was no stopping him. I could see it in his eyes. His mind was made up. I had a feeling my world—the one I'd been sort of building in Justice—was about to come crashing down, something I didn't need him bearing witness to. But I didn't see another choice.

"Fine. But don't protect me."

Finn huffed. "Fat chance there."

"I mean it."

"Are you crazy?"

"No, I'm realistic." I took a deep breath before facing the door. Readying myself for what I knew I was about to walk into. "And really fucking unlucky."

Before I could yank the door open, Finn had me in his arms. He kissed me brutally, the sort of kiss that rocked your soul and left you unable to figure out up from down. The sort that shattered your world and rebuilt it in a way that could only include the other person. The sort of kiss that led to long nights of sweat and sex and pleasure.

The sort of kiss that nearly knocked me to my knees.

"Jinx Reid," Finn said as soon as he pulled away. As soon as he took those wicked lips of his back. "Meeting you was the luckiest thing that ever happened to me. Now, let's go out there and see if we can hold off this swarm of bikers, yeah?"

"Yeah." I licked my lips and took a deep breath, trying hard to focus on the parking lot where that rumbling had never stopped. Where those bikers were waiting us out. Where my past and present were likely about to slam together and cause irreparable damage. Where I could lose Finn if he didn't play by the rules. "Just don't get yourself killed."

"I'll do my best."

His best was going to have to be good enough.

Chapter Eleven

FINN

The rumble of our uninvited guests cut off as soon as we opened the door and stepped outside. All of the engines —silenced in an instant. The night air hung cold and sharp, making our breath something physical in the air, the tension something as tangible as the snow starting to fall around us. But that wasn't the worst part of the scene before me. No, not at all. Snow, I could deal with. What nearly froze me more than the night air was the number of machines facing us.

There were a lot of bikes in The Jury Room parking lot. Too many. Enough to block the view of the highway. They had to be ten rows deep and five or six wide, just sitting there facing the bar. Deacon and Parris had both texted that they were on their way, but until they got here, it was Jinx and me and one Beretta M9 with a magazine of seventeen bullets in it.

The guys needed to haul ass.

"Let me guess," a man straddling the bike that was maybe

three inches in front of all the rest said, smirking my way. "You must be the infamous Finn Kennard."

That statement brought a small amount of relief. At least they were focusing on me and not Jinx. I'd dealt with men like these during my time inside—tough, alpha men who showed their worth through their fists. I knew how to play their game, and I'd win. I had to. "Who wants to know?"

The smirk grew, the arrogance shining through. "Name's Cash. I've heard a lot about you, kid."

"I'm not your kid, and unless you're here to tell me where Coyote from the local Soul Suckers crew is, we don't have anything to talk about."

"Don't know no Coyote. Do you, Creeper?"

The guy next to Cash shrugged with an exaggeration that made it clear he was lying. "Nope. No Coyote that I know of."

"Then I guess we can call this little drop-in visit over, can't we?" I kept my eyes on Cash but couldn't help but notice the guy behind him and to his left. The same guy from the night at the truck stop. The one who'd been staring hard at Jinx. The one I had a feeling she recognized. I didn't dare give him my full attention, but I could sense him watching the woman behind me. Again.

Cash, meanwhile, simply chuckled and turned to talk to the guy beside him, giving me a moment to let my eyes wander away. Fifty bikes, plus or minus a couple. And yeah, that guy was definitely staring at Jinx. Pure rage burned hot and bright under my skin, igniting my temper, but I kept my control over it. Kept my face stoic and forced my eyes back to Cash's location.

But that fucker wasn't coming anywhere near my girl.

Cash finally stopped jawing with his buddies and turned back my way, looking far too confident for my liking. "Who's your friend there?"

Translation: I know who she is, likely know more about her than you do.

"Who're yours?" I nodded my chin in the direction of their posse. "You say you know me, but you can't come talk to me without an entire crew behind you? What's got you so scared, Cash?"

Jinx's fingers brushed against my back, a signal for sure. Not that I needed one. I was skating on thin ice, and I knew it—there was no denying how outnumbered we were. But from my experience, guys like Cash didn't respect politeness and talking out their differences. They responded to strength. Arrogance. This wasn't a full-on attack, or they wouldn't all be sitting in the parking lot, wouldn't have waited for us to come out. This was a dick-measuring contest. And I could swing mine with the best of them.

Sadly for him, Cash was just beginning to figure this out. "What'd you say to me?"

But it was already too late for bravado. The guys around him —especially the ones wearing colors for clubs other than his own —were already chattering and whispering to one another. Already smelling the blood of someone weaker than them in the water. And Cash knew it.

"You think you've got one up on me, kid?"

I drew the Beretta, pulled the slide to disengage the safety, and held it straight out with one hand, arm locked and canted slightly, aiming for Cash's head while keeping my free hand brushing Jinx's hip. Keeping my face calm and my body in front of her. Not the best shooting stance, but one I'd practiced extensively over the years out in the hills around town. One I knew I could use to aim accurately and still keep what was precious behind me.

And then I let the cocksure, testosterone-fueled attitude I'd learned in prison—the one I usually kept tucked away in the deepest, darkest places of my mind—free. "I'll tell you this one last time. I'm not your kid. The name's Finn, and if you don't get it right, I'll carve it into your dead body as a reminder."

I heard Jinx gasp just as Cash moved as if to dismount his bike. An engine roared through the night, though—a truck screaming into the lot behind the bikers. Everyone turned, including Cash. That gave me a moment to grab Jinx by the elbow and shove her backward, almost pinning her against the door. Completely blocking her body with mine just in case. No way was I the only one carrying. If I couldn't make her hide inside, I'd wall her off myself.

By the way her fists connected with my lower back, I had a feeling she wasn't a fan of my plan.

"Settle the fuck down," I hissed just before Deacon's truck slid to a stop. He opened his door and hopped out, grinning widely at the bikers even as the tension tightened the skin around his eyes.

"Gentlemen. I hate to be the bearer of bad news, but The Jury Room is closed for the foreseeable future."

I had my eyes on Cash, so it wasn't until the sound of a second set of footsteps to my left caught my attention that I looked behind Deacon. A man stood with him, one I only vaguely recognized. The badge hanging around his neck I knew at first glance, though.

Deacon had brought the law.

And me? I was fucked. Being an ex-felon with a gun in his possession wouldn't fly with a county sheriff. But if I dropped the Beretta or tried to hide it, I'd leave Jinx exposed. Her life, or heading back inside—the choice was an easy one.

I tightened my grip on the pistol and kept my aim true.

"We were just chatting up old friends," Cash said, eyeing the man with the badge. "You bring the sheriff in on us?"

"Who, this guy?" Deacon nodded toward the man with the badge. The one who stood silent and still as he looked over the dozens of bikers before him. "This is my old friend Zane. He was helping me with a home repair project when we heard y'all had made the trek out here. I figured he could come along, seeing as he knows the county a little better than I do. Maybe he can direct you to a more fitting establishment for your needs."

Cash laughed. "I don't think we need a sheriff to tell us where to go."

The sheriff clapped his hands once. "Well good, then. So we can all get back to whatever we were doing. Right, fellas?"

Cash glared my way, but I didn't flinch. Didn't look away either. I got the message from that look—I'd made him look weak, so he'd be coming for me. That was fine. I'd be ready for him.

"We've done what we came to do," Cash said, glaring my way. "I'll see you around, Finn Kennard."

"Anytime." I didn't drop the gun, though. Didn't relax for even a second. Cash kept looking my way, the two of us in some sort of staring contest. One I refused to back down from.

Thankfully, Cash's own crew called an end to it.

"Let's ride," Creeper said just before he started his engine. The other bikers followed suit, the noise level rising from near silent to cacophonous in an instant. They revved those engines a few times, the sound near deafening, but eventually started to peel off. To leave. Jinx grabbed on to the waist of my jeans, pressing her body against mine. Resting her head between my shoulder blades. Safe...for the moment.

Once the bikers were all gone, having driven down the highway toward wherever they were staying, Deacon headed our way. Dragging me into the bar with nothing more than a hard look tossed over his shoulder toward his *old friend* Zane. "You two okay?"

I had other things to worry about at that moment, though. "You brought the sheriff?"

"Undersheriff Grogan, yeah. I figured you needed all the help I could get."

"Gee, thanks for the vote of confidence."

The man looked ready to roll his eyes, but smartly didn't. "You know that's not what I meant."

I didn't, but whatever. "Why are you hanging with the law?"

"Some things you don't need to know right now. You planning on letting me see her?" Jinx. He meant Jinx, who was still tucked behind me.

Deacon raised an eyebrow, holding it until I stepped to the side and exposed Jinx for the first time. He looked her over from head to toe, smiling softly. "You okay, lucky one?"

Even scared out of her mind—which I could tell she was— my girl was pure attitude. "I'd be better if this big ape hadn't tried to stuff me into a corner. I'm not helpless, you know."

Deacon shot me a look, one that said he was just as impressed by her as I was. "Better than throwing you to the wolves."

"You don't need to throw me to them—they come when I call."

This chick was something else. "Next time, I'll let you hide me instead, okay?"

She narrowed her eyes and glared. "No, you won't."

"You're right, I won't." I gave her hand a squeeze, then refocused on my boss as I held out the Beretta. "That undersheriff going to give me a hard time about this?"

Deacon shook his head and took the gun, double-checking

the safety was on before handing it to Jinx. "What gun? I didn't see you with a gun. You mean the soda gun head? That just needs to go back under the bar. Right, Jinx?"

"Sure. Yeah," she said, palming the gun before heading across the room for the bar.

Well, that was one less thing to worry about. "What's the plan?"

Deacon grimaced before blowing out a harsh breath. "You two get the fuck out of here for a day or so."

"Out of here...as in the bar?"

"Yep. We're closed until this shit is handled."

That wasn't anything I'd been expecting, and my chest tightened up at the thought of my routine being thrown so far out of whack. But I still had Jinx, and my need to protect her overrode just about everything else. "What about Jinx? She's staying at the motel."

Deacon shot a glance at the girl in question, the one walking toward us. Who would likely hear his answer even if she didn't know the question. "Parris is still staying there. Jinx should be fine."

"Jinx is always fine," she said, looking from Deacon to me and back again.

Her confidence wasn't soothing, and "should be" wasn't good enough. I sure as shit wasn't arguing with Deacon in front of her, though. "And you?"

"I'll be working the angles. Like always." He turned toward the door as Zane walked in. "Time?"

The undersheriff gave me a solid look-over, those sharp eyes seeming to take in every detail in a matter of seconds, then refocused on Deacon. "Definitely."

My boss nodded. "Get out of here. Both of you. And don't

do anything stupid. Parris or I will be in touch when we're ready to make a move."

With that, he literally herded us through the kitchen, allowing me to stop and pack up the vegetables I'd brought for Jinx that morning, and pushed us out the rear entrance where my truck was parked in its usual spot. Locking the door behind us as soon as it latched. The Jury Room closed because Deacon had given up on his business. Something I hadn't thought possible. That alone told me how much trouble we were all in.

"Well, now what?" Jinx asked, sounding way smaller than I'd ever heard her.

There was only one answer. "Now you come to my place."

Chapter Twelve

JINX

Fear made you do strange things. I hadn't planned on leaving the motel with Finn. I hadn't planned on jumping into Finn's truck and letting him drive us off into the mountains in the middle of the night. I hadn't planned on the gut-wrenching need to physically touch another human being that swamped me the second we were alone in a closed space together.

I hadn't planned on Finn Kennard at all, but I had a feeling he was going to shatter my entire world.

And after being terrified my life was over, I was ready to let him.

"This is it," he said softly as he turned into an almost invisible driveway between some trees. A small, single-level house sat on a slight rise, the porch light glowing softly in the distance.

"It looks peaceful." Because it did. Everything about the house seemed calming. The straight lines, the tidy flower beds, even the driveway that curved toward a detached garage. Nothing out of place. Not a beer can on the grass, a cigarette butt on the asphalt, or a bag of garbage to be seen. This was what a home was supposed to look like. Such a stark contrast to what I'd been exposed to over the last few years but a nice reminder of what had come before.

Finn shut off the engine but didn't leave the cab of the truck. Instead, we sat in darkness, both breathing just a little too hard. Did he feel the same anticipation and nervousness pounding through his body that was raging through mine? Did he notice the tension growing between us? How could he sit in silence and just...not talk? Because I couldn't.

"Finn, I—"

"I don't bring people here."

Direct. Blunt. That, I would have expected, but not the harshness of his tone. Not the feeling of anger I could sense in his words. "I'm sorry. We don't have to—"

"Don't apologize, Jinx. This is my fault. I need you to know that I don't...do this. I don't bring people—women—home with me."

I couldn't say that I minded that particular declaration. I also couldn't say that I understood where this conversation was going. "Okay."

"It's not okay. This is really far from okay." He gripped the steering wheel so hard, I could hear it creak. "Jinx, can I touch you?"

As if he needed to ask. "Of course."

He turned toward me, circling his fingers around my wrist and leading me across the bench seat. Pulling me close but not overpowering me. Not wrapping me up in his arms the way I wanted him to. Not yet, at least.

And then he sighed. "Almost no one comes here. Not even my family. It's my space, and I'm not the most welcoming person to guests."

My poor Finn. "We don't have to go inside—"

"But I want you here." He sighed and squeezed me closer. "I'm sorry. I keep interrupting you, but I really wanted to get that out. I want you here, but I don't know that I'll do everything right once we're inside the house."

I tugged on his hand until he looked at me, until I knew I had his eyes locked on mine. And then I said the only thing I could in that moment. "Okay."

He jerked back. "Okay? That's all you give me is okay?"

"What else is there to say?"

"I have no idea, but I was expecting more...something."

Silly Finn. "It's almost four in the morning, we worked all night, and fifty bikers showed up looking ready to kick both our asses. I don't have *more* in me right now. If you're worried that you might somehow insult or offend me once we get inside with your lack of social graces, forget all that. I'm a big girl—I don't need a welcoming party. If you're afraid me being in your space will throw you too far off, I promise to be quiet and virtually invisible."

"Not what I wa—"

I put my finger against his lips, quieting him. "Whatever you need, just tell me, and I'll figure out how to give that to you. You said you wanted me here, and I'm glad because there's no place I'd rather be right now than with you."

Without a word, Finn pulled me into his arms and wrapped me up tight, breathing into my neck as I clung to him. As I spider-monkeyed the heck out of his body as best I could. Even when he opened the door and started sliding backward out of the truck, I didn't let go. Couldn't. I needed him to anchor me. Needed the touch and smell of him to lock me in the present and not let me go back to those moments at the bar when I'd first seen all those bikers. When I'd seen a couple who would definitely recognize me. When I'd had a sudden and terrifying thought that they were there to take me back to the Soul Suckers.

Take me away from Justice and the man holding me.

Take me back to hell where I knew my life would end.

Finn never stopped his retreat out of the truck. He simply took me with him, dragging me across the seat then hefting me up his body once his feet hit the ground. I wrapped my legs around his waist and draped myself over him. Enveloping him.

He never said a word about my sudden clinginess as he walked to the front door of the ranch house and unlocked it. As he carried me inside. Not until he had me secured, the door locked behind us once more, and a dim light glowing in his foyer did he say a thing.

"Jinx."

My name. A single syllable whispered into my hair practically undid me, laid me out bare for him to do whatever he wanted to all the broken and damaged parts of me. That one word was more terrifying than anything else he could have said, and it left me feeling vulnerable and shaky. Needy. Unable to hold back as I said, "Don't let go."

"I won't. I just need to figure out where you'll—"

"Finn." Because it was definitely my turn to interrupt him.

He didn't seem to mind. "Yeah?"

"Take me to bed."

He paused just for a moment, a slight beat of time where he stood stock-still before everything kicked into place for him. He toed off his shoes and hung his keys on a small hook by the door. His change went into a bowl beneath them, and the knife from another pocket went with it. No wallet, though, oddly enough. He turned off the light and walked down the hallway, his bare feet padding softly across the wood floors. I got the impression the house was very neutral—in color, in style, and in feel. Neutral and calming, nothing to excite an ex-con addict who probably avoided chaos. And there I was, nothing but chaos, interrupting his peaceful little life.

When we got to his bedroom—soft blue, a lighter shade than his eyes, with gray accents—he paused. Still holding me.

Still far too anxious for me to ignore. "What are you trying to figure out?"

"I still need to grab the produce and your bag out of my truck. And before I go to bed, I usually do...stuff."

"A bedtime routine." Likely born of habits learned in prison as well as from his need to control the chaos of addiction. "So do it."

"I'll have to put you down."

Calm. Find your calm. He needs this. It was as if he could sense the tension inside of me, the fear and need and want building and burning bright. As if he knew the very thought of him taking his hands away from my body caused that burn to spike, to flare. To hurt.

But I had to deal because Finn needed something. "That's okay. You can put me down."

Such a lie.

Finn must have heard the tremor in my voice, the uncertainty, because he shook his head. "It's okay. I can skip it all for one night."

I couldn't let him do that. "Finn."

"Yeah?"

"You bought all that green stuff, and I fully intend to eat it. Plus, I know you have your rituals. I've seen you do enough of them to recognize your need for control and your focus on tasks to fulfill it. Don't worry about me—just take care of you."

He dropped his hands a little lower, squeezing my thighs. Bringing his lips to my neck in a soft, quiet kiss as he whispered, "I want to take care of you, though."

My sweet, sweet Finn. "You will. Once you're done. Go on." I pulled myself away from him, letting my feet drop to the floor. Letting my body release his. I hated it, hated the cold that overtook me as I stepped back from him, the beast that roared inside of me at the very idea of being separated from him. But this was necessary. This was what Finn needed. And it wouldn't take long... I hoped. "Please, Finn. Do whatever it is you usually do. I don't want to upset your routine."

His smile was both sad and sweet at the same time. "You already have."

Ash. That flame inside had left me nothing but ash. "I'm sorry."

"Don't be. I sort of like it."

Sort of. I'd take that over not at all any day. I could come back from the ashes with a *sort of.* "Why don't you do whatever it is you need to do before you go to bed? I'll just..." I twisted my lips into a pucker, hating every word or phrase that came to mind. Despising the very idea of being apart from this man for even a few moments. I was weak, but I wouldn't tell him that. "Hang out. I'll hang out here and wait for you."

He held out his hand, a question in his eyes as he said, "Come with me."

Not a question and yet the option to say no was right there, plain as day. Obvious, Finn didn't boss me around or make demands of me—he gave me options. Choices. He let me decide what I wanted to do. And what I wanted was to go with him —anywhere.

I grabbed Finn's hand and followed along as he moved through the house. He left me in the hallway when he hurried outside to grab my small bag of clothes and the box of produce. Once back inside, he dropped the produce in the kitchen, then set the bag in the doorway to his bedroom. His steps quick and his movements efficient, he started what I had to assume was his regular routine. Locking doors, checking windows, emptying the trash into a bin in the garage, and wiping down his sink. So precise. So ritualized. So calming in a weird sort of way. And I'd been right about the house—neutral and calm, with gorgeous smoky gray and tan hardwood floors throughout. Perfectly Finn.

I couldn't get over the floors, though. I slipped and slid over them, following the swirling gray patterns in the boards as Finn put away the produce he'd bought me. Traced patterns with my socked feet until I ended up back in the kitchen. "This wood is so pretty. Why is it gray?"

"That's beetle kill pine. It's what my family harvests and processes. We own the mill in town."

"Your family owns a mill, but you work in a bar?"

He shrugged one shoulder as he cut an apple, handing me a slice before saying, "I help out when I need to, but I didn't want to take advantage of the situation."

Sweet and tart, the apple flavor exploded over my tongue and made the back of my jaw tingle. Perfect. But that couldn't distract me from Finn's words. Take advantage? That threw me a bit. "What situation?"

He glanced my way, frowning as he finished chewing his own slice of apple. "Ex-cons don't always find work easily. Coming home, relying on my family to help me, putting them in danger should I relapse—I didn't want that."

"So you went to work in a bar."

"I like a challenge." He shot me a wink and handed me more apple slices, making my heart flutter just a bit. Charmer. I stepped away from the counter, checking out the rest of the room. A little scene sat on a table in the sitting area, a light shining on it. Shadows stretched along the walls, tall and thick. Almost...human-sized.

"What's this?" I sat down next to the lit display, inspecting it without touching. People. They looked like people carved from the same wood of the floor. "Did you make this?"

Finn came up behind me, quiet and slow. "Yeah. I did. It's what I think my mom's funeral was like."

Oh. *Oh.* My gut clenched, and my eyes burned. "What you think it was like?"

He reached out, running a finger down one figure. A larger, masculine shape close to the center. "Alder told me what it was like. I wasn't allowed to leave the prison to attend."

"Oh, Finn."

"They let me come home for my dad's. With a full police escort, of course. But at least I got to see it. This one..." He sighed, adjusting a couple of the figures. "I had to miss it."

Because he was in prison. For dealing drugs. Which he hadn't done. "I'm surprised you didn't kill that sheriff who set you up."

"You are?"

"Yeah. Because I would have."

"Don't think I didn't want to." He leaned down and placed a soft kiss to the top of my head. "I'm a better wood-carver than killer."

No doubt. "I would hope so. These are gorgeous."

"Thanks."

I stood, following him back toward the kitchen. "Have you always carved?"

"Yeah. My dad taught me when I was a kid. It relaxes me."

I reached for a slice of apple, crunching loudly as I looked around at all the little wood touches. Trying to determine which had been carved by the man himself and which had been purchased. My guess was that Finn had made them all. Impressive. The man had talent.

Once we'd finished the apple and the main areas of the house were cleaned and secured, Finn led me back through to his bedroom and into his attached bath. There was no shyness, no delay, as he grabbed a toothbrush—from a carved wooden holder, no less—and started brushing. At least not until he caught me watching him in the mirror. He froze for a moment then reached into a drawer and pulled out a second toothbrush. One just like his but unopened. He didn't say a word, just handed it to me and went back to brushing.

"Thanks," I said. He nodded once, his fingers trailing over the razor sitting in a wooden block to his right as he brushed. So much personality in this house, so many little handmade touches. It was pure Finn, and I loved it.

Teeth clean, face washed, and everything put back the way it had been when we'd walked in—plus the addition of my toothbrush in the holder against the mirror—Finn ushered me into his bedroom and stopped. Frozen in place as he looked around the room.

"What?"

He ran a hand over his head, mussing up his hair a little. "You can sleep in here."

"We. *We* can sleep in here." I leaned into his side, hating the very thought of being separated from him. "I don't want to be alone after tonight."

"Me neither, but I didn't bring you here to put you in a position where you felt as if you had to..."

He didn't need to finish that sentence. "There is no had to with you, Finn. Only want to."

A nod was my response, and then he was moving again. He opened a dresser drawer and pulled out a black shirt, looking so darn serious as he handed it to me. "It's not pajamas, but it should be big enough on you to make you feel comfortable and covered. And it's soft enough to sleep in."

"I brought some clothes."

A pause, a blink, a simple moment of something going on behind those stormy eyes. "I like the idea of you in mine."

Okay then. I took the shirt, bringing it to my face. It smelled like him. Perfect. I headed into the bathroom once more to change and give the man a little privacy. Give myself some too. I wasn't ready to be naked in front of Finn just yet. Privacy was still a good thing.

I pulled on Finn's shirt, snuggling into the soft cotton. The shirt hung all the way to my knees and swallowed my frame, but I loved it. Loved having Finn wrapped around me even when he wasn't in the same room. But he could be, so I took a deep breath and opened the door.

Finn sat on the edge of his bed with his head down and his hands clasped together. Obviously nervous.

"What's wrong?"

His shrug was more endearing than anything else could have been. "Nervous, I guess."

Bingo. "About me being here?"

His fingers moved against each other, the anxious fidget showing up. "About you likely wanting to leave."

"Why would I want to leave?"

"I've never...not that I'm implying we have to do anything, but I've never..." He took a deep breath. Frustration evident in his face. "This is so awkward."

But it didn't need to be because I already knew. Or at least could guess. The tension radiating off him, the edginess. The fear. "You've never had sex before."

"No. I have. Just..." He paused, then shook his head. "Not like this."

"You're going to have to explain that answer to me."

He looked massively uncomfortable. "I've been with women in the past, but..."

Realization might as well have been a slap to my face. "But you were high."

More fidgeting, those hands of his unable to hold still. "Yeah."

"You don't...remember?"

"I remember some, but I wasn't sober. Everything is sort of as if it happened to someone else." He shook his head. "I'm not sure I know how to be intimate while also being sober."

I couldn't stay away a second longer. I crept closer, my bare feet making no noise on the soft, plush rug covering the wood floor. My hand rising of its own volition to trace the edge of his ear once I reached him.

"You've been out of prison and sober for a long time."

He leaned into my touch, still pinched and obviously uncomfortable. "I haven't dated."

"Why not?" But I didn't need to ask. "Because it's too chaotic."

"Yeah."

I could understand that. In Finn's world, chaos was the enemy. He needed structure, routine, a firm handle on everything in his life just to feel anchored and secure. I could understand it, and I appreciated the admission.

Quid pro quo. "I've never not been coerced...into sex. It's never really been my choice to have it."

His head jerked back, his eyes wide. "I wouldn't do that to you."

"I know." I did. I truly did. Finn always asked permission, always made sure I was not just accepting of his advances but enthusiastic for them. He was a good man, and I was totally going to deflower his sober self. I straddled his lap, placing my hands on his shoulders and leaning in close. "So maybe this is a sort of first time for both of us."

"Oh fuck, Jinx." His harsh whisper was practically an aphrodisiac all on its own. "Are you sure? I don't want to touch you if you're not sure."

"I'm sure. Are you? Because I'm chaotic, Finn. I'll bring that into your life."

"I know. But I like your brand of chaos." His hands landed on my ass, gripping tightly. Pulling me so our bodies were pressed together. So I could feel his heat and his hardness through the cotton shirt I wore. "Anything you don't like or feel uncomfortable about, tell me. Okay? We can stop. I'll always stop for you."

I had a feeling I'd never want him to stop. "Kiss me, Finn."

But he didn't. Instead, he brought a hand up to push my hair behind my ear, staring into my eyes as he whispered, "I'd never make you do anything, Jinx. Not one damn thing."

"I know."

"Good. Because I'm going to kiss you now. And that kiss may lead to more. Are you okay with that?"

If I were any more okay, I'd be soaking through the thin cotton between us. "I'm totally okay with that."

He pressed his lips to mine, sweet and slow and soft. A brush of his tongue along my lips to ask for entry, a slip of his fingers under the shirt I wore to find my bare flesh. Nothing rushed or forced, nothing scary. Just Finn and me and first times of need and desire and sweetness.

Starting over...together.

Chapter Thirteen

FINN

Soft. Everything about Jinx was soft with an almost hidden strength beneath the surface. Every scar on her body, every sarcastic retort and harsh word. All of it was an act—a veil to disguise her inner self. A wall keeping all that softness hidden. But she showed it to me in her kisses and the way her body melted into mine. Made me feel it in the way her hands ran over my flesh, grounding us together. This was the true Jinx, alone with me in that intimate, vulnerable moment. And I never wanted it to end.

"Can I take this off?" She tugged at the shirt I wore, her breaths heavy and fast, matching mine perfectly. She wanted my shirt off? That was easy. I didn't answer her with words because there was no need to delay; I simply reached behind my neck and yanked the garment over my head. Baring myself.

I had no secrets from her. "Anything else?"

Those lips—so pink and plump and kiss-swollen—tipped up. "Quid pro quo. You take it off, I do as well."

I fingered the edge of the shirt she wore. My shirt. I liked her in my clothes far more than I was willing to admit. "Do you have anything on under this?" I nearly groaned when she shook her head all slow and teasing.

"Not a thing."

Death by Jinx. I could see that coming for me. "Then we'll leave this on along with my pants. For now."

I went back to kissing her, stroking up and down her back and over her hips. Keeping my pressure light. I'd seen her flinch when she moved certain ways, had felt her recoil when something touched her back. She had pain there—something I didn't want to exacerbate. So I held back, tried to stay gentle, tried not to hurt her even though every roll of her hips nearly killed me.

Seriously. Death. By Jinx. It was going to be a thing.

"Finn?"

I needed to hear her say my name about six thousand more times. "Yeah, baby?"

"I want you to take your pants off."

I almost came at her words, almost spilled right there with her in my lap. "Are you sure? We don't have to—"

She leaned back, taking her weight away, stealing her warmth and closeness from me. "Off, Finn. Take them off."

Done. I pushed my sweats down, pulling them off and tossing them into the laundry basket across the room. Leaving me naked in front of her. Naked and hard and so ready for whatever was about to come next. Jinx's smile grew, and she took the time to look me over before rejoining me on the bed. Before straddling my naked body once more. She even leaned back and ran her hands over my chest and stomach, teasing me. Riling me up.

My turn.

"Is this okay?" I ran my hands up her thighs and under the shirt she still wore, keeping them low on her hips. Not pushing her decision but letting her know what I wanted. "Can I take this off?"

She froze for a moment, her hands stilling on my chest. "Yeah, it's just... I'm not as whole as you are."

"Whole?"

"I have..." She turned her arms over, showing me her battered wrists. She didn't need to say the word for me to know what she meant. Scars. She had scars. I'd seen the ones on her arms a hundred times, knew they were there. I'd assumed she had more. But if she was reluctant to show me, they must have been bad.

Not that it mattered. "You can trust me."

She sat still as a statue for a handful of long seconds, then slowly—glacially slow—rose to her feet and took one step back. Just one. With a deep, measured breath, she crossed her arms over her body, grabbed the bottom of my shirt, and pulled the fabric over her head in one smooth movement before letting it drop to the floor. The move itself didn't catch my attention, though—the marks all over her body did. Round, long, deep, thin...they nearly covered her flesh. From her breasts down to her hips and side to side, there wasn't a patch of skin unmarked. Not a piece of her left intact. Some were obviously marks from cuts—long or short, deep or shallow, straight lines formed patterns across her skin. The ones that killed me were not straight or thin. Not scars from blades at all. They were round. Circles of mottled flesh standing out against the paleness. Perfect fucking circles smaller than a dime.

I rose to my feet, wrapped my fingers around her elbow as gently as I could, and stepped closer, dropping a kiss onto one such mark. "Cigarette burns?"

"Yeah." Nothing more than that. No story, no history. No true Jinx. You got what you saw with her—nothing more. And at that moment, that simple answer had to be enough because she didn't need me pushing her. What she needed was to know that the scars didn't change my opinion of her. I hated them—hated what they stood for and what they meant she'd apparently endured—but they changed nothing. I still felt a need to show her kindness. To take care of her.

Naked and alone, the two of us locked up together for the night, I could show her how much her past didn't bother me. I could give her something good after what was obviously a lot of bad. I could remind her that not all people would hurt her.

"You're beautiful," I said, tugging her close again, nearly shivering as our warm skin came together. "So damn beautiful and perfect."

She huffed a laugh even as her arms rose so she could clutch at my hair. "I'm far from perfect."

"Perfect for me."

Jinx stopped laughing. Stopped moving and breathing too. She simply stood and stared at me, those deep, gray eyes locking on mine. Telling me everything I needed to know without words. She was ready. She wanted more.

Me too.

I leaned in for another kiss, keeping my hands steady on her hips. Keeping my movements slow so she could refuse me if she wanted to. She didn't hesitate or pull away, though. Instead, she dove in and took control of the kiss, demanding more from me. Giving herself to me in the most obvious and enthusiastic way.

So I took what she offered.

Guiding her, I turned us and moved toward the bed. Laying her down as I followed her. Bringing our bodies together with me on top of her smaller form. So soft and hot, so willing. There was no holding back with her, no stopping.

At least not until she hissed and arched away from the mattress.

"Are you okay?" I pushed up onto my arms. "What's wrong?"

"Nothing. It's just..." She bit her lip and turned her head, hiding from me. "My back bothers me sometimes."

Knowing that I needed to look, that I had to understand what had happened to her, I rolled to my side and nudged her over. She turned willingly though not without pause. And not without hiding her face from me.

"Jesus." Rage. It burned under my skin. This girl...her back... someone had really done a number on her. Someone who deserved to die. "These aren't old."

"No."

"When?" I ran my fingers over the slashes across her back, afraid to do more than brush them for fear of causing her pain. "And who?"

"Before I came here. Some Soul Suckers guy got off on whipping women." She rolled back a little, finally meeting my eyes. "Your brother saved me."

"In Vegas?" I sighed as she looked away, confirming my suspicions. "There was no Vegas trip."

Jinx shook her head. "I didn't know the guy who had me. Didn't know your brother or Deacon when they came in either, though they seemed the better bet than going back to the Soul Suckers."

No fucking doubt. "I'm glad they got you out."

"I'm glad they brought me here." She rolled the rest of the

way, curling back into my arms. "I'm glad they brought me to you."

So many thoughts and questions raced through my head—who'd whipped her? Where was he? How soon could I rip his hands off and beat him with them? All things that could wait. Jinx was with me—safe and secure and needing comfort, not cruelty. Needing my time, not my vengeance.

She'd get both. Eventually.

"Don't let me hurt you," I said, rolling her on top of me. "Ever, Jinx. I don't care what it is—never let me hurt you."

"You would never."

"Not intentionally, no. But sometimes, I don't know how far to push. I don't always know the rules."

She stayed silent for a second, holding me. The tension in her body slowly easing under my touch. "So you choose not to push at all."

"Yeah."

"I can see people thinking that's a weakness." She leaned down, rubbing herself over where I was so hard for her as she kissed me. As she brushed her lips against mine and rolled that sweet, hot wetness all over me. "That restraint takes so much strength."

I thought about all the times I'd held back—with Alder, with Bishop, even with Deacon. All the times someone had pushed me a little over the edge and my temper had flared. Hell, Bishop had punched me square in the jaw, but I'd let him walk away without once raising my fists to him. Without a word either. I'd let him think he'd won that fight because I knew, if I let go, I'd hurt him. Yeah, that took strength. No one had ever noticed before, though. They'd always assumed I was just quiet. Maybe a little meek.

If only they knew.

But all that could wait. All the people in my life who doubted or underestimated me could disappear for the moment. I had a hot, willing female ready to ride me, and I was going to enjoy every second of that trip. So long as she was ready to go on it with me.

"You feel so good," I said as I gripped Jinx's hips and helped slide her back and forth over my cock. "So soft and wet. I just want to lick you up."

"I'd rather we skip that. For now." She reached between us and wrapped her hand around me, gripping tight and tugging as she stared down at it. As she made my eyes roll back with such a simple touch. "Do you have any condoms?"

Words were too hard, so I fumbled instead for the nightstand drawer, grabbing the unopened box from where it had sat all year. I tossed them on the bed, groaning and closing my eyes as Jinx pulled harder. As she jacked me off with her hot little hands. As she teased me closer and closer to the point of no return. So long. It'd been so long since I'd felt this much. Since I'd *let myself* feel. She was going to kill me, and I hadn't even gotten inside her yet.

Hips rising into her stroke, I murmured a rough, "If you don't stop, I'm going to come."

Her giggle lit up my entire world. "I think that's sort of the point."

I jackknifed up, grabbing her hand and stilling it. "Ladies first. Just hop on board."

With a roll of her eyes, she reached for the condom box, taking the time to rip it open and pull out one foil packet. She took care of sheathing me, keeping her eyes on mine as she worked her hands between us. Keeping me enthralled in her very presence as she took care of the necessities. And when she was done—when our protection was in place—she smirked.

"So...unlike the bikers I grew up around, you're going to let a pussy ride?"

Fuck me, that filthy mouth. "Baby, trust me when I say I'd love to roll you over and fuck you right through the floor. But I have a feeling your back would make that less than pleasant for you, and I want you to enjoy this. So yeah, ride me. I'm man enough to let a woman be in charge."

And take charge, she did. Rocking and rolling and groaning and angling her hips until we were lined up. Until she was so wet and ready that the tip slipped in easily. Until I had to grab hold of her thighs and hang on as I lifted my hips off the bed so I could nudge my way inside where she was so fucking hot for me. And tight. My god was she tight.

"Finn," she called as she sank lower, dropping her head to watch where we were coming together. "I can't stop."

"So, don't." I arched higher, pushing deeper. Hanging on tighter as I fought the instinct to simply ram myself home and bunny-hump to completion. I wasn't a fucking kid—I could hold on. Could do better for her than that. I had to. "I'll give that greedy pussy all she wants. You don't have to stop."

It took about four thrusts to slide all the way inside of her, about another three to work out our rhythm so we could move in tandem. After that, it was game on. I bit my lip to keep the curses at bay as I fucked up into the heaven of my girl, as I lost myself to her heat and her smell and the bliss of being completely surrounded by her.

Jinx didn't hold back for a second either. Rocking and bouncing and teasing her nipples as I worked her clit with my fingers. I needed her to come so badly. Needed to see her fall apart before I could do the same. I might have been man enough to truly enjoy a woman being on top, but I wasn't the type of guy to get mine without making sure my partner was satisfied first. Later, I'd get her off on my tongue. This time, it needed to be on my cock with my fingers backing me up. This time was all about Jinx.

"That's it," I said as she began moving faster and more erratically, chasing her own high. "That's the way to do it. Give it to me."

"Finn," she said, gasping and rolling her shoulders forward as she shook her head. "I need...I need..."

She needed all right, and I had an instinct of what that was. I moved my hand along her pussy, circling harder and faster against her clit. Working her over until she finally broke. Finally came with a shudder and a cry that would have woken everyone in the house had we not been alone. Milking my cock with every pulse.

So good, so good, so good.

I followed right behind her, unable to wait a second more. So thankful that I'd made it through her orgasm after so many years of nothing more than my hand. I felt like a fucking rock star for holding out, like a king for making her go limp in my arms. I'd satisfied my girl.

And I totally planned to do that again and again and again.

Chapter Fourteen

JINX

Waking up wrapped in Finn's arms may have been both the most amazing and terrifying moment of my life. The warmth of him, the gentleness was something I craved. Something I loved so much. Something I'd never experienced before. Something I knew better than to get used to.

"Morning," he mumbled as he pulled me tighter against his chest. "What are you thinking about so early in the morning?"

How much I'll miss you when this is over. "Just this whole situation."

"You mean this situation—" he ground his hips against my ass, gripping my breast tight in one hand as he did "—or the Soul Suckers situation."

Soul Suckers and Black Angels. I wasn't sure who to be more afraid of anymore. Not after last night when they'd both come rolling up together. I hadn't taken the time to really think that through yet—Finn had kept me pretty distracted after we'd left

The Jury Room—but it was bad. Those two clubs working together was really, really bad. Specifically, for me. Something Finn still didn't know about, and that I wasn't ready to tell him... yet.

"Definitely the clubs," I said, curling into his hold. Craving more of his touch to keep me centered, calm, and distracted. "Though I could switch my train of thought if you want me to."

He kissed my neck and held me tight, sighing into my neck. "It's not about what I want. It's about you."

Typical Finn. The words were so sweet, so kind, that they physically hurt my heart to hear. I couldn't even think of an answer other than, "I'm fine."

"'Fine'? That's not what I want to hear." He pulled back a little, not taking his touch away but giving me more room to move. "How about we do something else? Give you a chance to get past fine."

"Like what?"

He rolled me over, looking down into my eyes with an earnest expression as he asked, "Are you hungry?"

A serious question called for a serious answer. "Always."

"Good." He patted my ass and gave me one more kiss. "Get up, Lucky. Let me feed you."

Ten minutes later, I sat at his kitchen table as Finn moved about the space. Scrambled eggs and toast were on the menu this morning along with coffee—his with lots of cream and sugar. I had a feeling this was his usual breakfast meal, that he didn't vary the menu very often, if at all. Consistency had nothing on Finn Kennard.

I sipped my own coffee—cream, no sugar—and watched the man move through his kitchen. Watched him set up pans and pull out bread to toast, stared as he dug through his refrigerator —all that produce really did take up a lot of space—for things like butter, strawberry jam, and eggs. I watched, and I grew hungry for more than just food. The man was cooking for me, taking care of me. That was surprisingly sexy.

"What's wrong, Jinx?"

My eyes darted to his almost of their own accord. Did he know I'd been thinking about him? Naked? In the kitchen?

I shook my head and tried to clean up my dirty thoughts. "Nothing. Why?"

"You've shifted in that seat at least five times. Are you not comfortable?"

Consistent and observant. "I feel weird sitting on your furniture half naked."

He gave me a grin and raised his eyebrows, something that seemed much more like an invitation than it should have. "You're welcome to be fully naked if you prefer."

Which would lead to sex. On counters. And tables. And maybe chairs. *Is it getting hot in here?*

Distraction time. "I'd rather go in the opposite direction and be fully clothed. I mean, your shirt is quite comfy, but I need to get dressed. Do you think we can go to the motel after breakfast so I can grab more of my stuff?"

He frowned, turning his attention back to the eggs he'd cracked into a bowl. "I don't think that's a good idea. At least not without letting Deacon and Parris know what we were doing in case we ran into trouble. I have stuff you can wear, though."

The way that last sentence came out—a little quieter, a little more shy—piqued my interest. "You do?"

Finn turned all the way around, still whipping those eggs. Totally avoiding me. "Yeah. Check out the shelves in the laundry room for whatever you need."

I followed where he pointed, wanting more than his sweats or shorts and a cotton shirt but not saying anything. The threat to us was real enough to have me looking over my shoulder, so I knew better than to do anything that might put us in danger. Still, a pair of undies and a clean bra would have been nice at the moment—things I was pretty sure I had forgotten to grab. We'd had to leave so quickly that I'd thrown what I could into a bag, not thinking to the practicality of the garments. I hadn't grabbed any of my undergarments or my dirty clothes, which would have been much more reasonable than the jeans, shorts, and hoodies I remembered snagging. What I wouldn't give for fluffy socks and yoga pants. I dreamed of them sometimes, of how comfortable I used to be in them.

Which was why I nearly stumbled to a stop when I saw the clothes on the shelves. Not just panties and bras but skirts and blouses, jeans and long-sleeved shirts, sweaters, what looked like yoga pants. A veritable department store of clothing. And when I approached, a bit fearful of what this all meant and why these were here, I found them all to be in my sizes. All looking new enough to make me wonder who they belonged to. Jealousy raged hot and bright under my skin, an emotion I had no right to feel, and yet—

"Find them?" Finn stood in the doorway, looking very nervous. As he should.

"You just collect women's clothing in case someone decides to spend the night?" There was no way that could have come out in any way other than accusatory, and Finn's frown told me he heard that tone in my voice.

"I told you—I don't bring anyone here. No one's ever spent the night, and the only person I brought clothes here for was you."

That set me back on my heels. "Me?"

"Yeah. You came to Justice with nothing. I wanted to make sure you didn't stay here in that same boat."

He'd bought me clothes. He'd been buying me *clothes*. I thought over everything that had magically shown up at the motel or bar—shirts and jeans, underwear and socks. A thick winter coat with hat and gloves, even. I'd assumed Deacon had been stocking the bar with stuff specifically for me. Had I been that wrong?

"All the stuff at the bar," I said, reaching out to touch one pair of pants in particular. Yep, yoga pants. Soft and stretchy and more comfortable than anything I had in my bag. I was wearing those for sure. "The wardrobe malfunction stuff..."

"For the customers, usually. Though I've been feeding the pile for you." His frown deepened. "Parris had told me when you first got here that you lived in shorts and T-shirts, so that's what I got. But I noticed you always seemed a little cold. That's why I started bringing pants and long-sleeved shirts for you. There's more of that stuff in the pile. I hadn't brought them all to the bar yet."

"You bought yoga pants."

"My sister practically worships at the altar of them, so I thought you might like them as well. You're always tugging at your waistband like your pants are uncomfortable."

Had I mentioned he was observant? Still, though—he wasn't psychic. "How did you know my size?"

"I paid attention to what you picked and then made sure to restock with the right size."

For some things, that would work, but... "You bought bras and panties."

"Yeah." He blew out a breath and ran a hand over the back of his neck, looking horribly uncomfortable. "Don't hate me."

"Why would I hate you?"

"I...those things make no sense to me size-wise, so I asked for help."

"You asked for help in picking out bras for me?"

"Yeah."

"From who?"

"My sister."

I'd never been more relieved even if I wasn't sure why. "But I've never met your sister."

"She worked in the lingerie department of a high-end department store during her undergraduate years. She jokes that she can tell the right size bra for a woman from fifty paces. I sent her a couple of pictures of you to help me out."

Holy shit. "That's a lot of effort."

"Not really."

I shook my head and crossed the floor, crowding him. Rising up onto the balls of my feet to press my lips to his. Once. Twice. A little added tongue just for the hell of it as his hand landed on my hip. I couldn't get enough of this man.

"You're sweet."

"And you're cold." He kissed me once more, tugging me into him. Tangling our tongues together in a slow dance meant for lovers before backing away. "Get dressed. Eggs are ready when you are."

But I couldn't let him leave. Couldn't stop myself from calling out, "Finn."

He turned and raised his eyebrows. "Yeah?"

"Thanks. For making the effort."

"You're worth it, Jinx."

Those words slammed into my gut like a fist. No one had ever thought I was worth the effort. No one but my mom, and even she had put the club and the men in her life before me. Finn barely knew me, but he put time into making me feel comfortable. Put effort into making me feel cared for. I didn't deserve him. I didn't deserve any of this—and there was no way

I'd ever be able to pay him back for his kindness. I would owe him instead, and I hated owing anyone anything. That's what had gotten me into this mess in the first place—a debt of sorts. A need to pay for something I couldn't afford.

After getting dressed—yoga pants and a sweater that felt about as soft as clouds looked—I walked back into the kitchen still stuck on those thoughts, wondering when the debt collector would come for me. When I'd lose everything to mistakes that weren't mine. When the happy little rug Finn had laid out for me would be ripped away by the men who'd scarred my body and left me with nothing. I thought so hard that I didn't even notice Finn until he set a plate of eggs in front of me with a side of toast—already buttered. So damn caring.

But for how long?

"So, I was thinking," he said, settling in across from me with his own eggs and toast. "How about we go back to our quid pro quo?"

Like last night—you take off, I take off. I pointed my fork at him and raised an eyebrow. Just one, because people said I looked dangerous when I did that. "If you wanted me naked, you shouldn't have shown me all those comfy clothes you've been hiding. I may never take these yoga pants off."

He coughed a laugh. "Not that, though watching you walk around in those pants for the rest of my life doesn't seem like such a bad thing. I want you naked whenever you're ready to remove them temporarily, but I also wanted to ask you something."

Oh. That sort of quid pro quo. "Okay. Ask away."

"How do you prefer your eggs?"

That...wasn't what I'd been expecting. "Over easy. I like to dip my toast in them, but these are delicious."

He nodded, loading up his fork. "I don't think I've ever made eggs that way, but I'll learn."

Sweet, sweet Finn. "Scrambled is fine."

"I hate the word fine. You deserve better than just *fine*."

I couldn't deal with that statement. Not right then. "You wasted one of your remaining four questions to ask me about eggs?"

"That was sort of a warm-up." He blew out a breath, looking almost nervous. "Can you tell me about your mom?"

Bomb. He'd just dropped one in my world. One that sent ice exploding throughout my body. "What do you know about my mom?"

"Nothing except that apparently she's important in some way."

"Of course she is—she gave birth to me."

He set his fork down, his plate still half full. "I'm doing this all wrong."

"Is there a right way to interrogate someone?"

"I didn't mean to interrogate. I just...Parris mentioned—"

"Ah, so this is Parris' fault." I was going to kill that man.

"Fuck no." Finn pushed back from the table and tossed his napkin over his plate before sliding closer. Bringing his chair to face mine so he could place his hands on my knees. "Jinx, I want to know about you. That's all."

Knowing about me meant dragging him into something I didn't think I could get him out of, and that wasn't going to happen. So instead of answering him, I stood up and closed the distance between us. Straddled his lap right there at the table and pulled him in close. Held on as I let the ice melt and the tension release.

"Sorry," I said, locking my past down tight so I didn't slip up and admit everything to him. So I didn't drag him into a world he was so much better than. "My mom is a sensitive subject for me."

He pushed a lock of my hair over my shoulder and settled one hand on my hip. "I can see that. But I'd like it if you shared that with me at some point."

I had a feeling that would never happen. Or at least, we'd never have the time needed to get to that point of trust. I'd never get there, at least. A thought that hurt. "Some point...but not today."

"Okay. I'll wait." He gripped me tighter as I began to move, to tease, to roll over his lap. "Jinx?"

"If you ask me to have sex, my answer would be more than just fine."

"Yeah?" He pushed up against me, his hands sliding up to cup my breasts over my sweater. "What would it be?"

"Yes." I leaned in and bit the side of his neck. "A very enthusiastic yes."

He groaned as I rocked my hips over his lap, as I ground myself against where he was so hard for me.

"So, no quid pro quo today," he said as he picked me up and lifted me, carrying me easily across the room. "Not right now, at least."

"Not right now." I grabbed his shoulders when he laid me on his counter, holding on to stay upright. "Finn?"

"Lie back," he said, his voice deep and sultry, his eyes burning into mine. "Lie back and let me spoil you."

Well, that didn't sound too bad. I did as I was told—lying back along the counter. A sort of human offering in his kitchen. Finn tugged on my yoga pants, yanking them down my hips and legs. Tossing them onto the chair behind him before returning to bring my heels to the edge of the counter and kiss my knees. Exposed, I felt so exposed there. Legs spread and body on display. But this was for Finn, was with him, so that feeling didn't roll into discomfort. Instead, it morphed into desire. Wantonness. I wanted him to see me. Wanted him to look me over. I wanted.

"Is this okay?" he asked, rubbing up and down my inner thighs. Pushing my legs farther apart even as he seemed to fight to keep himself restrained. "Are you more than fine?"

"Yes," I said, reaching out to grip his hair and tug him closer. "So much more than fine."

"How's your back?"

"Fine." I grinned when he glowered at me. "Better than fine. So much more than fine. I'll let you know if we drop down to fine."

"You're sure?"

Was I ever. "Yes."

"Thank fuck." He yanked my panties down and off my legs, leaving them hooked over one ankle as he pushed my knees back and brought that talented mouth of his to my pussy. To where I was soaked for him. Tonguing, licking, sucking, biting...he worked me over good. Teasing me with flicks and laps and flat-tongued licks that made me see stars in seconds. Made me come twice before he finally stood and dropped his own pants. Not before digging a condom out of one of the pockets, though.

"You came prepared," I said, watching as his long fingers worked the latex down his length. "Were you a Boy Scout?"

"Not for a single day, but no way was I missing out on feeling you wrapped around me again." He nudged his way inside, lifting my sweater and sucking on my nipples as he kept up a slow, easy rhythm. As he worked his way deeper and deeper, filling me with an unending patience. Making me claw at his shoulders and chant his name.

"My lucky girl," he said, groaning long and deep as his hips finally pressed against mine. "I'd do anything for my lucky girl. Gonna make this pussy feel so good. Gonna make you scream my name again."

And he would. I knew that. Felt it. Yet there still seemed to be an end date on our relationship. I had a tiger by the tail, and it was only a matter of time before it turned on me. A beast that would use my sweet Finn as leverage if it knew how much I felt for him. Telling Finn about my mom—bringing him into my life —meant putting him in danger. And there was no way I could do that.

But I could care for him. I could use my body to bring him pleasure. I could do *this*.

"Again, Finn," I whispered as he thrust harder. "You feel so good deep inside me. Do it again."

He did. Over and over and over, pushing me along the counter until I had to hold on to the end of it. Bringing me right to the precipice of pleasure then throwing me over the side of it. Making me come with his body and his words. Shaking and groaning and pressing deep as he came too.

This I could do. This—sex and playing house and letting him in close to me—was only dangerous to one thing...my heart.

JINX

I had never been a late sleeper. Growing up, I'd always been up early for school or whatever activities were going on in the neighborhood. As I got older, work had forced my body from bed at an earlier and earlier hour until it was hard for me to sleep past sunrise. I still used an alarm, but it really hadn't been a necessity in my daily life before I'd gotten involved with the Black Angels.

Finn obviously woke up even earlier than I did and was a much better alarm clock than any I'd ever used.

"Oh god." I arched off the bed, reaching down to fist my hand in his hair as he attacked my clit with his tongue. There was no other word for it—what he was doing was pure aggression. Slashing, licking, flicking, giving me no relief from the impending orgasm heading my way. Waking me up in the most arousing way possible. "Finn."

"So sweet and wet," he murmured against my flesh as he

slipped what felt like two fingers inside me. "I can't get enough of this pussy."

I wanted to respond, to tell him I couldn't get enough either, that he was going to make me come if he didn't stop. To beg him not to stop. But words failed me as pleasure crashed through my body. Every nerve firing, every inch of skin and muscle and flesh singed by the explosion within me.

Tugging hard, I dragged the man up my body, wanting more than his mouth. Wanting to feel him fill me. To see his face as he came with me again.

"More," I said, kissing him deeply, groaning as I tasted myself on his lips before pulling away. "I want more."

"Anything you want, baby." He reached into the nightstand and pulled out a condom, taking care of wrapping himself before lining us up. "Anything you need."

"Just you. I just need you."

He pushed his way inside, filling me as he moaned my name. As he cursed and bit his lip, his eyes locked on mine. The moment almost too intimate to handle. But then he was moving, thrusting into me with harder and faster strokes, and I was lost to the pleasure again. And again. And again.

———

"What is this?" I tapped the wooden figures on the shelf in Finn's dining room. The ones surrounding a carved wooden... something. Was that perhaps a pile of pieces? And the rest... "Is that a llama?"

"Yeah." Finn came up behind me, kissing my shoulder and wrapping his arms around my hips.

"But...why a llama?" Finn's carvings were all over the house —figurines, handy gadgets, boxes, bowls, coasters. Everywhere sat little works of art. But these were different. Abstract animals, if I had to guess. A handful of them all standing together.

"My sister had a bit of an obsession with them for a while. I carved a ton of the beasts because of her, so they're sort of scattered about. These ones represent all my siblings." He frowned when I turned in his arms, looking completely out of sorts. "It's weird, I know."

"Not weird. What's the thing in the middle?"

"It's a broken Lady Justice. My dad carved it, but somewhere along the way, it broke. I hope to figure out how to fix it someday."

Lady Justice...from a man who lived in Justice. Funny. "Your dad was the one who taught you how to do that?"

"By that, you mean carve things? Yeah, he whittled wood at night while watching the news. It's a habit I picked up, I guess. Minus the news."

"That's right, you don't—"

Before I could finish my sentence, Finn's phone rang, breaking the silence around us.

"That'll be Elijah," he said, frowning toward where the device sat on the counter. He'd made that same face yesterday when his brother had called. He'd cut that call short as I'd escaped to the bathroom, something I doubted was his normal. I was beginning to understand that look—his habits and rituals were being disrupted. By me. By my presence. That concern was his indecision over what to prioritize—his routines or taking care of me. I couldn't make him choose.

"Answer it," I said, pushing him in the direction he needed to go. "I can always go take a shower."

He grabbed his phone off the counter but didn't let me go, tugging me along with him.

"Stay," he said as he tapped the screen a few times. A voice came over the line before Finn could say anything more, the person not bothering to issue a greeting.

"You're about to get a nice warm front. I hope you'll be taking advantage of it."

Finn set the phone on the table, pulling me into his lap as he dropped onto a chair. "You have so little work to do that you check the Justice weather reports daily now?"

"Of course not. I get an email."

"There's an app for that."

"Precisely. How's your day going, brother?"

Finn grinned, squeezing my thigh. "I've got a girl with me, so it's going great."

Silence stretched, pushing at me in a way that felt uncomfortable. Anxiety-inducing. At least until the man on the other end—Elijah, Finn's twin brother—laughed.

"Well, well. Is she listening right now?"

Finn nudged me, so I said, "Hi, Elijah. I'm Jinx."

"Good morning, Jinx. What's a nice girl like you doing with my favorite brother?"

"I'm not always so nice, but Finn feeds me vegetables and makes me tea." I grinned down at the man in question before dropping a quick kiss to his lips. "I like that about him."

"Vegetables and tea are all it takes to make you happy? She's a keeper, Finn."

"Yeah, I sort of figured that out already."

I gave him one more kiss then rose to my feet, laughing when he tried to pull me back down. "Shower," I whispered as I headed for the hallway toward the bedroom. "I need one."

"I could join you," Finn said, his phone already in his hand. But I knew better—he needed his routine, and that included a morning phone call with his brother. A nice, long one—not like yesterday's.

"You stay and chat. I'll be there when you're done."

"Deal."

I was halfway into the bedroom when he hollered, "Dress warm, Lucky. We'll be heading out for the afternoon to enjoy the weather."

Elijah's voice was the last thing I heard before I closed the bathroom door. "See? It's a good thing I check your weather reports."

———

Finn definitely liked seeing me naked, though I couldn't help but notice how his eyes tended to fall to my scars.

"Stop it," I said before reaching for a sweatshirt to cover myself with.

"Stop what?"

"Looking as if I'm in some sort of pain. They're not new—they don't hurt anymore."

Finn frowned, reaching out to trace the burn marks on my arm—the perfect circles left by a particularly cruel man. His fingers moved higher, running along the slash marks. Nice, neat, straight lines crisscrossing my arms.

"What are these from?"

My stomach rolled, and the half-truth I'd been telling for the past year rolled off my tongue even though it burned my throat. "Cutting. I...used to deal with that."

"Used to?"

Past tense. Before I left the Black Angels the first time. At least, the man who'd given me those scars hadn't added any new ones since. "Yeah. Not anymore."

He tugged the neckline of my sweatshirt to the side and kissed the scar that blew my secret apart. The long, S-shaped one on my shoulder that there was no way I could have done myself. "Okay. I'll leave it alone for now, but you can revise your story whenever you're ready to."

I did not deserve someone so sweet. I also wasn't even close to being ready to tell him the truth about the past year of my life.

"Where are we going?" I asked as I followed him outside to his truck.

He opened my door for me with a smile. "I figured we could head into town for breakfast, then maybe take a short hike along one of the ridges."

"Into the mountains?"

"Sure. Why not?"

"Uh, because there are bikers all around."

Finn shrugged. "I texted Deacon my plans. He seemed fine with it."

"He did?"

"Sure."

"And what exactly does fine with it mean in terms of Church?"

"It means he didn't tell me not to go."

"Sounds like permission to me." I looked out the window at the vista before me. Peaks rose in the distance, creating almost a wall of rock and imposing forests. "I've never been in the mountains."

Finn turned onto the highway, grabbing my hand once he had a long, straight patch of road before him. "Let's change that, then."

We pulled up outside The Baker's Cottage within minutes, Finn parking the truck with ease in one of the pull-in spots.

"Does this place make you scrambled eggs with toast and strawberry jelly?" I asked as he grabbed my hand and led me to the sidewalk.

"Of course. I wouldn't eat here if they didn't."

"Your lack of flexibility in your breakfast choices makes me a little sad."

He opened the door, staring down at me with an intense expression as he said, "When you know what you want, there's no point in trying anything else."

My heart dropped then raced, my skin flushing warm under his stare. There was a double meaning there, a subplot to those words. And I liked it.

"Hey, you two." Shye—the blonde who'd brought me the best pot roast sandwich ever—hurried over, a couple of menus already in her hands. "C'mon in and snag a seat wherever you like. I'll grab some coffee for you."

"Tea," Finn said, stopping the woman in her tracks. "Jinx here prefers tea."

Shye smiled all slow and sweet, looking from him to me and back again. "Tea, it is. I'll put on the kettle for you."

Finn directed me to a table by the bar, pulling out my chair for me like a gentleman. "I assume this is okay."

It didn't escape my notice that he'd put us in a spot facing the door, or that he had his back to a wall. A lot of the Black Angels did the same—the men who'd seen war. Who'd fought in the military. Finn might not have been a veteran, but he had been to hell. I had a feeling he'd learned to protect his back while inside.

"This is fine." I reached for his hand once he took his seat, smiling across the table at him. "Thank you."

"For what?"

"Being you."

Finn looked ready to say something when the bell over the door rang and he glanced up. His smile fell, his expression flattening fast. I turned, not at all surprised to see Alder Kennard striding our way.

"How are you two doing?" he asked as he pulled out an extra chair at our table and took a seat. "Everything good over at the motel?"

I blinked, glancing at Finn. His expression didn't change, his eyes never leaving his brother's as he said, "Yeah. Everything's fine."

Apparently we were lying to the man. Got it. "We were thinking about going hiking today."

"Hiking?" Alder looked to Finn. "You think that's a good idea—to go off into the woods?"

Finn shrugged one shoulder. "We won't go too far or for too long, and Deacon knows where we're going. She's never been in the mountains, so I told her I'd show her what she's been missing."

"Well, don't go too far off-grid. And call if you need anything." He looked away, a smile crossing his face as Shye hurried toward us. "Well, good morning, honey. I missed you."

She practically rolled her eyes. "You've said that to me about six times already today."

"So? Am I not allowed to miss my future wife when she's away from me?" He tugged her closer, kissing her cheeks as they reddened. As she blushed and giggled from his attention. Sweet. So sweet.

"Stop it," Shye finally said, smacking Alder on the arm in a weak sort of way. "I'm here to work. Jinx, what can I get you?"

I glanced at Finn and winked. "I'll have what he's having."

"A matched set," she said. "I'll get the order in and bring you your tea."

"Is Gage in the back?" Alder asked, still holding on to his fiancée. He grunted at her nod. "I'll come with you. I need to talk to him about something. It was good to see you out and about, Jinx. Try not to get into any trouble."

"I make no promises." I waited for him to disappear into the kitchen before turning to Finn. "You're a very different person around him."

"You think?"

"I know."

He huffed, rearranging the silverware on the table until it was perfectly aligned. "He treats me like a child at times."

"Because you were an addict."

"Am," he said, holding my gaze. "It never goes away. The want...the desire to block out the world with some sort of self-medication. I am an addict in recovery and will be for the rest of my life."

Shye dropped off a cup of coffee for him and a kettle of hot water along with six different tea bags, giving me time to formulate my response. To let his words percolate through my mind for a minute.

"I would think your brother would respect you for lasting so long in such a hard battle." I grabbed a tea bag—green tea with citrus—and poured hot water into my cup. "Addiction is a hard beast to beat back."

He took a sip of his coffee, meeting my eyes over his mug. "He sees the flaw first, not the win of the recovery."

"Well, that's just stupid."

Finn laughed, setting his mug down and reaching for my hand. "I'm really glad you're here, Jinx."

I felt my cheeks warm again, felt my body responding to his proximity. To his sweet words. "I am too. And, Finn?"

"Yeah?"

"Let's make this hike a short one."

"Why's that?"

I ran my foot up his inner thigh, grinning when I reached his lap and his hand dropped to grab my ankle and stop my progression.

"Jinx." Ooh, those eyes were stormy gray.

"You don't have many neighbors, do you?"

He swallowed visibly, his Adam's apple bouncing as I wiggled my toes against where he was obviously hard for me. "No. No one else lives on my stretch of road."

"Good."

"Why is that good?"

"Because it's a beautiful day outside, and I think we should open up your windows."

He frowned, still rubbing my ankle. Still breathing a little harder than normal and not pushing my foot away from him. "Why would it matter if I have neighbors when I air out the house?"

I tugged my foot away, leaning over the table to run my finger up his arm as I dropped my voice a little lower, a little softer. A little sultrier...I hoped. "Because I intend to make you groan my name again today, and I'd prefer if no one else got to hear how sexy you sound when you do it."

He stared at me for a long minute, not even breaking the connection when Shye showed up with our food.

"Here you go," she said, setting two plates down on the table. "Is there anything—"

"The check," Finn said, making my lips quirk. "Just the check."

Shye looked from me to him and back, likely frowning when neither of us even glanced her way. Not that I cared.

"Yeah," I said, cocking my head and giving Finn all of my attention. "We're sort of in a hurry."

He grinned. "A big hurry. Lots to do today."

"It'll take hours."

"I hope so."

"Okay," Shye said, drawing out the word. "I feel as if I'm missing something here, but no matter. We have your card on file, Finn. Just head on out when you're done."

"Bonus," I said as I picked up my fork. "Eat up, Fish. You're going to need your strength."

Chapter Sixteen

FINN

Three days, countless orgasms, and more naked Jinx than I'd ever thought possible. That's how long I let the girl play her little distraction sham before I figured out how to beat her at her own game. Because, yes, I knew what she was doing. I wasn't an idiot. I might not have been wise to the ways of people in a relationship when she'd come to me, but I knew manipulation when I saw it. Jinx used sex as a weapon—no, as a shield. I asked a question she didn't want to answer, and she found a way to twist the moment into something enticing. Something sensuous.

Yeah, I saw it. And I let it play out for a bit while I found a way around her.

"You ever read *Where the Red Fern Grows*?"

Jinx looked up from the book she'd been reading—a Stephen King classic I'd read a hundred times while in prison—and frowned. "Is that the one with Pony Boy?"

"That's *The Outsiders*."

"Huh. I read that one in school, but I don't recognize the name of the other."

When opportunity knocks, you open the door. "Really? We read both. Where'd you go to school?"

Her eyes tightened. "Vegas."

That actually fit what I knew of her, except for one thing. "Your mom was from Wisconsin, but you grew up in Vegas? You come from a long line of Cheesehead gamblers?"

"Cheeseheads and Packer fans, yes. Gamblers, no." She went back to her book, tangling her legs with mine. "Drunks, addicts, and losers, but no gamblers."

More pieces to her puzzle. I hoarded the crumbs she dropped like a squirrel prepping for winter. I'd learned a few things over the past couple of days. She was from Vegas, had never met her dad, and had gone to community college there. She was handy—could fix things a lot of people couldn't—which was apparently something she'd picked up from one of her mom's friends. The way she'd spat the word friend had made me think there was more to that story, but I hadn't pushed her. I didn't want her shutting the door again. Or using sex to distract me. Don't get me wrong, the sex was amazing. And plentiful. But I wanted something deeper, wanted more from her.

I was a starving man standing before a buffet, and no fucking way was I settling for just an appetizer.

Which reminded me—I needed to go to the store. Well, not really. I had food in the pantry, but I drove to Rock Falls on the same day every week to hit the big grocery store. This week should have been no different, but it was. Because of Jinx.

"You're edgy."

I sighed. "Sorry."

"What's wrong? Did I leave a light on again?"

I flinched, wishing I'd have handled that moment better. "I apologized for that."

"You did. You apologize for too much." She rolled to a sitting position and set her book on the table. We'd been on the couch for two days—reading. Chatting, watching movies. If there hadn't been the specter of a motorcycle club hunting us down outside the walls, it would have been perfect. Well, as perfect as she'd let it be considering she kept that veil between us.

Still, as she crawled over my body and lay on top of me, I couldn't complain. I had my girl in my arms. That was something I'd never thought would happen.

"Are you wanting to work on your carving?"

Because she'd become obsessed with watching me take my knives and chisels to the piece of wood I'd been working on. The one I'd started the first day we'd been in my house together. The one definitely inspired by her. "No. Maybe later tonight, though."

"Do you need to call Elijah or Lainie?"

"I already did this morning."

"But it seems to help you calm down when you get upset."

She'd really paid attention to my habits. "No, I don't need to talk to them."

"Then what do you need?" She grinned up at me. "Want me to go down on you again?"

So hard. Instantly hard. This girl—she'd dropped to her knees just the night before while I'd been washing dishes and had sucked me hard and deep. I'd come in mere seconds, too surprised by her actions not to. Too turned on to even hope for more control. Yeah, I wanted those plump, soft lips wrapped around my dick. I also wanted them telling me all her secrets.

But the fact that it was grocery day and I was supposed to go to Rock Falls wouldn't stop distracting me.

"As much as I'd love that, I'd rather slide inside that soft pussy of yours and let you ride me again."

"That could be arranged." She frowned and tilted her head. "But there's still something bothering you."

Fuck. "It's grocery day."

"Yeah?"

"I grocery shop in Rock Falls every Monday. It's…"

"A ritual." She looked down, eyes unfocused as if lost in thought. "Why not here in Justice?"

"We don't have a grocery store."

"Damn small towns."

"You get used to it."

She gave me a kiss and rose to her feet. "So, let's go shopping."

"I don't know if we should."

"It's one trip to another town. We'll go and get back real quick."

My hands practically shook with my need to acquiesce. I needed to buy my groceries, needed to stay somewhat on track with my weekly tasks. I couldn't go to work, so my schedule had been shot to hell already, but I could at least keep my home life in order. Maybe. "I should text Deacon."

"You do that. Let me get dressed, and then we'll leave." She leaned down to kiss me. "It'll be fine."

Famous last words. "You're awfully brave."

"No, I'm empathetic. This will drive you to distraction if we don't do it. Why torture yourself when we can just head to Rock Falls, do the shopping, and hurry back instead? It's broad daylight outside, and we'll be together. Strength in numbers."

Or larger targets, but whatever. I needed to get this task done, and she was more influential than I'd given her credit for. "Let's go."

But it took far longer than it should have to get out the door mainly because Jinx decided to torture me. Nearly naked, she bent and wiggled her way through brushing her hair and putting on the little bit of makeup I'd hidden away for her. And how she dressed herself? Pure torture. No one needed to bend themselves in half to put on jeans, but she did. With her ass practically in my face as I sat on the bed. I couldn't help myself. I grabbed her and pulled her into my lap, grinding up into that cotton-covered pussy as I sucked on her neck.

"You're so naughty."

"In the best way."

"Yes. The best."

Twenty minutes and two orgasms—one for her, one for me—later, we finally stumbled out of the house and into my truck. Jinx's cheeks were flushed from our activities, and the smile on her face only grew as I turned onto the highway.

"I love this song," she said, reaching to increase the volume. "Did you go to many concerts before?"

Before I went to prison. "No. We're too far from anywhere to really get much more than half washed-up country acts. I went to one when I got out as a test, but I didn't last long."

"Too much drinking?"

"Too loud. I prefer the quiet."

"I'm not surprised."

"What about you?"

She sat back, her voice going all wistful. "My mom was a huge Eagles fan, and she used to drag me to see them every time they came through Vegas."

"Did you enjoy it?"

"I did. I missed going when she decided to take whatever man was shacking up in our house instead."

More breadcrumbs to hoard. I reached across the console to

grab her hand. "That had to suck, being left behind when it was something you enjoyed."

"Yeah, it did. But when I got to go, it was fun. Just the two of us, you know? A rarity at times."

"You love her."

Jinx nodded, turning away to stare out the window. Putting that wall back up. "I did, yeah."

Past tense. Another piece.

"Did Deacon ever text you back?" Jinx asked, pulling me from my thoughts.

"I don't know. Why don't you—" I practically froze, staring unseeing at the highway before me. "Fuck."

"What's wrong?"

Cold like I'd never felt ran through my veins, making my heart race and my muscles go stiff. "I left my phone on the counter."

An impossibility. My wallet stayed in my glove box because I'd forgotten it so many times, but my phone? Never. I always had it with me, always remembered to put it in my pocket before I left the house. This wasn't like the razor thing where it was such an innocuous item that forgetting was a possibility. This was like forgetting my name—just as rare and upsetting.

Jinx stared at me for a long, quiet moment. "Finn."

I couldn't even focus on her. "I left my phone. I always have my phone. It's not like the razor or the light. I *always* have my phone. How did that happen? I must have forgotten—"

"We just got off track," Jinx said, reaching across the seat to place her hand on my arm. "I'm sure everything's okay."

I didn't feel okay. "What if I didn't turn off the stove?"

"You did. I saw you—the stove was off and the dishes were washed before we left the kitchen to read."

"Did I lock the door?"

"Yes. I watched you."

But I doubted. The possibilities of having forgotten something vital—of leaving something out that shouldn't have been—plagued me. Jinx must have felt my unease because she held on to my hand and brought it to her mouth to kiss the back of it.

"Everything is fine at your house. I would have stopped you if you'd done something like leave the door unlocked or the stove on. Let's get the groceries, and we can be back in no time."

An hour minimum, but the only other option was turning around, and that would only irritate me more. "Sounds like a plan. Just...we need to be quick."

"Absolutely understood. Speedy grocery shopping. Totally doable."

We drove the rest of the way in silence, tension in a slow rolling boil between us. If anything happened today, it would be entirely my fault—I couldn't let go of how stupid I was to leave my phone behind. What if we broke down on the road? What if we needed Deacon or Parris? What if Alder's house was set on fire and he needed our help? With the way things had been going in Justice lately, all those seemed quite possible. But there was nothing I could do except cling to Jinx's hand and hope this trip would go by quickly.

We made it to the store without issue, a fact that appeased me enough to breathe normally again. I scanned the parking lot just in case, but nothing seemed out of the ordinary—no motorcycles, just the usual collection of junker sedans and pickup trucks. Totally regular day.

T-minus twenty minutes until we should be able to leave. "Ready?"

Jinx smiled my way. "Yup. You know what you want? Or do you buy the same things every week."

I frowned, which only made her smile.

"You do," she said, nodding. "You buy the exact same items every week. I bet you already know how much your bill will be."

"No." Because they had sales and sometimes even coupons. "I like order."

"Will it bother you if I buy things outside your normal?"

"Of course not." I hurried around the front of the truck to help her down on the other side. "Is my house lacking Jinx-approved snacks?"

"Not snacks, no. Though now that you mention it, I could go for some pretzels."

"Pretzels we can do."

"And tea."

I paused, my hand on the handle of the cart I'd grabbed. "Tea?"

"Yeah. You're a coffee drinker, but I like tea."

"I bought tea."

Her face darkened, and she looked away. "Yes, but it's black. I really prefer green. Not to be difficult or anything."

Well, now I felt like an ignorant ass. I should have bought her different kinds of tea. Or asked her what she preferred. "We'll get you as much tea as you need. You should meet my brother Bishop's girl, Anabeth, by the way."

"She a tea drinker?" Jinx turned as she walked through the doors, her eyes catching mine.

"Addict would be a better word, and I don't use that term lightly."

"I think I'd like her. Why haven't I met her yet?"

I stumbled, remembering Bishop's fury the last time I'd seen him. The sting of his fist connecting with my jaw. "We don't have the best relationship. Plus, they live in Vegas most of the time. She's a performer."

"Exotic?"

There was no holding back the laugh that busted out of me. "No, not at all. Paranormal shows. She reads tarot and stuff."

"Huh." Jinx grabbed a bunch of bananas and set them in the seat of the cart. "Why the bad relationship?"

"That's a long story."

"Quid pro quo."

"You'd have to give me something deep for this one. It's... Let's just say, it doesn't make me look good."

She chewed her lip as we walked through the vegetable section, grabbing a bag of salad and jar of dressing from the display, along with some precut broccoli. "I think my mom was a sex worker, though I never have been able to wrangle the truth on that."

I couldn't even consider that a breadcrumb. It was an entire slice thrown at me at once. "That's deep, all right. You think she participated in that profession all your life or..."

"Participated in that profession?" Jinx raised her eyebrow— just the one—and gave me a saucy sort of grin. "That's a really nice way to say turned tricks."

"I'm trying to tread carefully here."

"I can tell. And yeah, I think most of my life she was being paid for sex. Mostly with the bikers she hung around with. Now it's your turn—tell me about this beef between your brother Bishop and you."

I'd set up the quid pro quo thing—it was only fair to follow the rules. "In high school, I talked his girl Anabeth into using with me, then almost killed her with an overdose of meth."

Jinx froze, eyes wide as she stared at me right there in front of the deli counter. "Whoa."

"Yeah. Do you like ham? I usually buy that for sandwiches."

"Sure. Ham is fine." She frowned at the display of lunch

meat as I made my request to the lady behind the counter, waiting until I was done to say, "So... She's still angry about that, I assume."

"Actually, no, but my brother is." I accepted the packet of meat—twice as much as I usually bought—with a nod. "Anabeth left Bishop not long after that incident without telling him anything, and they spent a lot of years apart. She only recently came back and told him what had happened."

"And he got mad at you for it."

"Punched me right in the face and told me to keep my addiction away from her."

Jinx grabbed a tub of vanilla yogurt as we rounded the dairy case. "But...you're not using anymore."

"Haven't since before I went in. My family seems to think I'll crack and fall back into old habits at any moment, though."

"Do you worry you might?"

"Of course. I'm not arrogant enough to say it'll never happen, but deep down? I know it'll never happen. I won't let it."

"You don't seem like the type to fall off the wagon again and again. You're too—"

"Crazy?"

"Regimented. And strong. You're so damn strong."

I grabbed her hand, stopping her. Tugging her closer. "I think the same thing about you, you know."

"I'm not strong. I'm just determined. There's a difference." She gave me a quick kiss, then dragged me down the cereal aisle. "Come on. Let's get some Lucky Charms."

"I don't eat cereal."

"I do, and Lucky Charms are my favorite." She grabbed the box in question, smiling up at me. But her smile faltered as her eyes focused on something over my shoulder. I didn't turn though because three guys had just come into the aisle from the far end, guys in jeans and leathers. In club colors.

"Shit."

"You can say that again." Jinx nodded behind me. "We've got company."

We sure the hell did. Three guys stood at the other end of the aisle, six altogether. Blocking us in. But it was the one in the middle on Jinx's side that caught my attention. That made my stomach drop and my blood run cold. He looked familiar, and he was staring at Jinx as if he knew her.

The same guy from the truck stop. And from the lot at The Jury Room the other night.

He stopped a few feet away from us, looking Jinx up and down as he said, "What's up, Luckless?"

Chapter Seventeen

JINX

Dead. I was dead. This was it—I was going to be killed while standing in a grocery store aisle with a box of Lucky Charms in my hands. Fitting.

Ravel leered my way, totally ignoring the man at my side. A gift, in my mind.

"Prez wants to talk to you."

The squeal of another cart in the store sounded from what seemed like far away, which meant we had company. Not exactly calming considering it was probably some housewife with her kids in tow, but I'd take what I could get. No one wanted witnesses when they planned to murder someone. "I've got nothing to say to him."

"You might want to rethink that." Ravel finally took notice of Finn, obviously playing some sort of game with me. "Who's your friend?"

Yeah, he could fuck right off if he thought I was playing with him in regard to Finn. "No one."

I immediately wished I could take those words back as Finn stiffened at my back. But I couldn't—if Ravel or the other guys knew Finn was important to me, he'd be used against me so the prez could get what he wanted. But Ravel wasn't dumb—no matter what act he put on. He must have noticed something because he smirked at Finn as that damn squeaky-wheeled cart grew louder.

"You thought you mattered or something? I've heard how good this particular pussy is, but never trust your heart to a whore, son."

Finn didn't miss a beat. "I'm not your son."

And I wasn't letting this devolve into some sort of dick-measuring contest between the two of them. "You tell Prez I'm not interested in whatever he's selling."

"He's not selling, kid. He's buying," Ravel said, those dark eyes I knew far too well meeting mine once more. "I heard Parris was putting out feelers within the Soul Suckers for you—looking for the right price to bring you back to the Black Angels since Prez was pretty pissed when Zed lost you. Fucker lost his patch for that mistake."

Bastard deserved that after all he'd done, but I couldn't say that. Not with Finn behind me. Not without seeming heartless and cruel. I was neither, but I also wasn't one to care about someone who saw me as property and threw my life into a card game like nothing more than a hunk of plastic. Zed deserved to lose his patch. He also deserved a good, swift kick in the balls and a few nights on an ant hill covered in honey with some sort of spinal block in so he couldn't move or scream. He deserved a lot. None of which I would admit to wishing for.

But wish, I had.

"Good," I said, practically spitting the word. My hatred for

Zed likely obvious to the men around me. "He didn't deserve to wear those colors, not with how he went against orders. And Parris can do what he wants, not that it matters—he doesn't own me."

Why the hell wasn't that shopper getting another cart? The squeal seemed practically endless at this point. It grated on my nerves and made me jumpy. Like some sort of horror movie soundtrack playing through the store. Closer, louder, closer, louder.

"You're right," Ravel said. "Parris doesn't own you, no matter how many nights he spent in your momma's bed. Prez owns you, or he did before Zed fucked up. He's going to want his property back." Ravel grinned at Finn. "Preferably unharmed and untouched, though he might accept payment for services rendered."

Finn just couldn't keep his mouth shut after that one. "Unless Jinx herself asks me for payment, there will be no money changing hands."

"Didn't you know?" Ravel asked, looking downright ready to strike. "Nothing is free with this girl. If she spread her legs for you, there was something she wanted in exchange. She might not ask for cash, but she's a whore nonetheless."

"You smoke?" Finn asked, seemingly out of nowhere.

Ravel looked almost as confused as I did. "No. Never have."

"Then for today, you live."

"Stop it, Finn." I knocked him with my shoulder, feeling the tension running through his body against my back. Not wanting him to lose it and lunge at Ravel. Six against one was crappy odds. Even six against two—Finn and me fighting together— wasn't likely to net us a win. We were at the Black Angels' mercy, and they knew that. This was so bad. I'd mentioned my mom to Finn, but I'd never told him how I ended up dealing with the

Black Angels. Never explained how I went from college kid to biker bitch in the span of a few hours. I'd never wanted to tell him about the choices that had led me to be sold off like cattle.

But what I wanted no longer mattered. "Look. If Prez—"

Deacon suddenly appeared, pushing the buggy with the squeakiest wheel known to man and whistling something that sounded like a song from *Mary Poppins*. Big, strong, and seemingly oblivious to the standoff before him as he walked down the breakfast food aisle in his faded concert tee, jeans, and flip-flops. All eight of us stared as he strolled right past the bikers, focusing on the shelves. Shoes thwacking and cart screaming that irritating sound. Interrupting us without a word.

That man had balls the size of cantaloupes.

He also had one hell of a poker face. "Hey, guys. What's up?"

Ravel glanced at his crew then asked, "What are you doing here, barkeep?"

Deacon seemed completely unfazed by the fact that Ravel knew who he was. "Looking for some Pop-Tarts. Ah, there they are." He grabbed a box off the shelf—strawberry frosted— making a big show of tossing the box in his noisy cart before smiling at Ravel. "Breakfast of champions. Y'all looking for something specific?"

Ravel smirked my way, glancing over my shoulder as he said, "Yeah. Prez sent us to hunt down his chicken and some fish."

The chicken was me—I'd compared myself to cattle. Apparently, the prez didn't see me as anything holding that much value. Fish... well, that could only be Finn. Ravel had just shown his hand, letting me know there was no saving Finn from whatever was coming from the Black Angels. No stopping it. His fate had been sealed, even if I went back willingly. Unless I dealt with the president directly.

That made me sick to my stomach. "You're a piece of shit."

"And you're property of the Soul Suckers, though not for long. Consider yourself lucky that we caught up with you before they did. Not that you've ever been lucky." Ravel glanced at Finn, his eyes dark and his scowl firmly in place. "Expect a visit from the prez, and you'd better be ready to do some serious groveling for your friend here. You know what'll happen when Prez finds out someone was playing with his toys without his permission."

Yeah, I did. They'd kill Finn. Likely in front of me as a lesson since his death would be my fault. Something I couldn't let happen.

But it was Deacon who responded. "You tell your prez to come talk to me about anything related to Jinx. Her tie to the Soul Suckers has been severed, so she's mine now."

His words hit me right in the gut, much like a sucker punch. Still, I kept my mouth shut.

Ravel didn't. "My boss isn't going to like that."

If Deacon's grin got any wider, he'd look like the Joker from *Batman*. "Put up or shut up. I put up what the Soul Suckers wanted and got Jinx in return. She's no longer for sale. Period. Now get the fuck away from her before I call in my crew. No one wants to bloody up the cereal aisle. Tony the Tiger's watching us." He pointed at a box of Frosted Flakes, shaking his head solemnly. As if he was serious about a cartoon character monitoring us.

Balls. The size of cantaloupes.

Ravel practically growled. "I'll see you soon, barkeep."

"Name's Deacon. Come see me anytime, son."

He waved. The man waved at the bikers, practically shooing them out of the store. And it worked. They definitely didn't like it, but they left. I couldn't believe it. I also couldn't stop shaking. I kept my back straight, though. Kept my eyes on Ravel and his crew as they headed for the exit. Kept Finn behind me and Deacon at my side as ideas and thoughts and plans ran through my head. Bought and sold again, even if it was to Deacon. This shit had to stop.

Once the bikers had left, Finn turned and walked off down the aisle, leaving me alone with Deacon.

Leaving me. I'd messed up. Big-time. But maybe that was for the best. Maybe—

"Hey," Deacon said, grabbing my arm before I could follow Finn. "You okay?"

Nope. "I'm used to their threats, so I'm fine."

He frowned. "Is he?"

Finn. I didn't have an answer for that. Not really. "I don't know. What did you mean—my tie has been severed?"

Deacon took a deep breath, his eyes not quite meeting mine, then headed after Finn, dragging me with him. "We'll talk about that another day. Just know that they no longer own you, if they ever did. Personally, I'm not a fan of the whole owning people thing, but your situation with them was a roadblock we had to take care of. So I took care of it. Now, I want to get you back to Justice. You two gave me a heart attack when I couldn't reach you."

We caught up with Finn at the butcher counter. The man appeared fine—not calm, but solid. Unafraid. Though he wouldn't even look at me.

"You good, Finn?" Deacon asked.

"I forgot my phone at home."

Deacon definitely seemed taken aback by that answer. I was as well. But of course, Finn would focus on that when things had gone so wrong. He'd obsess over the mistake he'd made and how that had thrown off his day. He liked order and despised chaos. I brought him nothing *but* chaos. And not the good kind.

It took Deacon a full ten seconds to absorb Finn's words and respond with, "Is everything all right?"

Finn lifted one shoulder in a halfhearted shrug, still purposefully not looking at me. "Yeah, I just didn't get a chance to double-check things. It won't happen again."

Somehow, that felt directed at me. My distractions wouldn't happen again. We wouldn't happen again. A statement much like the one I'd tried to play off with Ravel about Finn being no one. A wall to hide his hurt behind. I knew walls—knew how to build them, how to reinforce them, and how to block myself off from all other people with them. Finn had never blocked himself off from me. Not until right then. Not until I'd hurt him enough for him to feel the need to.

My poor, sweet Finn. I'd broken him.

"It was my fault," I said, wishing Finn would at least look at me. At least acknowledge my existence. "I've been upsetting his routines for days."

"But you two are okay?" Deacon asked, looking from Finn to me and back again. "No trouble out at the house?"

"No trouble," Finn replied, finally glancing my way. I'd never seen his blue-gray eyes so dead. So...stormy. A hurricane building off the coast, bearing down on land without mercy. A thunderstorm preparing to terrify all who lay in its path. I'd really hurt him.

A fact that might just play into my hands.

"Yeah, no trouble. Are we going to be able to come back to work soon?"

Deacon stared at me, his face stoic but his eyes—they betrayed him. He didn't believe our story, didn't buy that things were fine. His trust in me was gone. "Not until we take care of the threat and run the Soul Suckers out of town."

Wonderful. "Are you planning on letting us in on what's going on with that?"

"Not in the least, but plans are in motion."

Jerk. "Fine. Then we hole up for a few more days."

Finn nodded. "Sounds like it. Grab your cereal, Jinx. I'm ready to go home."

That was a dismissal if I'd ever heard one. "Yeah. Okay. I'll meet you up front."

I grabbed our abandoned cart from the cereal aisle, then headed toward the checkout lanes. Stopping in the aisle with cleaners and household hardware supplies to grab one extra thing. Something I needed if I was going to enact the plan weaving itself together in my head. If I was going to save Finn from having to face the Black Angels head on. I tucked the package into my waistband and under my shirt, figuring petty shoplifting was better than trying to explain to Finn why I needed it. Not that he'd listen to me in his current mood anyway.

The drive home was one long exercise in silence and trying hard not to break down. I wanted to talk to him, to tell him how I'd been trying to protect him by saying he was no one. But I bit my tongue and thought through my plan over and over again. All my knowledge of the Black Angels—and specifically of their president, a man who went by the road name Edge when he wasn't being called Prez—coming together to help me figure out the best way out of this mess. For Finn more than for me. This was how things needed to be. This was the rug being pulled out from under me as I'd expected. Finn would be mad for a while, but that would fade. He'd forget about me.

It was my job to make sure Ravel would forget about him too.

Chapter Eighteen

FINN

No one.

I was no one.

Deep down, I knew Jinx had been fronting when she'd said that, but the words still gutted me. Right there in front of danger, she hadn't let me help her. Hadn't even pretended to need me. I'd been rendered useless by her, and those two words had cemented that fact. *No one.* I had no idea how to get over that, not without a serious conversation. One I wasn't up to having yet.

"I need to take a shower." I tucked the Lucky Charms she'd wanted—the cereal she'd been holding while that asshole had called her a whore—into the cabinet, all groceries put away. Kitchen back to rights. Life in complete chaos. I hadn't said a word since we'd left Rock Falls, so it shouldn't have surprised me that she jumped at the sound of my voice. Still sucked, though. I didn't want to be the one to scare her. Not ever.

"Sure. Sounds good." Jinx walked out of the kitchen without a look back, her shoulders stiff and her head up. Whether she was mad or hurt, I couldn't tell, but I'd fix it. I just needed a few minutes to get my head on straight. To figure out what to do about this whole situation and how to reassure Jinx that I could take care of her. That I wanted to be more than no one. That she definitely was to me.

I stripped down in the bathroom and turned on the shower. Hanging my head and letting the hot water pound my shoulders. Letting my mind wander as I tried to look at this thing between Jinx and me with logic. I liked her. I was attracted to her for sure. I cared for her and wanted to take care of her. I also wanted her in my bed every night, wanted her feet pressing between my thighs when she got cold. Wanted to see her smile when I added cheese to her eggs and hear her laugh when something funny happened in those movies she loved so much. I wanted all of her. The broken bits too.

I wanted to heal her and have her be the balm for my soul that I needed.

I wanted forever. Because I loved her.

"Motherfucker," I hissed, turning off the water and jumping out of the shower as the need to tell her, to grab her and apologize for being an idiot and make amends pushed me to move hastily. Fuck drying off. Fuck cleaning up after myself. My girl was out there hurt and needing me, and I couldn't stand that thought.

"Jinx," I yelled as I rushed into the kitchen. No dice. I turned and headed for the living room, dread pushing down on my heart. Empty as well. "Jinx."

No answer. In fact, the house was silent. Almost eerily so. I was headed for the bedroom again when I noticed something out of place. A piece of white paper on the little table by the front door.

A note.

I approached it slowly, cautiously. Knowing what it was before I reached it. Before I saw the black slashes and loops across the pristine surface. Before I read the words that opened up a gaping hole in my gut.

I'm sorry, but this won't work. I'll get your truck back to you.

Gone. Left. Took my truck and everything as if we were somehow living in an old country song. But that didn't matter, what did was that she'd taken my heart with her. I hadn't been enough for her, so she'd left me behind.

I stumbled my way to the kitchen table and plopped into a chair, fighting hard to hold back the hurt. I wanted to drink, wanted to get high and erase all these emotions. Wanted the numbness I remembered from before.

Before...

When I couldn't think of anything except where I'd get my next hit.

When nothing really hurt because the drugs numbed out the world.

I'd have done anything to be numb again.

I reached for my phone—fucking thing that had become a symbol of my screwed-up day—and tapped a few times to pull up a number. A few times more to connect and put the call on speaker. And then I waited.

One ring.

Two.

Just a little longer.

Three.

Maybe not. Maybe I'd go to voice mail. Maybe—

On the fourth ring, I heard the click of the call connecting. "Finn? What's wrong?"

My brother's voice was the only thing I could hold on to at that moment. The only thing that could keep me grounded. "I want to use."

Elijah wasn't my sponsor, he wasn't my addiction counselor, and he wasn't my parole officer. What he was surpassed all of those. He was my lifeline to past me, the Finn before the drugs. The responsible guy who'd wanted to go to school and earn a degree and do something with his life. That guy was dead— buried under guilt and shame and bad decisions—but Elijah remembered. He would always help me regain whatever little part of past me I needed. And right then, I needed his strength.

"Hang on." Elijah whispered words away from the phone— likely excusing himself from something far more important than I would ever do—and then came back to me with a breathy, "What's going on?"

What *was* going on? I wanted to use, yes. Wanted to get high and numb, totally. But that wasn't the right answer. Back when I was detoxing and trying to find my way through the drugs, a fellow inmate—one who'd been sober longer than I'd been using —took me under his wing. Had seen me struggling and chose to shore me up. He'd asked me one question—what's your problem? When I'd tried to tell him about my drug use and my cravings, he'd just shaken his head.

"That's not your problem, boy. That's just a side effect. What's your *real* problem?"

It had taken me a long time to figure that out. Loneliness. In a family as large as mine, it hadn't even seemed possible, but I had always been buried behind Alder and Bishop, lost the youngest status to Lainie—the only girl and therefore the doted-on princess—and had been the twin to the family clown. I'd never stood out, never had a place of my own. I'd been *one of the Kennards*, and that had led me to make some really bad decisions on the path to finding attention.

So today, wanting to use wasn't my problem. It was the side effect.

What was going on? Well, there was only one answer. "I think I fell in love."

Elijah was silent for more seconds than was comfortable. "With the girl, the one from the bar."

"Yeah. The one who's been staying with me." I couldn't say her name. I tried, but it got stuck in my throat. Got caught up as pain ripped through my chest again.

"Okay," Elijah said, drawing out the word. "So why—"

"She left."

"Oh."

Yeah. One syllable. What else could he say? The big, bad lawyer speechless struck me as funny, though. At least until I thought about that—big, bad lawyer. *Shit.* "You were probably busy at work. I'm sorry to bother you like this—"

"You got someone with you there? Alder or Bishop or Deacon, maybe?"

"No. It's okay, though. I'll track someone down to hang with. I won't use."

"Four hours, man. I can be there in four hours. I just need to know you'll be okay while I'm on my way."

Guilt burned, adding to my pain. Elijah had a big job to do, an important one. He had a life in Denver that I didn't want to be in the way of. "Don't come. You don't have to do that."

"Fuck you." The slam of what had to be a car door sounded in the background, my brother practically growling that curse. "You think I'm about to leave you alone when it's the first time you've ever reached out to me for help like this? I'm already driving."

I...wasn't sure what to say. Too lost in my own thoughts. Was it really the only time I'd reached out to him? I called him every day, spoke to him on the phone more than I spoke to anyone in person. That was me reaching out for help—for stability and comfort. I'd been solid in my sobriety since I'd gotten out of prison, though. Had never wanted to use as bad as I did in that moment. Even after Anabeth had come back and stirred up all those memories, after Bishop had punched me in the face for what had happened between us all those years ago, I hadn't wanted to be numb.

Today was different, I'd give him that. Today, I wanted to get high and pretend the world around me didn't exist anymore. Today was a struggle. "You don't have to come here, though. I can call Alder. I will...I'll call Alder. He'll come over and stay with me."

"Alder isn't the one you called first, though. I was, so I'm coming."

"People need you."

"You need me, and you're my brother. You outrank them."

"I shouldn't."

Elijah was silent for a long moment, the only sound coming through the speaker the rumble of the engine in his fancy car. The one he'd gotten right after he'd started his own practice. The one he'd bought with the money he made defending people who'd been wrongly accused or convicted. Like I had been. Trying to help people the way he hadn't been able to help me.

If my old friend from prison had asked Elijah what his problem was, my brother would likely say he worked too hard. But that wasn't the problem—that was the side effect. Elijah's problem was wrapped up in my imprisonment. Was a giant ball of guilt sitting heavy on his shoulders. I knew that feeling. Knew that ball well. Mine may have moved into place for different reasons, but we both carried the burden of them. We both suffered.

Elijah broke the silence, issuing a quiet, "Finn?"

"Yeah?"

"Talk to me."

I sat back, leaning against the wall. Not sure when I'd dropped to the floor in the first place, but feeling right in that spot. "About what?"

"The girl. Tell me about the girl."

Jinx. I sighed. "It's sort of a long story."

"We've got four hours."

Yeah, we did.

"Her name is Jinx."

Chapter Nineteen

JINX

It wasn't hard to find the clubs once I made it back to Rock Falls. Bikers were everywhere—they practically swarmed the small town like ants. The weather hadn't warmed up much, so most of them wore their winter riding gear. Once the snow really fell, they'd all be stuck in cars and trucks. Cages, they'd call them. These guys weren't hobby riders—they were hard-core bikers. A little cold wouldn't stop them from staying on two wheels.

There were two different crews in town, Soul Suckers and Black Angels, both national clubs with members wearing different house patches. Arizona, Colorado, Utah, Nevada—I saw indications of bikers from many places. Guys from all over the southwest had come to town, it seemed. That fact might make my job harder, but I had to try.

I headed for what I figured was the safer of the two clubs, looking for the patch that indicated they were from my hometown. The guys who were supposedly Parris' *brothers*. The ones who would likely kill me at some point along the way. The Black Angels of Las Vegas.

Surprisingly, I found them without too much trouble. A small group of Vegas Angels stood in an abandoned fast-food joint's parking lot, surrounding their bikes, drinking what had to be hot coffee from the truck stop next door. The same one where Finn had taken me for an ice cream sundae. Where he'd first held my hand. That seemed like a lifetime ago.

No time to worry about the past. I pulled into the lot, drawing every bit of attention from the crew. Good. Time to get this over with.

"Hey," I said to the Vegas bikers as soon as I had the window rolled down. "Where's Edge staying?"

One guy stepped forward—road name Knuckles. "What are you doing out here, Luckless?"

That was a question even I couldn't really answer. "I need Edge. You know where he is?"

Knuckles locked eyes with me, looking almost wary. But Edge—the president of the Vegas chapter of the Black Angels— had likely told all his guys to keep an eye out for me. Knuckles knew better than to deny the prez what he wanted.

And what he wanted was me. Always.

"Nash and the prospect here can take you in," Knuckles said before turning his back on me to talk to the other guys. That was fine with me. I rolled up the window and sat in the warm truck, waiting. Biding my time and doing my best not to throw up all over myself. This was my decision. My way to help Finn and the rest of the town of Justice. My sacrifice. But this time—almost a year after I'd attempted to do the same thing for my mom—I knew exactly what that sacrifice entailed.

The two Black Angels started their bikes and headed out of the lot, one riding ahead of me and one behind. Trapping me between them, of course. A few turns, a few stretches of blacktop with nothing around but nature, and a camp appeared in front of me. Lots of recreational trailers, mostly those pop-up ones, small wooden structures that had to be rentable cabins, and bikes of all types littered a piece of land with a stunning mountain view as a backdrop. Beer cans and whiskey bottles were piled high at the side of the entrance road, right beside a boulder proclaiming this some sort of park. Protected land. The club had taken it over and trashed it right there under the glory of nature. Typical.

"Jinxy girl. Such a surprise. Where ya been?" Tiny, the huge, body-building enforcer of the Vegas Black Angels, strolled over, probably having known I was coming from the time I hit the Rock Falls city line. No way was he actually surprised to see me. I knew better than not to play his games, though. He'd put chains on me for less.

"Playing barkeep over in Justice. Is Edge around?"

Tiny looked me up and down, considering. Likely examining the handiwork of the scars Edge had left me. The slashes and lines Finn had thought were self-inflicted. The ones I definitely hadn't done myself and had made sure to show off for this particular trip. Tiny was probably hoping he'd get a chance to see me bleed and scream again. That was fine—let him look. Let him see those marks. Didn't matter. I'd take them all over again if I had to, and I had a feeling I was going to have to.

"He's not in the greatest of moods," Tiny said, surprising me for the first time since I'd left Finn's house. Tiny had never warned me when he was going to hurt me or when Edge had been in one of his moods. He'd never even hinted at what was to come until I was trapped in the middle of it. That comment about Edge's mood was a warning if ever I'd heard one, but I couldn't turn around now. Couldn't give up. I had one shot at making things right, and I needed to take it before I lost my nerve.

"I can handle him."

"Yeah, you can. But it's likely going to hurt."

Not the first time. "Just tell me where he is."

He nodded toward a trailer—a big, drivable unit with extendable parts pulled out and what looked like a picnic table sitting outside of it. As if this were some sort of family vacation. I headed that way, fighting to keep my breathing smooth and my heart from thumping out of my chest. I kept picturing Finn —all serious and sweet, kind and caring. I didn't want to, didn't want to bring such a happy thought into this hell, but he was the only way I'd make it through this. Knowing my sacrifice was for him.

I knocked twice when I reached the trailer, not even giving myself time to wait. *Just act. Don't think.*

"Well, what do you know," Edge said as soon as he came strolling to the door. He wore a faded pair of jeans that hung loosely from his hips, likely because he hadn't buttoned them, and nothing else. Bare feet padded across the carpet, and his muscles bunched and pulled as he opened the screen door for me. "Jinx has found her way home."

Home, my ass. "I want to talk to you."

"Come on in, then, darling. Make yourself comfortable." I brushed past him, stepping up into the trailer and heading for the back. I knew the setup of these things—knew where the bedroom area was. Knew exactly where I needed to be. This negotiation was going to take place where Edge was most vulnerable whether he liked it or not.

A blonde lay across one of the couches in what must have been considered the living space. I paid her no mind, at least not until Edge did.

"Shelly, go on back to Tiny now. We can play some more later."

"But I thought we were going to get high and fuck," she said, her voice soft and almost whiny. Her craving for the drugs Edge had obviously been denying her clear as day. He did love to make women beg for what they needed.

"Tiny will take care of you. Tell him I said to give you the good stuff and then treat that pussy real nice." He smacked her on the ass twice as she headed for the door, though that didn't stop her from throwing a serious glare my way. Whatever. She didn't have any scars yet—that bitch didn't even know what would be coming for her if Edge decided to claim her.

"You in some sort of hurry, Jinx?" Edge asked when I'd passed into the bedroom. Yeah, I was, but only because this needed to be done. This deal needed to be locked down.

I sat down on the bed, and I turned my arms just so. Just the way he liked me to so he could see the burn marks from his cigarettes. The ones he'd been giving me for almost a year. "I've got a proposition for you."

"You." He grinned and slithered closer. "Have a proposition. For me?"

"Yeah, and I think you're going to want to pay close attention to it."

"Well, I'm all ears. Hit me."

I wished. "I'm offering the one thing you've never been able to get from me. The one thing you've been trying to get since I first walked into your club. What you've lied and cheated and manipulated to get, not that I ever gave it up."

"I've had that pussy, Jinx."

My stomach lurched at his crass words, but he wasn't wrong. He'd had me before—had coerced me into letting him take what he wanted in exchange for what I needed. And I was about to make a similar deal, but on a much bigger and more dangerous scale. "I'm not talking sex. Sex is simple—you can get sex anywhere. I'm talking *more*."

If I hadn't studied him as long as I had, hadn't made sure to learn everything I could about him over my year with his club, I wouldn't have noticed the tic in his jaw. The way his eyes sharpened and his nostrils flared slightly. He was interested—far more than he wanted to let on. "I'm listening."

This is it. No turning back now. "I'll give you my surrender."

He blinked, staring. A single muscle twitching in his jaw the only sign he'd even heard me, but I knew he had. Knew this was just what he wanted. Me...not fighting back. At his mercy voluntarily. Unlike what he'd done to most women around the club, he'd never been able to break me, and I knew it ate at him. I knew this—Edge knew this as well. For a guy who loved control as much as he did, I was offering him his grandest wish. To control the one thing that had been uncontrollable.

No way was he turning me down. "What's your price?"

"The Black Angels go home. All of them leave Justice and the people there alone, no matter what the Soul Suckers ask you for."

"That's a steep cost, Jinx. I expected you to ask me to find your mom for you. That's all you've wanted since you came walking into my club a year ago."

He was partially right. That had been all I'd wanted. That's why I'd come back into the club world after avoiding it for so long. Why I'd been hanging around for the past year, letting them do whatever they wanted to me in exchange for information. To find out what had happened to my mom. But I already knew her fate—always had—I'd just spent a long year refusing to believe it. "I know my mom's dead. I also know Ravel probably killed her with your approval. She's not what I want in the exchange."

He nodded all slow and deliberate. Taking up time. Likely trying to figure out a way he could get more from me. "Did you come with a backup deal? With something more to negotiate with in case I don't see this as even?"

"Nope. Just me. That's what I've got."

"Abandoning the Soul Suckers is a hefty price," he said, clucking softly. "There'll be retaliation."

Which meant he was at least considering my deal. I just had to close it. "I'm worth whatever might come. I'll make it worthwhile. Besides, since when do the Black Angels bow down to those bastards? I thought your crew was stronger than them?"

His face turned hot, his glare pinning me in place. "We are. The only reason we're here is because you got their enforcer killed."

Ah, that actually made sense. "I didn't kill him."

"No shit. You're not exactly the killing kind, are you, Jinxy?"

Not yet. But I didn't say anything—not one word. I stayed silent and let him stew over things for a few seconds. Let him consider the angles. I was close, though. I almost had him.

Edge leaned against the wall, a thoughtful expression on his face. "What's got you giving a fuck about some nothing town in the mountains?"

Finn. Not that I could tell him that. "They saved me from Pistol, the Soul Suckers enforcer. They got me out of there before he put too many scars on me."

"Zed never should have put you up in that card game." He ran a cold finger down my arm, pushing at one of the marks he'd given me. Making me flinch. "He got his ass beat for that one, and he lost his patch."

He deserved more than that. "Good. He brought me into

that game as if I was property, then lost me to the Soul Suckers. They gave me to Pistol to use as a toy."

Edge looked me up and down, his eyes harder. Showing more interest. "I heard he liked to hurt women."

The excitement in his voice, the obvious pleasure at the idea of watching someone inflict pain, made my stomach roll. "He did. I'm proof of that."

"How bad?"

I knew what he wanted, so I stood up and pulled my shirt over my head. Showing him my back. The scabbed-over mess of flesh that would scar soon enough. The evidence of what Deacon and Alder had saved me from.

"He does such nice work." Edge traced a fingertip down my spine before pushing. Hard. Making me gasp at the sting he incited. "But you weren't his to scar like this."

Nope. I'd belonged to Edge since my mom had gone missing and I'd come looking for her. He'd claimed me, took me as his property, and placed his own scars all over my body as I'd fought him. As I'd refused to totally bend to his whims. Always promising me info on what had happened to my mom but never giving me enough. Never telling me exactly what had happened and where her body was so I could find peace and closure. Breaking me down until I hadn't thought escape was possible, until I'd resigned myself to a life of pain and abuse, even though I'd still fought back. He'd taken my body a hundred times in a dozen different ways, but he'd never really had me. Never got me to be willing. That was about to change...if he accepted my deal.

"Let me talk to Tiny. See what sort of fallout this deal would cause." He pressed his lips against my shoulder where a long, thick scar made an S. The one he'd carved into my flesh. His mark of ownership. For Shawn—his real name. "It's good to have you back, Jinx."

"I'm only back if you accept the deal. If not..."

I let that statement trail off, let the warning land and grow. If he didn't agree, I'd leave. And this time, I wouldn't come back.

I'd never wanted to return once I'd gotten out.

But I'd had to...to save Justice.

To save Finn.

"You've got twenty-four hours to decide. After that, I'm gone." I reached into my pocket and pulled out what I'd stolen from the grocery store. The little pack of razor blades meant to be used in some sort of box cutter or something. Meant to slice open packages and score cardboard.

Which wasn't what I knew Edge would do with them.

"Here," I said, handing the blades to him. "You accept my deal, you can use these on me. Just like you like to. But this time, I won't try to stop you."

Edge took the blades, rolling them in his palm. Staring at me with a dark, desirous expression. He liked my deal, wanted to take what I offered. He wanted me broken and willing to let him do anything to my body. That's what got him off—not my struggling and fighting—my surrender. I'd just offered him the ultimate toy, and I knew, deep down, he'd take it. Eventually. He wouldn't be able to turn it down.

"You know I could just force you."

I did. He'd been forcing me to do what he wanted since the day we'd met. "That's not what you want. Besides, without the deal, I'll leave."

"Tiny will chain you up if he thinks you'll run."

"Never stopped me before."

He laughed, then leaned over and bit my shoulder hard enough to draw blood. Hard enough to make me jump no matter how hard I tried not to react.

"I've missed you, girl. It's nice to have you back."

I couldn't say the same because this would be death for me. But if Finn and his friends and family were safe at least from the Black Angels, I'd take it. And then I'd work from the inside to make sure the Soul Suckers left the town alone as well.

I owed it to them.

Chapter Twenty

FINN

Once he made it to Justice, Elijah shadowed me the entire day. A blessing or a curse, depending on how you looked at it. Considering we were at a closed Jury Room so I could keep up with my usual cleaning tasks and was super sick of him on my heels, I'd say curse for the moment.

"I just need to take a piss."

My twin—who I had to guess looked exactly like I would if life had turned out a little differently for me—shrugged. "I'm not stopping you."

"No, you're following me."

"You said you felt like using."

I did. I still did. "It's fading."

"You can't lie to your brother."

"I lie to my brothers all the time."

"Not your twin."

True. Lying to Elijah had never come easy. He was the first to know something was up when I'd started using, and even then, I'd known he hadn't believed me when I'd told him I was fine. After I'd almost killed Bishop's girlfriend, he'd been the only one I'd told. The only one who'd known that secret other than Anabeth and me. He'd never said a word—not to Bishop, not to Anabeth, and not to anyone else who had wondered over the years why the girl had just up and left town. He'd kept that secret for me.

No sense lying now. "Fine. I still want to use, but I've got a decent hold on it."

"Decent isn't good enough. You felt the need to come into work even though the bar is closed, so now you've got access to all sorts of liquor and who knows what else that might be hidden around this place. Your control is being tested by the environment you put yourself in. I'm stuck on you until you've got this back under control."

No sense arguing with a lawyer, especially not one as stubborn as Elijah. I pushed past him into the men's room and headed for the urinal. "Fine. Just stay over there."

He leaned against the wall by the door, looking toward the ceiling. Silent until I'd finished and was zipping up. "How long until the gossip mill works against me?"

As in, how long did he have until Alder found out he was home. "My guess is he already knows."

"We should go say hi."

"Go right ahead." I washed my hands, meeting his eyes—so much like mine, they still set me back on my heels at times—in the mirror. "I heard Bishop was in town, and I'm not interested in pushing any more of his buttons."

"Still haven't dealt with the whole Anabeth thing yet?"

That *I almost killed Bishop's girl, so he decked me* thing. "No."

"You need to confront him about it and just lay everything out on the table."

I grabbed some paper towels to dry my hands. "Not my style."

"No shit," he said with a laugh. "You're the most nonconfrontational Kennard. You couldn't even do your twelve-step apology in person. You wrote letters."

I had. Telling my brothers and friends how much of a loser I was in person had seemed impossible at the time. And now...my thoughts went to Mercy Bell. How I usually avoided her. How she seemed very much on her own in town and could probably use a friend or two, but I couldn't deal with my stuff enough to offer. A true relationship with Bishop and Anabeth, family members, seemed out of reach as well. And Alder treated me as if I might break at any moment. Never mind that he could be right.

I sighed, my thoughts dark and swirly like a stormy sky. Like Jinx's eyes that I already missed so damn much. Something like a knife to the chest stabbed through me, making me ache all over. Making me practically tremble at the pain. If only I could be numb...

Not possible. "I apologized. That's what was important."

"Maybe it's time to face your past and let the two warlords know you're not the weakest link."

But I was. Everyone knew it. "Yet you're here because?"

He stared at me hard, a look on his face that was pure Elijah. Inquisitive, intelligent, and sure of himself. "Because you were strong enough to know you'd hit your limit and needed help. That's not weakness...that's brains."

I shook my head and pushed past him, needing to get back to work. Sort of regretting calling him in the first place. But only sort of. I'd missed him. I'd do anything for any one of my siblings, but Elijah and I had a different sort of bond. A closer one. I'd called him because I'd known there was simply no one else I trusted like him, and of course, Elijah had set everything in his own life aside to come help me. It was what he did. I was simply tired of needing the help.

When I walked into the main area of the bar, though, all thoughts of not needing my brother's help went right out the window. Mercy Bell stood in the center of the room, staring at me. As if called from my own thoughts of her and waiting for me to acknowledge her. Which I did with a, "What's wrong?"

She scrunched her nose for a second before smiling at Elijah. "Hey, Finn. Hi, Elijah. I didn't know you were home."

"Gossip mill—defeated," he whispered before heading her way with a smile. "Good to see you, Mercy. I'd heard you were back."

"My dad needed someone to run the store, so here I am." She looked my way, seeming a little nervous. "I was just wondering if anyone had seen that asshole you brought back with you. The guy who showed up at my store the morning those bikers came through."

Elijah raised an eyebrow at me. "Some asshole who isn't a Kennard in Justice? I'm intrigued."

"The guy works with Deacon and Alder. Has some sort of link to Jinx's mom." I could only shrug when his other eyebrow joined the first, surprise practically radiating from him. I was far more worried about Mercy, though. "I haven't seen Parris in a couple of days. He's been working—"

"For Deacon. Yeah, I know." A deep frown cut across her face. "He'd promised Beckett he'd take him over to Crystal Falls to look for a new bike, but then he disappeared."

Probably hunting motorcycle clubs. The ones Jinx had likely

run back to. Fuck, that thought burned. "I can tell him you stopped by."

"Sure. Thanks." But instead of leaving, she sidled up to the bar and took a seat. "I know you're not really open, but do you think I could get a drink?"

I refused to even glance at my brother. This was my job—I could handle pouring one or two. "Of course. No problem. What'll you have?"

She squinted across the bar, looking over the row of bottles along the mirrored back. "Gimme a gimlet."

My moratorium on looking at Elijah lasted exactly three seconds before I had to glance his way. He shook his head, offering me no assistance. Great.

"You might need to help me with that one."

Mercy jumped up and headed behind the bar. "No problem. I've always wanted to tend bar."

That took me by surprise. Mercy had been all about business and commerce when we were younger. Bartending didn't seem to fit what I knew of her at all. "Really?"

"Yeah. It's always looked like fun." Mercy set about making a drink with lime juice and gin as Elijah and I sat and watched. Her moves were quick and efficient, not a single extra step required. She'd make a good bartender, to be honest. Like Jinx.

Fuck, the pain. It burned so bad. I really needed to stop thinking of her, which didn't seem likely to happen anytime soon.

"How's your store doing?" Elijah asked, distracting me from the ache coursing through me. "There can't be much business left in this town."

"You got that right. I do more online selling than anything. I've got a good thing going with some local artisans—they make, I advertise and sell for a cut of the money. Win-win."

"You should sell some of Finn's carvings."

The hell she should. "I don't sell them."

"Never understood why."

Because selling them added pressure where none was warranted. Whittling and carving were stress-relievers, and I didn't need to complicate that hobby by trying to turn it into something more. "Because I don't want to."

Mercy huffed a laugh. "Trust me, Elijah. I tried when I first started that aspect of the business. He gave me a strong and vehement no." She took a sip of her finished drink and sighed. "Now this is just what I needed. So, anyone going to tell me why you look like someone kicked your puppy, Finn?"

She always had paid attention. "No one kicked—"

"His girl left him." Elijah—the traitor in my midst—shrugged at my glare. "Well, she did. Think you can make me one of those, Merc?"

"Sure thing." Mercy frowned my way. "You were dating that new girl in town, right? The one I saw you with the other day. What's her name again?"

"Jinx." *Blinding fucking pain.* "But we weren't really dating."

"I heard there was an ice cream at the truck stop date."

Gossip mill back on the board with a point scored. "Yeah. One night. But that was just us hanging out. Not a date."

She cocked her head. "*And* I heard she'd been staying with you for the past few days. Sounds like more than friends to me."

Mercy always had been tenacious. A trait that hadn't been turned on me in a number of years. I hadn't liked it back in high school, and I still didn't.

"Does everyone know my business?"

Elijah and Mercy both stated "Yes" in unison.

"Fucking perfect."

"You know how it is," Mercy said as she handed Elijah his drink. "There's no hiding stuff around here. Hell, remember in high school? They had us married off and raising like six kids after our first date. I swear, when Beckett was born, half the town was certain he was yours even though we hadn't been together in years. The other half hated me for—" she raised her hands, making air quotes "—breaking you. Never mind the fact that we'd broken up in high school, almost three years before you went—"

She froze, her eyes going wide. Unable—or unwilling—to say the words.

Luckily, Elijah had no trouble reminding me of my faults. "Prison. He went to prison."

She flinched. "Yeah. Sorry, I know you don't like to talk about that."

"It's fine." It wasn't, not really. My gut certainly didn't think things were fine with talking about my time inside in front of Mercy Bell. But there was nothing I could do about that now except redirect the conversation. "I'm sorry the townspeople were rough about all that. You didn't deserve any of it."

She waved her hand and took another sip. "Not your fault. It's just how this town is. I remember being so pissed off because we'd never even had sex, yet they were certain—nine years after we'd ended things—that I'd had your kid and was keeping him away from the glorious Kennard family."

I jerked back, my hazy memories of times so long ago trying hard to come to the surface. "Wait, we never..."

How the hell did one ask *that*?

Thankfully, Mercy knew what I meant. "No, we didn't have sex. Did you think we had?"

"Yes." God, I was an idiot.

"Well, if you were having sex back then, it wasn't with me."

She practically grinned over her glass. "Looks like all the old biddies in town should have been gossiping about your extracurricular activities instead of mine."

"Oh hell," Elijah said, raising his eyebrows and turning away from the bar. "They gossip enough about our family."

Mercy didn't seem upset by my memory lapse, though. Instead, she was looking at me as if I was a puzzle she wanted to figure out. "How much were you using back then?"

Too much. "Enough to have not remembered if we'd ever had sex."

"Yeah, okay. So, a lot." She huffed a laugh. "Why didn't you just ask me if you didn't know?"

I shrugged a shoulder, suddenly far too uncomfortable in my own skin. "I don't know—"

"Because he's the most nonconfrontational man on the planet." Elijah grabbed his glass, raising it at me as if in cheers. "He prefers avoidance to actually dealing with things."

He might have been right, but that didn't mean I was going to admit that. "You're an asshole."

"Fact." Elijah grinned over the rim of his glass. "Anything else we need to know about one another?"

Mercy took that one. "Were you having sex with Anabeth back then?"

I nearly stumbled backward. "What? No. She was Bishop's girl."

"You two spent a lot of time together. It was one of the reasons I ended things."

That I hadn't known but had always assumed. "I never cheated on you with Anabeth. I'm positive about that."

"Huh." She downed the last of her drink. "Well, that changes nothing but is good to know. Thanks."

"That's it?" Elijah asked, looking from me to Mercy and back again. "Thanks?"

"What? Did you expect me to see Finn with new eyes and fall in love right here in this bar?" Mercy scoffed, her eyes finding mine again. "I liked you, Finn, but I never loved you. That's not about to change today. Besides, you've got a girl."

A girl who had left me with this gaping, burning hole in my chest. "Jinx and I aren't—"

"Do you love her?" Mercy asked, blunt as ever and not giving up.

You could have heard a pin drop with how silent Elijah and I went. For different reasons, I was sure.

"That's not really the issue here."

Mercy downed the rest of her drink and slammed the empty glass on the counter. "I call bullshit."

Elijah grinned. "Damn, I like her."

"Shut up," I hissed, ready to toss him on the floor.

Mercy ignored us both and leaned forward, all intense expression and surety that I'd never seen before. "The pain and sadness radiating off of you tell me the answer, but I want to hear it from your lips. Do you love this girl? Jinx."

The answer hung heavy in my heart and on my tongue, making it practically impossible to deny. "Yeah. I think I do."

"Then quit being an idiot and go get her."

As if it were that easy. "She left me, not the other way around."

She focused on Elijah. "He really is nonconfrontational."

"Told you so." My brother finished his drink and grabbed both their empty glasses. "He needs to quit worrying about upsetting people and use that big dick energy he's got for his own good."

"Big dick energy?" I asked, looking from one to the other. "Is this a thing now?"

Mercy put her hands up. "Don't look at me. We never had sex, remember?"

"It's in our blood. All Kennards have big dick energy," Elijah said, looking cocky as fuck. "Even Lainie."

"Stop." I put my hands up. "I don't need to think about big dicks and our little sister at the same time."

"Fine. No more talk about big dicks. So, what are you going to do?" Mercy asked, as if that topic were any better. "If all Kennards have this energy about them—and I'll admit I've seen it with Lainie, Alder, Bishop, and even smarty-pants Elijah here—how are you going to use it to your advantage?"

I didn't feel any sort of special Kennard energy. Especially not in regard to this particular arena. "What if she doesn't want me back?"

"What made her leave in the first place?"

Bikers. Her past coming back. Me being no one to her.

Me giving her the silent treatment after that altercation in the grocery store instead of talking to her.

Me failing to see how much those guys had likely scared her and she'd tried to protect me.

"I fucked up."

Mercy didn't seem surprised. "So, go fix it."

"I don't even know where she went."

"Sure you do," Elijah said. "She may not have told you, but you know."

Whether or not I wanted to admit it, he was right. I *did* know. She'd gone back to the bikers who'd owned her. Not the Soul Suckers—I had a feeling she was more scared of them than anything. No, she went back to the Black Angels. To what she knew, even if that world was hell. The devil you know and all that.

"He's going to go get her," Mercy whispered, leaning into Elijah's shoulder.

"I sure hope so. He's boring as fuck when he's mopey."

"Who's boring as fuck?" Deacon came strolling into his bar, looking all sorts of worse for wear. Tired, dirty, and with bags under his eyes the likes of which I'd never seen on him before. "I heard a rumor that Elijah Kennard was in my bar. Looks like Vol's wife was right on the money again."

Score two for the gossip mill, but they no longer mattered. Not to me, at least. My mind was made up, my path forward growing more and more clear with every second. I knew what I needed to do. "We were just leaving."

Deacon frowned. "Where are you going?"

Big dick energy time. "Jinx and I had a little issue, and she left to go back to the Black Angels. I think. I'm pretty sure."

"Be sure," Elijah said, to which I gave him the international symbol for shut the hell up. Also known as a middle finger pointed straight up in the air.

"I'm sure. It's the only place she'd go other than to Parris, and no one seems to know where he is."

"He's busy," Deacon said, looking at the three of us in turn. "So you three were going to...what? Drive into a biker camp, throw the girl over your shoulder, and carry her out?"

Mercy stepped back. "Don't look at me. I'm just here looking for an asshole."

"Parris," I said when Deacon raised an eyebrow. "She's looking for Parris."

"Like I said, he's busy. He'll be back in a day or two."

"I'm not really one for waiting around. Not when my son is involved." She moved beside me and gave me a quick kiss on the cheek. "I'm glad we talked. Go get your girl. And come see me more often. I don't bite."

She didn't and having her back as a friend might add a little levity to my life. Something I seemed to need more of. "You okay to drive?"

"Of course." She grabbed her coat and headed for the door. "Tell Parris not to bother coming around anymore. Beckett doesn't need another man in his life who'll do nothing but disappoint him."

"He'd be there if he could," Deacon said, sounding weary. "You and your son have been on his mind, I can promise you that."

"Yeah, well..." She shook her head. "Actions speak louder than words—or thoughts, as this seems to be. And his actions are saying it's time for me to walk away." She yanked open the door, letting in a swath of bright, late afternoon sunlight. "See you guys later. Stay safe out there."

Deacon waited until the door had closed behind her to refocus on me. "So...what's the plan?"

"I don't have one, but I'm going to get Jinx back."

He nodded once. "Let's go."

"Just like that?" I asked, glancing at Elijah. "We have no idea what we're walking into."

"We weren't prepared when those fuckers took out Camden's house and killed Leah, but we know more now. Not everything, but more." He rubbed a hand over his face, eyes unfocused for a second, looking more exhausted than I'd ever seen him. "Sometimes you have to brass-ball a mission, and this seems like one of those times." He slipped behind the bar and grabbed a large metal lockbox from under the counter. "So long as you're prepared."

Elijah watched as Deacon opened the box and pulled out five

guns, his lips growing tighter with each one. "What about Alder?"

Deacon sighted down a pistol as he replied, "What about him?"

"He's your usual partner," I said, jumping onto Elijah's train of thought. "Aren't you going to call him to help?"

"Alder's not the only Kennard in town who can shoot. You and I will do just fine, Finn." He looked to Elijah. "You in, counselor?"

My twin didn't even hesitate. "I'm in."

"So we go." Deacon stopped and looked me square in the eye. "So long as you trust me to help you get your girl back."

As if there was any question. "I trust you."

"Then let's do this."

Chapter Twenty-One

JINX

I was going to throw up.

There was something so stifling about the RV, something so cage-like. It reminded me of those first few days with the Soul Suckers. When they'd tied me down in a dark room. When they'd threatened to take turns with me if I didn't behave. I knew that wasn't what Edge wanted—he didn't usually like to share. And yet, that feeling of impending terror hovered around me all day.

As the sun finally began to set, the feeling grew stronger. I didn't want to do this. Didn't want to once again give up my freedom. But then I thought about Justice. Thought about Alder and Shye. About Deacon and the menagerie of locals he'd collected and cared for at the bar. They were all in danger. They still would be with the Soul Suckers around, but not as much. The Black Angels weren't as vicious as the Soul Suckers, but they were more trained. More militaristic in their operations. Put their sort of smarts behind the Soul Suckers' sociopathy, and they'd be unstoppable. I had to give Deacon and Parris the chance to stop them. That meant taking the Black Angels—and therefore Edge—out of the equation.

I didn't turn on any lights as the rooms darkened under the incoming night sky, choosing instead to become one with the shadows. To sit in the deepest ones and let my mind wander. To my past, to my childhood, to my mom. I'd been hunting for her for close to a year, had given up everything I'd loved to try to find her. All the while, deep down, I'd known she was dead. Edge not denying it had only cemented that knowledge. My mom was gone. Likely over drugs or for having a loose mouth. Secrets ruled with the Black Angels, just like any other biker club. They were vital to each member staying alive and out of prison. My mom might have said something she shouldn't have or seen something Edge knew she wouldn't be able to keep to herself. Hell, she might have simply been in the wrong place at the wrong time or charged the wrong John too much for what she'd given him. Whatever—she was gone, and Ravel had killed her. Eventually, I'd pay him back for that.

But not right then. I needed to focus on getting the club out of Colorado. For good.

Which was why I didn't jump when the door to the RV opened and Edge climbed inside. I was settled, decided and ready. Dead inside so that what I knew was coming wouldn't hurt so much.

Just don't think about Finn.

"Your price is a little steep, Jinxy."

But not impossible or he wouldn't be talking to me about it. "My offer is worth the price."

"Maybe." He stepped closer, pulling me to my feet and capturing my chin with his hand. Squeezing hard and slipping his thumb between my lips as he practically growled, "You going to bite me, bitch?"

I waited for him to remove the offending digit, to release his hold enough for me to speak again. "I might. I'll likely fight back until I know my offer has been accepted."

He took a step back, watching me. Sizing me up. A shark on the hunt. "Maybe I want to try this new Jinx out. Take you for a test drive."

Don't throw up. "I'm not spreading my legs until we're on the road home."

"We'll see about that." He leaned closer, the smell of the beer on his breath almost making me gag. "Don't bite."

And then he kissed me. I squeezed my eyes tight and tried my hardest not to think of how wrong this felt. How much I hated it. My friends had to be protected, Justice needed to be saved. I could help them. Could take some of the danger out of their path. I just had to be willing to let Edge do more than kiss me. Had to be able to take his abuse and deal with his lust. I had to die inside so he could have the outside. And I would, because there was a man back in Justice—

Don't think about Finn.

Edge broke the kiss with a groan, tilting his head and staring down at me. Looking for any sign of resistance, I assumed. I wouldn't give him one. This was his game, his rules. He'd shown me what he wanted when he'd chased after me, when he'd tied me down and sliced into my skin. When he'd gotten more and more interested the less I fought back. He wanted me to submit, and I could do that. For now.

I stared back at him, chin up and eyes locked on his. I would not fail. "What's your decision?"

The man almost smiled. "I'll take your deal, Jinx. On one condition."

"I'm the one—"

An explosion of pain spread across my cheek as the flat of his palm made contact, and my words died on my tongue. This was the Edge I remembered, the one who hated disobedience. The one who would tape my mouth shut if I argued too much.

Mistake number one was talking back.

"You think I'm just going to play into your hands?" Edge asked, grabbing me by the arm in a harsh, bruising grip. "You want us to leave this place, so we will. I'll pull the fucking national club out of Colorado for good because I get you— completely submissive to me in every way when we do. But that's not enough."

I really was going to be sick. "What's your condition?"

"I want your suck."

"I told you, I'm not—"

"No one said anything about spreading your legs. Just your lips. Besides, this isn't for me." Edge smirked as Ravel stepped up into the trailer and closed the door behind him, looking dark and mean and absolutely terrifying. "It's for him. I want to see you on your knees for my friend here. I want to see you thank him for taking care of our club so well."

Taking care of the club...by murdering my mom. My stomach lurched hard, and I had to lock my muscles down to keep from shaking. Ravel had gotten his hands on me a few times, had given me some of the scars on my skin, but this was different. Edge had never let him touch me in a sexual way. Never made me do anything with him. The man had murdered my mom, and I was going to have to—

Finn and Deacon and Shye and good soup and all the things that made a place a home. Don't think about anything else.

I swallowed down the sick rising in my throat. "And then we can leave?"

"Yeah. Then we can leave."

"Tonight?" Because if we stayed any longer, I'd break the deal. I'd run back to Justice. Back to the little ranch house with the pretty floors and the wood carvings decorating just about every flat surface. I'd go back to Finn if this didn't move quickly.

Edge took my question as something it wasn't, though. "She's so fucking anxious, Ravel. Maybe you should give her something to calm her down a little first."

Drugs. They mean drugs. I jerked away, yelling my refusal, but Edge held me tight. He twisted my arm and yanked me into his hold as Ravel approached, pulling a syringe from his pocket.

"Don't worry, Jinx. This won't hurt."

Hell yes, it would. It would break me in a whole different way than I was prepared to deal with. It would kill any chance of ever getting back to Finn.

Something I hadn't even allowed myself to consider yet.

Something being taken away before I had a chance to even contemplate the option.

"I don't need that," I said, pulling against Edge and trying to break his hold. "I promise—I'll behave."

Ravel scoffed. "I doubt it."

"Please don't," I yelled, jerking my hardest to pull out of Edge's hold and failing miserably. Tears ran in fiery rivulets down my cheeks as I stared at the needle. That gateway to a life of addiction. I'd never been drugged before, not even when I'd first made my way to the Black Angels looking for my mom. They'd threatened me with it, of course—hung the thought of their injecting me with some unknown substance over my head as a way to make me compliant. They'd also drugged other women while I was around. I'd seen what happened to them—how they went from saying no, no, no to accepting all the attention the men gave them. All the touching and kissing and...more. I didn't want that. I at least wanted the illusion of consent. I at least wanted to know there was one line I wouldn't have to cross.

"Please don't give me that. I promise I'll be good."

"Oh, you'll be better than good." Ravel grabbed my arm, and I screamed. Unable not to. Unable to hold in the fear coursing through me as he twisted and pulled and brought that needle closer. As Finn's stormy eyes exploded in my mind.

My sweet man. My former addict. He'd never want me after this. "No. Don't do that. I don't need it. Stop."

But they didn't listen. Instead, they forced my arm down onto a counter and held it in place as I screamed long and loud and hard. As they wrapped a rubber tube around my bicep and tapped on my elbow crease.

As I felt the prick of the needle poking through my skin.

As I lost myself to the swirl of light inside my own mind.

Gray. Lots and lots of gray.

Finn.

Chapter Twenty-Two

FINN

The campground where the Black Angels had taken up residence in Rock Falls looked a little too suburban-vacation-getaway for my taste. Lots of little wooden cabins, RVs, and pop-up trailers sitting close together in a multilevel circle. If it weren't for the beer and whiskey bottles stacked near the entrance and the sheer number of motorcycles parked across the frosty grass, one might have thought that's exactly what it was.

"Is it just me, or are you waiting for some kids to bust out the Slip'N Slide?" Deacon asked, staring out the window and frowning.

I glanced across the truck cab. "You reading my mind now?"

"Nope. We must be on the same wavelength, though."

"God help us all," Elijah said from the back of the crew cab. "Do we have a plan yet?"

Deacon shrugged, sitting in the driver's seat of the parked

truck and looking at the mess of campers and RVs before us. "Walk in, find Jinx, get the fuck out."

"Wow," Elijah said. "That's some thorough planning you got there. I thought you Special Forces guys were supposed to be the experts at this."

"We are, but we usually get more than a few hours to research, recon, and plan a hit. I'm flying by the seat of my pants over here."

"Here's to hoping we all stay airborne, then." I opened the door and stepped out into the grass. The sun had begun to set, the shadows deepening throughout the woods and across the campground. We'd passed about fifteen bikes going in the opposite direction on the way in, so the number of people in camp would likely be smaller than we'd anticipated. Still, Deacon had come prepared.

"Do we need a reminder lesson on how to shoot, Finn?"

I took the semiautomatic pistol from him, sighting down the barrel and getting used to the weight. "Nope."

"What about you, Eli? You been shooting recently?"

My brother put his hand out for a pistol. "It's Elijah, and no, but I'm a good shot."

"You sure?"

"I've outshot Alder every year since we learned to hunt."

"You're sure. Got it." Deacon handed Elijah a gun similar to mine. "I've got explosives in the bag and a few other party tricks up my sleeves. Things go wrong, get Jinx and yourselves out of there and leave me be."

I shot a look at Elijah. "You want us to leave you behind?"

"Yeah. I do. I can take care of myself." He grabbed an assault rifle from his bag of tricks. One that looked bigger and much more dangerous than the guns Elijah and I carried. "Though, once you get out, call your fucking brother and tell him to come save my ass, okay?"

That made more sense. "Done."

"You ready, kid?" Deacon said, looking at Elijah. My brother had his phone out and appeared to be texting, which seemed like the worst idea ever considering what we were about to do.

"Elijah," I said, glancing purposefully at him and then his phone when he looked up. "What's up?"

"Nothing, I'm ready." Elijah tucked his phone back into his pocket. "You realize Alder's going to kick your ass for taking us on this mission, right?"

Deacon shrugged. "Wouldn't be the first time. Now, how are we going to find Jinx in this mayhem?"

I didn't have an answer for that one. We headed into the camp with our guns drawn and our eyes open, slipping around the sides of campers and past parked bikes quietly. It seemed as though very few people were around. The camp sat quiet and still, the night broken by nothing more than the sound of insects calling to one another.

At least until a scream pierced the air.

"That's Jinx," I said, my stomach dropping like a lead balloon. "That's my Jinx."

I was running before I could finish getting the sentence out, focused solely on following that scream. It didn't take me long to track her down—a huge RV sat toward the back of the camp with no lights on but the door open. And Jinx's voice coming from inside. Words I couldn't understand found their way into the night, and then nothing. A long silence before a heartbreaking scream. One that sent me hurtling toward the camper door.

"Let me," Deacon said, jumping in front of me and hopping up the steps. He stopped right at the top, leaving Elijah and me just enough room to follow him onto the steps but not inside. Blocking my way when I would have rushed forward.

At least until I'd had enough. I shoved him forward, forcing him farther into the trailer and hopping up the last two steps. Scanning the interior until I found her.

Jinx.

She lay on the floor by the kitchenette, looking pale. Looking dead. I wanted to fall to my knees and crawl to her, but Deacon had me stuck behind the bench seat. Elijah scooted in behind me and pressed his shoulder to mine. Supporting me. Looking from Jinx to the men standing over her. The ones who definitely weren't happy to see us.

"I believe I heard the lady say stop," Deacon said in a calm voice. Far calmer than I felt.

"Who the fuck—" The bigger man turned and smiled, looking positively deadly. The same one from the truck stop the night I'd taken Jinx for ice cream. And from the grocery store. The one who knew Jinx. "Barkeep. And Finn, the Soul Suckers' friend. I can tell by looking, this other fellow must be a Kennard as well. You grow them close to the same cut, don't you?" He huffed a laugh, setting his hand on the counter where a syringe sat. *Had he drugged my girl?* "I don't remember inviting you into our house."

Deacon brought his rifle up to his hip, still looking far too casual but armed and deadly as fuck. "We were out for a stroll and heard the commotion. Figured we should step in."

"There's no commotion. Just a little difference of opinion, isn't that right, Edge?"

The other man turned, and I caught sight of his vest. President. The patch sat right above his road name. This was the guy who'd made all the choices for Jinx. The one who'd been pissed about her sale to the Soul Suckers. The one who deserved to die for what he'd done to her. I had to have patience, though. I needed to make sure Jinx was okay first, then dole out whatever punishment her situation called for.

Death. Certainly death. Quick or painful was the only question at that point.

"Get the fuck out," Edge said, breathing heavy and leaning over to pick up Jinx. "This ain't none of your concern."

"Well, now…that's where you're wrong." Elijah stepped in front of me, practically holding me back as if I might rush the fucker for touching my girl. Which I might have, except that would have solved nothing and left us open to attack. My brother sometimes forgot that I'd made it through seven years in prison. I knew a lot more about surviving in a sea of sharks than most people. "See, that girl there is ours. And we're taking her home with us."

Edge scowled and hissed a hard, "Fuck you."

"No thanks. You're pretty and all, but not my type." Elijah inched his way across the floor, setting us up into a perfect V. Readying our positions for optimal firing accuracy with little chance of being hit with friendly fire.

The other guy—Ravel—cracked his neck. "The prez said to get out. I think it's time for you boys to leave."

As if we'd just walk out and forget what we'd come for. "Not without Jinx."

Ravel looked my way, sizing me up. "You're the one she's been staying with the past few days. You been fucking her?"

"That's none of your concern."

"Yeah, I bet. Look, Prez. This guy thinks he can steal your toys, use them like they're his own, and then keep them after you've reclaimed them. What do we say to that?"

"We say fuck off and die," Edge said, a definite threat in his words.

"Right." Ravel pulled a gun from the back of his waistband. "We say fuck off and die."

I didn't give them the opportunity to fire first. My finger squeezed the trigger without delay, popping off a shot into Ravel before he even had a chance to take a breath. Elijah shot as well, both of us hitting our mark. Two shots leading to one dead biker with no way to know which of us fired the kill shot. My twin backing me up in every way as he always had.

That just left the president.

"I got him." I nodded toward Elijah. "Alone."

My brother grunted his acceptance but didn't drop his weapon.

Deacon looked my way. "You sure about that?"

Keeping my gun on Edge, who had already taken a few steps back, I slipped closer to Jinx. "What did you give her?"

"A cocktail," Edge said, as if drugging women was a totally normal thing to do. "Keeps her calm so she doesn't get feisty on us."

"You mean so she can't beat your ass?" I bent over Jinx and brushed the hair from her forehead. "You okay there, Lucky?"

She moaned and blinked her eyes open, unable to truly focus them. "Fish?"

That word, that single syllable, filled the hole in my chest like nothing else could have. "Yeah, baby. It's me."

She scrunched her face, looking sick. "They drugged me."

And they would die for that. Or Edge would—Ravel was already taken care of. "I know."

"I'm so high." Her giggle turned to a moan. "And sick. So sick."

"I know that too."

"I don't like it."

"Good, because this is the last time. Okay?" Because I

couldn't go back down that road. Because two recovering addicts in a relationship would be a mistake of epic proportions. Because I didn't want her to have to deal with the stuff I did on a daily basis. Because there was no way I could be with someone who used, and I wanted to be with her. Forever.

"Okay," she said, sounding much more confident than I'd expected.

"Good. Give me a minute, and I'll get you out of here. We'll go back home, okay?"

She closed her eyes and curled into a ball, looking far too pale for my liking. "Cool. But hey, Finn?"

"Yeah?"

Those gray eyes I loved so much opened, clear and bright and completely focused on me. Clear for just one moment as she said, "Kill that bastard for me."

I raised my gun and pointed it at Edge, meeting his surprised eyes. "Anything for you, baby."

Edge threw his hands up and took another step back, running into the wall as he did. "Now, hang on."

"I don't think so."

He looked all around as if seeking escape, of which there was none. "She came to me, man. She offered herself to me."

She had. I knew that. I had a good idea of why too. "In exchange for what?"

"The Black Angels breaking our agreement with the Soul Suckers and leaving Colorado."

Sacrificing herself to save my town. My family and friends. Probably me as well. Damn her. "Hey, Deacon?"

My boss didn't hesitate. "Yeah, kid."

"What do you think will happen to this club when their top two guys disappear?"

"They'll leave the area—head back home to regroup."

"My guys are smart," Edge said, his voice loud but weak. Fake bravado against our attack. "They'll stick around to figure out what happened to us."

I raised my gun a little higher. A little more in line with his head. "You sure about that?"

"There's a solution for that possibility," Elijah said. "We don't make them disappear. We leave them right here in their campground. Set the bodies up outside and use them as an example of what happens when you cross the Justice town line."

Elijah was such a badass. "I like that plan. Very Vlad the Impaler."

He shrugged. "I'm a fan of the classics."

"Take the whore," Edge said, keeping his hands close to his sides. His fingers twitching. Calling my attention to his yellowed fingernails. "I don't need her. You take her, and we call it even."

But I couldn't stop looking at his hands. "You smoke?"

Everyone stilled, silence falling fast. When the guy didn't answer, I rose to my feet. "I asked you a question. Do you smoke?"

"Yeah."

Circle marks up and down her arms. Perfect scars from cigarettes pressed against her soft skin. "You're the one who burned her."

Deacon practically growled, jumping forward a step as he said, "You sick son of a bitch."

"Look." Edge licked his lips, unable to focus on any one of us for long. "You take her and go. I'll pull my club. We'll leave your fucking town."

A day late and a dollar short. "Oh, I plan to take her. And your club will be leaving Justice, too. For good."

"Finn?" Jinx's soft voice was about the only thing that could have stopped me at that point.

"Yeah, baby?"

"I think I'm going to be sick."

"I got it," Elijah said, rushing past me to grab a towel off the counter and kneel beside Jinx. Taking care of her as if she were family...as if she were mine.

Which she would be the second she agreed to be.

"What exactly did you give her?" Elijah asked as Jinx began to shake.

"Special K mixed with Amytal. Should have just made her sleepy." He frowned when Jinx began vomiting into the bowl Elijah had found for her. "Look, just take her. I'll handle the mess and get my guys to clear out. We'll call it even."

Even wasn't Jinx walking away with scars all over her body.

Even wasn't him leaving to do to another girl what he'd done to her.

Even wasn't a possibility at this point.

"Up to you, kid," Deacon said to me, still pointing his rifle at Edge.

"Finn," Jinx said, her eyes finding mine once more. Looking so damn weak and sick and tired as she whispered the three most perfect words ever. "I love you."

Joy unlike any other erupted in my chest, and I nearly grinned. In the middle of the hell we'd found ourselves in, she still cared. Still found it in herself to let me know I wasn't no one.

It was time to get her home. "I love you too, baby. Which is why he can't walk away from this."

"Wait," Edge said, but it was far too late for more waiting.

I raised the gun and aimed at his chest. I fired one shot.

And much like my twin, I never missed.

Chapter Twenty-Three

FINN

I'd killed a man. With intention. Not by accident or even in the heat of the moment. I'd gone into that camp knowing what the end result would be. Planning on it.

Premeditated.

That thought ran through my head the entire way back to Justice. The guilt of having ended a life, the niggling doubt that we'd left too much evidence to escape from the consequences of the act, rolled through me with no end in sight. And yet, with Deacon and Elijah safe and whole in the front seat of the truck and Jinx lying across my lap, I couldn't regret my actions. Lord help me, but I'd go to my grave knowing those deaths had been totally justified. Especially because of what the men had done to Jinx. I'd killed them, and I'd pay my penance for the rest of my life so long as I got to keep her away from people like that. And if I got caught—if I went back to prison for what I'd done—the only thing I'd be losing was any future with the girl I'd only just found. I'd survived my time inside once. I could do it again.

Elijah, though...

"Hey," I whispered as I set my hand on his shoulder, knowing there were no words strong enough to impart how much this day had meant to me. "Thank you. For everything."

"No thanks needed. I'm your brother, and I'll always be there for you." He patted my hand and looked back at me. "Next visit, how about we try to keep the murders to a minimum, though?"

"I'll do my best."

"Good enough." He sighed and stretched, practically taking up the entire front half of the cab with how he spread his arms. "I don't know about you guys, but I could use a little something to take the edge off."

Deacon frowned his way for a second before turning his eyes back to the road. "What exactly are you talking about?"

I could practically feel Elijah's grin as he said, "Ice cream, man. I could really go for some ice cream. A sundae with hot fudge and whipped cream. That's what I need after killing a man and watching my brother kill a second one."

Deacon sat silent for a minute before busting out a laugh. "Well, kid—I think I can handle that request. You two and your fucking ice cream."

"It's our thing," I said, fist-bumping my brother. "Always has been."

"Always will be."

It was also Jinx's and my thing. That had been our first pseudo-date—ice cream at the truck stop. The evening hadn't ended well, but the memories were still something I liked to replay. I had a feeling that night would be one of my very favorites for the rest of my life.

"What about Jinx?" Deacon asked, checking his rearview as if he could see her. "You think she'll be sober enough to want some ice cream?"

"Her high won't last long, but coming down is going to be a bit of a bitch for her. I think I'd rather take her home to rest. We need to deal with some stuff tonight." Because we had things to talk about. Stuff to handle. Confrontations to have. I hated the thought of it, felt physically sick from the very possibility, but it had to be done. I wasn't losing my girl to my inability to confront my past. Or hers.

But first, I needed to make sure she was sober.

"Whatever you want," Deacon said, glancing back once more. "Just be careful with her."

Elijah turned to look over the seat, taking a long inspection of Jinx. I knew what he was seeing—her little body curled up on the seat, her head in my lap. Her hand in mine. The two of us linked together physically, our comfort in that touch obvious. There was nothing about the position that didn't scream she was mine and I was hers.

He definitely saw that. "I'll stay at Bishop's tonight since he's back in Vegas. Give you two a little space."

My brother—the genius. "Sounds good. I'm sorry to kick you—"

"Don't. She needs you, and you need to pull your head out of your ass and tell her you need her, too."

I did. I really did. "I plan on it."

Deacon pulled up to The Jury Room, his headlights bathing the parking lot in light. Showcasing a single motorcycle.

"Parris is here." Deacon turned off the ignition and opened his door, staring at the door to the bar as the man in question appeared as if made from shadow himself. "I think we need to have a few words."

I woke Jinx with a soft hand to her back, shushing her when she startled. "It's okay. We're safe."

She tightened her grip on my thigh before murmuring, "There's no such thing."

No, there wasn't. Especially not with me around. But I'd do my best. "Come on. You can officially meet my brother."

"Another one?" She pushed up to a sitting position, looking far more rumpled than she'd probably want to be. "I still don't feel so hot."

No doubt. That post-high comedown would last for a few more hours. "Let me help you."

I hopped out of the truck and hurried around to the other side, opening the door and reaching for Jinx's hand.

She wobbled when her feet hit the ground, looking almost surprised by her lack of balance. "Walking seems really hard right now."

"Want me to carry you?"

"Can you?"

Challenge accepted. I scooped her into my arms and carried her across the parking lot. She didn't even try to fight me on it—simply curled up against my chest and held on, making me feel like a king. When Parris spotted us from his spot by the door to the bar, he gave me a glare that could have peeled paint off a building. Not that I cared.

I hoisted Jinx a little higher, held on a little tighter, and glared right back. "You got something to say?"

Parris ignored my question. "You shouldn't have gone in there hot."

Armed and ready to fire. As if walking in without guns would have been any better.

It was Deacon who set him straight. "There was no other way."

Parris crowded my boss, looking ready to throw punches. "I've been working them for five years, been selling my soul to the devil for weeks now to figure out how to get them the fuck away from your little pissant town, and you go in guns blazing to take out the prez and his vp. And for what?"

"For *what*?" White-hot rage flowed through me, so I set Jinx down, tugging her behind me as Elijah came to shore her up. To protect my girl while I dealt with Parris. "They had Jinx, and we weren't leaving her there to be tortured."

Parris froze, his brow tight. "They didn't have orders to bring in Jinx. I would have let you know."

"They didn't bring her in." I tugged her closer, hanging on to her hand with a grip that was probably just this side of too tight. "She went there to make a deal with them."

"She went there." He cocked his head, looking around my shoulder at the woman in question. "You stupid or something, girl?"

"Fuck you," Jinx said, still sounding way too weak to me. "I thought I could get them to leave."

"Yeah, well, you might have just set off a club war. What were you thinking?"

My turn. "It was my fault. She went there to protect the town because we had a misunderstanding."

"That's quite the misunderstanding. You know they'd likely kill you, right, Luckless?"

That name...it grated. A lot. "Stop calling her that."

Parris looked me up and down, appraising. "You grow a backbone or something, kid?"

Elijah huffed behind me. "He always had one. He just never had a reason to use it. He does now."

"Okay then." Parris glanced at Jinx then back at me before nodding once. "You look like shit, though."

"Is that what you used to say to my mom when she'd come home high? Because I have to tell you, I've got more of a temper than she did."

Parris went stock-still, staring at Jinx in a way that looked like trouble. "You don't know anything about your mom and me."

"I know enough." Jinx leaned her head against my back, gripping my shirt in her fists. "I don't feel so good."

"We're done here," I said. "She's had enough. You want to fight about this, fight with me."

"And me," Elijah said.

"You Kennards are all pussy-whipped." Parris sighed and ran a hand over his head. "Fine. I'm sorry I didn't think about Jinx's safety before I blew up. I'll deal with the fucking upheaval of two dead Black Angels."

"You think the other guys will leave town?" Deacon asked.

"I'll definitely plant the seed that they should. Maybe sow a little discord with their current partners. Make them think the Soul Suckers could have had a hand in this." He looked my way, obviously less angry but still not chill. "You strong enough to keep your mouth shut about what happened tonight? Confident Deacon, Jinx, and Elijah will be as well? Forever?"

There was no doubt in my answer. "Yeah. I am."

"Good. Then I'll deal with the fallout. You take care of Jinx."

"I can take care of myself," she said, though the wobble in her voice and the lack of conviction behind her words betrayed her statement.

"Anything you need us to do?" Deacon asked.

"Yeah. Quit murdering people."

Elijah jumped in with, "We make no promises."

Parris looked him up and down, his heavy brow pulled taut. "You the twin?"

"Yeah."

"You're a defense attorney in Denver, right?"

Elijah shrugged. "Among other things."

Parris nodded, looking oddly impressed. "A lawyer breaking laws. Guess I've seen everything now."

"Lawyers break laws all the time—we're just experienced enough to know how not to get caught. And if that fails, we know how to work the legal system to get out of trouble."

"You'd better. Because murder isn't going to get you a mere seven years like your brother got for selling drugs."

"No, it won't," Elijah said, standing a little taller. "I'm solid, though."

"Good. I need to get back to camp and deal with your mess. Keep out of trouble, would you?" Parris stalked to his bike, throwing a leg over the seat and grabbing the handlebars. "Oh, and Finn?"

"Yeah?"

"Does our deal still stand?"

It took me a second to figure out what deal he meant. Info on Coyote for a favor. The day we'd had lunch at The Baker's Cottage, I'd agreed to that. And I still had no idea where the Soul Sucker was. "Definitely."

"Expect a text from me." The roar of his engine covered any response I could have made, dimming as he drove out of the parking lot and back toward Rock Falls.

"I think I need to say no to the ice cream run and head home after all this," Deacon said, looking more exhausted than I'd ever seen him. Or maybe it was the parking lot lights.

"You okay?" I asked, trying to figure out if the bags under his eyes were really there or made of shadow. It was too hard to tell, though.

"I'm fine." Deacon turned to Elijah. "You need a lift to Bishop's?"

My twin shrugged. "If you don't mind."

"I don't. Besides, I want to take a few pictures hanging out in his house. Find some ways to irritate that bastard a bit. I need to bust Bishop's balls a little, and I haven't gotten to do that in a few weeks. The man gets a big head if we don't knock him down a peg or two now and again." Deacon shook my hand, then hugged Jinx. "Glad you're home, girl."

She gasped at the word home, as if she hadn't expected that. As if she hadn't felt like Justice was her home. Something I needed to be sure to fix.

Jinx looked almost ready to cry as she pulled herself from Deacon's hold and whispered, "I'm glad to be home."

Elijah was next though he only reached to hold on to her arm. "It was really nice to meet you, though next time try not to toss your cookies on my shoes."

"I'm so sorry," Jinx said, her face turning a deep pink color.

"I'm just picking on you. You didn't get my shoes. Just my pants." He patted her on the shoulder when she made a choking sound. "Stick around this time, okay? No running away. If this guy fucks up, just call me and I'll set him straight. No questions asked."

Jinx glanced my way. "Deal."

"Good." Elijah released her, stepping in my direction to give me a backslapping hug. "Good luck with this one, bro. Call if you need me."

I nodded, knowing I wouldn't need him. Not for this. Jinx and I could work out our own issues. I might not have liked confrontation, but being without Jinx was a fate worse than a lifetime of confrontations. I'd be as bold as fuck for her.

"Finn," Deacon hollered. When I spun his way, he tossed me a set of keys. "Bishop and I will round up Gage and deal with getting your truck home. There's an Oldsmobile in the rear lot. Take that for the night."

I flipped the keys over, running my thumb along the fob. "Thanks."

"Thank me if I get your truck back. There's no guarantee."

Because it was still parked in Black Angels territory where Jinx had parked it since we didn't want anyone to be forced to drive back alone. Safety in numbers and all that shit. I shrugged. "The truck would be a small thing in comparison to what could have been lost. I still call the mission a success."

He shot Jinx a wink. "Me too, kid. Me too."

Once Deacon had driven out of the lot with Elijah riding shotgun, I loaded Jinx into the passenger side of the sedan around back—big, brown, and totally giving off those undercover cop vibes—and headed for home. Trying to figure out my first move. What to say. What to fix first.

She beat me to it.

"You didn't ask Edge about Coyote."

The Soul Sucker who'd started the fire that had killed Camden's wife. "No, I didn't. Though I'm surprised you were aware enough to have paid attention to that."

"Your voice cleared some of the fog." She sat quiet and still for a moment, almost stiff. Nervous, if I had to guess. Finally, she sighed. "You ask all the bikers about this Coyote guy. Why not Edge?"

"I had more important things to worry about at the moment."

"But you always ask about Coyote. Why?"

I turned off the highway onto my road, slowing down on the curves as I stared out into the night. Remembering the fire. The words painted on the wall outside Leah and Camden's bedroom. The way my best friend had crumpled when he'd learned he'd lost his wife. Yeah, I always asked about Coyote...because I needed to find him. "My friend owes him something."

"Like what?"

"Death." I stopped in my driveway and turned to look at her, "Coyote helped light a fire that killed a friend of mine—a woman named Leah who was married to my best friend, Camden. I want to find him so Cam can get his revenge."

"Oh." She opened the door and stepped out, meeting me at the front of the truck. "That seems reasonable."

"It seems reasonable to kill a man?"

She paused just inside the door, her eyes locked on mine. "Yeah. Because if Edge had tried to hurt you, I would have done the same thing. Drugs in my system or not."

This girl. I shut the door behind me and herded her deeper into my house. Wanting so much to touch her, hug her, feel the solidness of her now that she was back where she belonged. With me. But there was still so much to say, and I had to pick where to start and how to handle the discussion.

In the end, I went with full-frontal honesty.

"I am the worst person in the world for you to be with."

She didn't even blink. "Okay."

"Are you okay? Like, do you feel—"

"I'm fine." She waved a hand when I scoffed. "I'm still feeling sort of sick, and I'm tired in a weird way. I don't ever want to take another drug in my life and I really need a shower and a toothbrush, but I'm fine to talk for a bit."

"Are you sure? You can go—"

"Talk to me," she said, looking far too earnest for me to ignore.

Here goes nothing.

"I'm the worst person in the world for you because I'm an ex-addict and an ex-con. I may never be able to get a job outside of Deacon's bar or my family's business, and I hate that. I may never earn back my family's trust, and I hate that more. I live in a world of rules and walls to keep myself from slipping backward. But you know all that." I settled us on the couch, grabbing both her hands and hanging on. Needing her to feel grounded. "I spent so many years high that I have no recollection of what I've done or not done, but I like the idea that I get a redo of sorts with you. I like the thought that we can have all sorts of firsts together."

She took a deep breath, clinging to my fingers just as hard as I did to hers. "You think I'm judging you for your past, when really, I'm more worried about you hating me for mine."

As if that were a possibility. "I could never hate you."

She pulled her shoulders back, seeming to shore herself up as if for a fight. "I chose to go back to the club because I knew if I offered myself to Edge, if I promised to submit to him, he'd leave Justice."

Just the thought of her having anything to do with that bastard had my stomach churning. "You didn't have to—"

"I know that, but it's not the first time I've done it." Her hands shook, and her eyes looked suspiciously watery. "My mom disappeared about a year ago. I was busy working and taking classes at the community college and trying to keep my head above water, so it took me a couple of days to realize she was missing. I knew she'd been hanging around the Black Angels— working biker clubhouses was how she earned her money. I had never wanted any part of club life, and she definitely tried to keep me away from that scene. But when she went missing, the only logical conclusion I could come up with was that someone in the club had taken her. I was so arrogant and foolish—I figured I'd walk right in there and demand answers."

"They didn't give them to you."

"No. Edge gave me the option of working for those answers, though. One I made the mistake of accepting. I lived for six months as their willing prisoner, sticking around for any scrap about my mom they would give me until I figured out they were playing a different game than I was. They don't abide by rules. I couldn't take the manipulation anymore, so I left. I'd tried to leave a few times." She rubbed the scars on her arms, the lines I'd assumed she'd given herself. "They didn't let me get very far."

Pieces of her puzzle started sliding into place, shifting and turning until the entire image changed. Until the life of Jinx as I thought I knew it flipped upside down. "You're not a cutter, are you?"

"No. These?" She ran a finger over one particularly dark scar. "There's a reason Edge earned that road name. He likes his blades."

I tugged her hand away from her arm, tracing the scars with my own fingers. Circling the burn marks as well. "He also liked his cigarettes."

"He did." Jinx grabbed my hand again, pulling it into her lap. "I was punished when I'd run, I was punished when I wouldn't do as I was told. I was punished for no reason but that Edge or one of the club leaders wanted to see me cry. I always fought them, but sometimes it was just too hard."

"Jinx, you not winning a fight wasn't accepting their behavior. That's not consent."

"I know that, but I still feel guilty. I should have known better than to go there in the first place. I should have known they wouldn't respect me. I should have known—"

"They should have known better than to treat another human being as property."

"Yeah, well, they didn't." She inched closer, resting her thigh against mine. "I got away a few months back. Made it past their net for two whole weeks and thought I was free of them. But then Parris showed up and made me go back. Edge owed him big for some weapons deal they'd been whispering about for months, so he sold me to Parris like some sort of farm animal. Parris...who'd spent enough time in my mom's bed for me to know not to trust him. But I was stupid. Still. He promised he wouldn't let anything happen to me and would help me find out about my mom. He knew that was a huge motivator for me."

"He took advantage of that."

"I think so, yeah. But he kept to his word—I was seen as *his* within the club, so the other guys didn't mess with me anymore. He didn't force me to do anything either. He had his things he wanted to find out, and I had mine—we usually worked sort of in tandem on them."

"What was he trying to find out?"

"I'm not sure. Something about a man named Wolf. His protection didn't last, though. Edge outranked him, and he started sending Parris out on more and more overnight missions for the club. When that happened, Edge and Ravel would make me come to the clubhouse. Ravel would put me in restraints, and Edge..." She broke, tears falling. Voice hitching. My god, I wanted to kill those fuckers again.

"I should kill Parris for his role in all this."

She snorted a sad-sounding laugh. "Yeah, good luck with that. The guy has nine lives or something." Jinx took a deep breath and blew it out, still clinging to my hands. Trembling. "Parris was on a job with Edge the night a guy named Zed showed up and told me I needed to earn my keep with the entire club. The night they used me as collateral in a card game. That's how I ended up with the Soul Suckers."

"Where Pistol whipped you," I said, an overwhelming sadness taking over me. My heart positively ached for all this girl had been through. "And you were willingly going back to all that?"

"To keep you safe. You and your family and friends. This town. I can't get the Soul Suckers to leave, but they're all brawn and no brain. I figured you'd have better luck against them if the Black Angels weren't around. They're brawny too, but most are ex-military. They're smart and strategic. It's why the Soul Suckers like working with them. I knew Edge wanted me as his. He'd been trying to break me since the day I walked in the club doors. And Ravel—he gets off on pain caused to other people. If I let them hurt me? I knew I could help you and your town."

And she would have died inside with every cut or burn or hit. "I wouldn't want you to help us that way."

"That's why I didn't tell you. I couldn't let you talk me out of it."

So stubborn, this girl. So independent and headstrong too. I liked that about her—loved it, really. Life with her would never be boring...if she even wanted a future with me.

Which led me to ask the one question I simply had to have an answer to before I could deal with the rest. "Do you want to go back there, Jinx?"

She sat deeper into the seat, a confused expression taking over her pretty face. "What?"

"Do you want to go back to them? This is your choice. No manipulation from me. Do you want that club life or to go back to dig a little deeper into your mom's disappearance?"

"No."

Strong. Firm. One word setting me up to ask the next question. The one I definitely wanted a different answer to. "If you don't want to go back there, what do you want to do? Wait. No." I shook my head, ready to kick myself for softening the question I wanted to know the answer to. Elijah had said I was nonconfrontational—it was time for me to stop that. "Do you want to stay in Justice?" Better. Not enough. "With me? Do you want to stay in Justice and be with me?"

Jinx stared at me for the longest five seconds of my life before giving me another strong and firm one-word answer.

"Yes."

Yes. She said yes. I almost couldn't believe it. Almost. "Jesus, Jinx." I grabbed her, pulling her into my arms. Finally giving in to my need to touch her. "I'll do everything I can to make you happy, baby. I promise. But I don't know how to help you find the answers for what happened to your mother."

She buried her face in my neck, snuggling close. "She's dead. I know she is—have known it since the beginning of all this, I think. I just didn't want to admit that to myself."

"And you'll be okay never knowing the whys and hows?"

"I think it'll always bother me, but Edge wouldn't have given them to me anyway. None of the Black Angels would have."

"Can you live with that?"

She nodded, her sigh long and warm against me. "Yeah. I'll have to."

I'd take that as an answer. "I know we haven't known each other all that long, but I want you here with me. I want to make a life with you. I'd follow you if Justice wasn't the place you wanted to be, though."

"I like it here," she said, pulling back to smile up at me. "Though maybe someday we can spend some time in a place without snow. And a beach. I like beaches."

Me and Jinx and a beach...sounded like heaven. Though, her sitting on my couch with me in Justice wasn't too far off.

"I love you, Jinx," I said, cradling her face in my hands. "I want you to know that."

"I do, and I love you too." She put a finger against my lips when I moved to kiss her. "Let me take a rain check on that right now."

Oh. Right. "You vomited on Elijah's pants."

She flinched back. "I did. He's going to hate me."

The very thought made me laugh. I tugged her to her feet, dragging her down the hall toward the master bedroom and the en suite bath where her toothbrush sat. Where it would be staying for the foreseeable future. I liked that idea, and I suddenly wanted to break out my carving tools to make us a holder that would hold both our toothbrushes.

"Elijah would never hate you."

"Good, because he's important to you. That makes him important to me."

"And the rest of my family?"

She pursed her lips as if thinking hard about it. "I mean, this Bishop guy sounds like a real asshole, but Alder saved me, Elijah let me puke on him, and Lainie seems like a nice enough woman. I think we'll get along just fine."

"Good." I tapped her on the butt, sending her toward the bathroom. "Clean yourself up, woman. I'm going to get you some ibuprofen and a big bottle of water."

"For what?"

I reached out and grabbed her arm, turning it over to run my thumb over the mark on her elbow from where they'd injected her. "What they gave you, the detox isn't bad at all, but you're still likely to feel a little off for a day or so."

"You taking care of me, Fish?"

"Absolutely."

And I always would.

Epilogue

JINX

I'd always expected bachelor parties to be like they were within the club—loud, raucous affairs where men drank themselves half to death and partook of the female entertainment provided. Alder Kennard was unlike any man I'd ever known.

"The bachelor and bachelorette parties are together?"

"Yeah. Why?" Finn turned his truck—which we still had no idea how Deacon had managed to get back—into a spot along Main Street, looking serious and focused as he parked.

If we weren't already committed to attending the festivities, I'd tell him to take me home and drag him back to bed. I still might before the night was over. "Won't Shye be upset?"

"About what?"

"Seeing Alder with the strippers."

Finn laughed, the sound one I was still getting used to. One I fell more in love with every time I heard it. "If you think there'll be strippers tonight, you don't know my brother."

I didn't. Alder was still a bit of a mystery to me. I hadn't even met Bishop yet, but Elijah, I'd gotten to know during his few days in Justice. Lainie, too, though over the phone either on a regular or video call. Finn still spoke to his twin and sister every single morning—it was a ritual of his that I refused to let him alter. I envied their closeness and was thrilled when the two Denver siblings welcomed me with open arms. They'd pulled me right into their little family, demanding to see me on the video calls and asking me about my new life in Justice whenever they could. They included me, and I would be forever grateful for that.

Finn helped me out of the truck, holding my hand as we made our way to The Baker's Cottage. The sidewalk outside glowed in a golden hue from the light pouring out of the windows, and the sound of men laughing and talking broke the usual silence of the small town. This was definitely an unusual event in Justice—a Main Street business open after dark.

I was just about to reach for the door—even though I knew Finn would rush forward to open it for me—when I felt a strong hand surround my arm just above my elbow. Finn pulled me to a stop, not saying anything. Just...watching me.

"What?" I asked, looking up into his storm-cloud eyes. "What is it?"

"Are you ready for this?"

A night with his family and most of the town? Probably not, but I'd do it. I had a feeling this wasn't about me, though. Tonight, Bishop and Anabeth would be at the restaurant. The brother I hadn't met yet. The one who'd punched Finn the last time they'd been in the same room. Yeah, Finn's concern definitely wasn't about me. "Are *you* ready for tonight?"

He looked pensive for a moment, obviously giving his answer a lot of thought. "I think so. I'm feeling stable."

"Then I'm ready too." I squeezed his hand a little tighter. "Give me a signal if you need me."

"I always need you."

Heart. Exploded. This man never failed to tell and show me how much he cared, never skipped the thoughtful things most men forgot about. I loved that about him.

"You know," I said, sliding closer. Pressing my body against his. "We don't have to stay for long."

Finn caught on quick. "You're right. We don't. We can say hello to a few people, congratulate the bride- and groom-to-be, then head back home."

I sighed as his hand landed on my ass. As he grabbed a handful and tugged me closer. "I am sort of tired. We should really spend a little time in bed."

Finn chuckled, leaning down to nuzzle my neck. To nibble on my earlobe as that wicked hand kept a firm hold on my backside. "Bed, couch, floor, kitchen table...all good options. Though I think my favorite might be the living room. I can start a fire in the fireplace, then lay you down on the rug." He nuzzled closer, pressing his hard cock into my hip. Inflaming my need for him with his soft, simple words. "I'd crawl between those thighs and spend a good long time with my face in your pussy. Make you scream my name."

I moaned, gripping his shirt. Rocking against where he was so hard for me. "You like to make me scream your name."

"No. I *love* to make you scream my name." He pressed his lips to mine, slipping his tongue against mine and kissing me deeply. Pinning me to the wall as he overpowered my mouth and owned my body.

I could hardly catch my breath when he finally broke away. "Hey, Fish?"

"Yeah, Lucky?

"How soon can we go home?"

"I say thirty minutes should do it."

"Let's go for twenty."

"Deal."

Finn kissed my cheek sweetly then opened the door, guiding me to walk in before him. The room was crowded with just about everyone I'd met since moving to Justice, plus more men and women I'd never seen. What stuck out, though, was the burliness of the men. Justice seemed to be the place where lumberjacks came to procreate. Lots of beards and broad shoulders, flannel and thick thighs. My girlfriends from high school would have been in heaven.

"There're my brothers." Finn pulled me along behind him, saying hello to people as he passed and introducing me as his girlfriend to every man who even thought to glance my way. An odd term to hear for sure, but one I relished. Especially since he seemed to be staking a claim. I liked jealous Finn. A lot.

By the time I met the fifteenth person who had stopped Finn to say hello, I was fully accepting of the fact that I'd never remember all these names. Except Rusty. That kid was as red as red could be, from his hair to his freckles. I wouldn't forget him. The rest? Eh...they'd have to introduce themselves to me again the next time we met.

Because there *would be* a next time. Justice was a small town, and I had no intention of leaving it. Not without Finn right beside me.

"Jinx." Alder held out a hand in my direction, calling us past the remaining ten flannel-clad men in the room and directing us over to him as he hugged Shye to his side. "It's like running the gauntlet to try to get to anyone in here."

Finn nodded, still holding on to my hand as if I might get lost. "Everyone is here to celebrate with you."

Alder grinned, practically radiating happiness. "These assholes just came for the free liquor."

Lies. All lies, and he knew it. "I think they're here to see Shye. You look beautiful tonight."

The blonde gave me a smile that practically glowed, it was so bright. "Thanks. You look great in that dress."

The one Finn had ordered for me...and promptly tugged off my body the first time I'd tried it on for him. It hugged every curve but flared at my hips, and Finn liked that. A lot. "Thanks. Finn picked it out."

"He's got great taste." Alder looked up as a redhead walked up with a man right behind her. One who looked an awful lot like a Kennard. "Jinx, have you met Bishop and Anabeth yet? They just came back into town again from Vegas."

Anabeth, whom Finn had almost killed. And Bishop, the brother who had punched Finn in the face when he'd found out. Yeah, I knew the story, and I didn't like the idea of anyone hurting my Finn. Ever.

But I had manners.

"Not yet." I leaned in, still hanging on to Finn. Offering my hand to the couple. "I'm Jinx. Finn's girlfriend."

The woman—Anabeth—smiled, nearly taking my breath away. She was stunningly gorgeous, with auburn hair and wide, bright eyes. Finn had said she performed in Vegas—I could see why she was so popular. Looks-wise, at least.

"I've heard a lot about you," she said, turning that megawatt smile on Finn. "I'm happy for the two of you. Bishop, have you met Finn's girl?"

"Not yet." A man who looked as if he was cut from the same cloth as Alder and Finn smiled stiffly. "Nice to meet you, Jinx. Welcome to Justice."

As Alder and Bishop began chatting about something to do with beetles, I felt Finn step away from me. When I turned, he had his phone in his hand, a frown on his face. That couldn't be good.

"Everything okay?" I asked, keeping my voice quiet and turning my back to his brothers just in case.

Finn hummed his affirmation as his thumbs practically danced on the screen. "It's Parris."

I'd barely seen the man in over a week, not since the night I'd gone to the Black Angels to try to save Justice. *God, it's only been a week with Finn.* The best week of my life.

Finn tucked his phone away, still frowning. Looking seriously distracted. "He found Coyote."

"Okay."

"We'd made a deal—he got me info on Coyote, and I gave him a favor for later."

Oh no. "You didn't lock him in on what that favor could be?"

"No."

"Finn—"

"I know." He sighed, shaking his head. "But I owe this to Camden. He deserves the closure."

"Parris will make you fulfill your end of the deal."

He pinned me with a look, his mouth set in a firm line. His eyes hard. "And I'll honor my promise."

Of course he would. "He's a shark, Finn. He'll pull you under with him if he gets the chance."

Finn wrapped his arms around me and dropped a sweet kiss

to my forehead. "I know that, but I've dealt with guys like Parris before. I can handle this."

I sighed because I had my doubts, but this was Finn's deal. Finn's decision to make. There wasn't anything I could do to stop him. "So, what info did he have?"

"Coyote's in town."

"In Justice?"

"Rock Falls, but yeah. Close enough."

Too close. Still. "Did you tell your friend?"

"Yeah. I sent him a message."

"Did he respond?"

Finn shook his head. "Not yet. C'mon, let's enjoy our remaining fifteen minutes at this party, then I'm taking you home and forgetting everything other than making you mine all over again."

Charmer, thy name was Finn. "Sounds like a plan to me."

We rejoined the other Kennards, catching up on the conversation going on between the four of them with ease. At least until Alder cut it short.

"Excuse us," Alder said, pulling Shye away. "Deacon's finally here, and we need to talk to him. Enjoy the party."

He and Shye headed across the room, leaving us standing with Bishop and Anabeth. Alone. An awkward silence fell over the four of us, Anabeth looking at Bishop, and Bishop...well, glaring.

I hated awkward silences, and apparently, so did Finn.

"I need to say something to the two of you," Finn said, sounding far more serious than this party called for.

Bishop and Anabeth exchanged a glance before he replied with a simple, "Okay."

"I know I wrote you both letters when I was in prison, apologizing for my past transgressions, but I need to say the words too. I'm sorry. I'm sorry I ever involved Anabeth in my drug use, and I'm really sorry I didn't say anything to you, Bishop, after she almost died. I never should have let that wound fester for so long." Finn stood a little straighter, lifting his chin. Looking so damn strong and confident in the face of Bishop's obvious anger. "I'm sorry for everything, and I can promise you that nothing like that will ever happen again."

Oh, my sweet man. Such a brave thing to do. I'd have to tell Elijah about this conversation in the morning. No way would he believe Finn had broken his nonconfrontational streak to be so direct with their older brother.

Thankfully, Bishop seemed to understand how big of a moment this was for Finn. He relaxed a little, nodding, looking thoughtfully at the man before him. Proudly too. "I accept your apology, and I know nothing like that would ever happen again. You're strong enough not to fall back into those habits, Finn. I know it." He tugged Anabeth closer, his frown turning in to one hell of a cocky grin. "Though I'm not sorry I punched you."

Finn shrugged, his hand finding mine and holding on. Tight. "I deserved it."

"It won't happen again, brother." Bishop yanked Finn into a hug, the two smacking each other on the backs. Two brothers mending fences and agreeing to move forward. I almost wanted to cry.

Anabeth simply shook her head. "I think you're good for him, Jinx."

"Maybe so, but he's good for me too."

And he was. So good for me. And as long as I had him on my arm, I knew things would be okay. With us, with the Soul Suckers, with life. We'd be just fine...together.

We'd be even better when we got the hell out of this party in exactly ten more minutes.

Acknowledgments

There's a lot to be thankful for in my life. My friends, my family, my children, my dog, the people who got me here, the ones who were kind enough to walk away when I needed them to, the support network I've built and the people I've found over the years to help me regain my footing when I couldn't do it myself. I owe everything to them.

To Lisa—my editor, my friend, and one of my favorite humans. I might like your cat more than I like you at times, but I'm pretty sure you can't blame me.

To my Bitches, my Flavortown Crew, my Chatty Whores, and my Future Commune ladies...y'all keep me sane. Good luck keeping that up.

Kristin Harte started off as a chemistry major in college but somehow ended up writing romances featuring ex-military heroes and the women who knock them to their knees...literally and figuratively. She likes drinking in the shade, snuggling under a warm blanket on a cold evening, and researching how to blow things up. Her children know nothing of what she writes, and her husband just hopes he's not at their Chicago-ish home the day the government shows up to confront Kristin about her Google search history.

When not writing good men doing bad things, Kristin can be found writing paranormal romance as Ellis Leigh, co-writing naughty novellas as London Hale, or taking her signature style into the mystery realm as Mille Thorne.

www.kristinharte.com
Kristin@KristinHarte.com